PUBLISHED BY BAISDEN PUBLISHING

MICHAEL BAISDEN

MAINTENANCE MAN II

MONEY, POLITICS AND SEX
Everyone Has a Price

PUBLISHED BY BAISDEN PUBLISHING

LEARN MORE BY VISITING WWW.BAISDENLIVE.COM
Follow Michael on Facebook at BaisdenLive and on Twitter @BaisdenLive

DEDICATION

To every woman who has come into my life
to teach me more about myself, I thank you.
Sometimes the lessons were painful, but those are the
ones that shaped me into the man I have become.

To every man who offered good advice and set
the right example, I promise to pay it forward
to the next generation of young men.

—Michael Baisden

MAINTENANCE
MAN
II

MONEY, POLITICS AND SEX
Everyone Has a Price

ACT I

PICKING UP THE PIECES

CHAPTER 1

The atmosphere around The W Hotel was chaotic. The entrance to The Wall Night Club inside the hotel was already roped off to control the crowd of overly tanned men and exotic women that wrapped around the corner.

"The lot is full!" the valet shouted in a heavy Spanish accent while frantically waving a flashlight. "Keep it moving!" His uniform was drenched in sweat from the humid 85-degree Miami heat. A symphony of horns echoed off the nearby buildings as the line of expensive cars began to back up down Collins Boulevard, blocking the intersection. "No hay espacio," he shouted at a belligerent man driving by in a black Maserati. "Don't you understand English?—rich assholes," he said under his breath.

Suddenly, a red Ferrari came speeding down the street against traffic toward the entrance. It cut in front of the line, barely missing the valet and came to a screeching halt.

"What the hell are you doing, Puta?" the valet yelled. "You could've killed me!"

The tinted back window slowly lowered and a familiar deep voice boomed from inside the car.

"If I wanted to kill you, you'd already be dead, mi amigo," Malcolm laughed.

"Mr. Tremell, is that you?" the valet smiled while reaching for the door handle. "Long time no see!"

"Glad to be back, Hector."

Malcolm stepped out of the limousine and gave him a brotherly hug. At six-four, he towered over the much shorter valet. His fitted short-sleeve shirt accentuated his muscular chest and arms. As he slipped on his white linen jacket, the women waiting in the long line for the club abruptly stopped complaining to take in the view.

"Um-Um-Um," one woman moaned loud enough for him to hear.

"So, are you moving back in with us?" Hector asked.

"No, I'm just staying overnight. I got a place at that new high-rise off Ocean Drive," Malcolm said. "Do me a favor and park my car out front. I'm meeting the movers first thing in the morning,"

"Of course, you know we always have a space for you," Hector said, lifting the trunk. "So, where have you been all these months? The ladies still ask about you."

"Let's just say I've been on hiatus," Malcolm laughed.

"I'll have your bags sent right up," Hector said. "Will you be needing your usual table at the club? The manager will be glad to see you again."

"No, not tonight, I'm beat. I just got off an eight-hour flight from London."

"Well, I hope you're not too tired; Miss Smith checked in

about an hour ago."

"Miss Smith, huh? Well, in that case, have room service send up an order of sushi and a bottle of Riesling to Miss Smith's suite." Malcolm discreetly slipped him a one-hundred-dollar bill. "It looks like the party's here tonight."

"Yes, sir. Looks like it!"

They shook hands and Malcolm made his way through the crowded hotel lobby, stopping along the way to shake hands with the bouncers and other hotel staff that he had come to know over the years. As he approached the elevator doors, there were two beautiful women wearing bikinis and wraps waiting to go up. Their demeanor was elegant. One of them was Caribbean with flawless dark brown skin and short natural hair. The other was unmistakably Cuban, with long blonde hair, light brown eyes, and full hips. Malcolm casually admired the perfectly round breasts that were bulging out of their tight tops. The Caribbean woman was holding a drink that was half empty. The night must just be getting started for them, too, Malcolm was thinking. When the elevator doors opened, he politely held the door while they filed in.

"After you, ladies."

"Why, thank you," the Caribbean woman said with a flirtatious smile.

The Cuban woman pushed the button for the tenth floor. Malcolm and the Caribbean woman he was admiring pushed the penthouse level at the same time, brushing against each other's hands.

"I hope you're not stalking me, Mr.—?"

"Tremell, Malcolm Tremell. And what man could resist stalking such exquisite prey?"

"Well, you know what they say in my country?"

"What's that?"

"What happens in Jamaica, stays in Jamaica," she replied while moving closer to him.

"Just in case you hadn't noticed, we're in South Beach."

"Use your imagination, Mon!" She smiled seductively. "My name is Marie, and this is my friend Jo Anna."

"Ladies, the pleasure is all mine."

Just then, the elevator doors opened onto the tenth floor. Jo Anna kissed Marie on the cheek and stepped off. "Don't do anything I wouldn't do better!" she laughed.

Just as the elevator doors were closing, a large hand reached through the crack and the doors sprung back open. A tall burly man clumsily stepped in. His eyes were glassy and he reeked of alcohol. He stood directly in front of the doors until they closed, then he looked over his shoulder condescendingly at Marie.

"Boy, this place is crawling with Kaffirs," he slurred in a South African accent. "It's hotter than an African jungle in here!"

"For your information, I'm Jamaican not African, you idiot!"

"What's the difference?"

"If I wasn't a lady I would show you the difference!"

"Well, come on little lady." He leaned toward her with his chin out and closed his eyes. "Give me your best shot!"

Malcolm slowly guided Marie behind him, then tapped him on the forehead.

"Hey, Adolf! Why don't you go sleep it off?"

The man opened his eyes and grabbed Malcolm by the collar. "And what are you gonna do—Kaffir Lover?" Then he took a swing.

Malcolm ducked and hit him with an uppercut, then three rapid punches to his stomach, the last punch lifting him off his feet and into the elevator wall. He was out cold! Malcolm held him up straight with one arm while looking over his shoulder at Marie.

"Is it just me, or are there more assholes than usual on South Beach this summer?" Malcolm said sarcastically.

When the elevator door opened onto the penthouse level, a bellman was waiting with an empty baggage cart.

"Mr. Tremell, everything ok?"

"Everything is fine; he just had one too many Red Stripes."

Malcolm laid him down on the baggage cart and stuffed a twenty-dollar bill into the bellman's pocket. "Tell Hector to put him in a taxi and have him dropped off in Liberty City!"

"Yes, sir!" he laughed to himself. He knew Liberty City was a mostly black area of Miami.

Malcolm offered Marie his hand and escorted her off the elevator. She stepped over the unconscious man's legs, which were dangling off the cart, and followed Malcolm down the hallway. They stopped in front of room 2018.

"Well, Mr. Tremell, you really know how to show a girl a good time!" She put her arms around his neck. "Is there *any* way I can repay you for rescuing this damsel in distress?"

"I wish I had time, but—"

"But, what?" She moved in toward him and kissed him on the lips.

"But, I had a long flight and I've got a busy day tomorrow, so—," he grabbed her arms and pulled them from around his neck. "This will have to be goodnight!"

He pulled away and began walking backwards. He paused in front of room 2020 waiting for her to go inside.

"Please tell me you're not gay!"

"Far from it. Good night, Marie!"

"I'll be damned, of all the nights to meet a fuckin' gentleman!"

Then she went inside her room, slamming the door shut.

Miss Smith's room was two doors down in suite 2020. Malcolm walked up to the door and put his ear close to it. He could hear the song "Sexual Healing" by Marvin Gaye playing from inside the room. The aroma of scented candles crept through the gap at the bottom of the door. This is definitely the right room, he said to himself. *Knock, knock!* He tapped lightly on the door and covered the peephole with his hand.

"Who is it?" a soft, sexy voice apprehensively inquired.

"It's the Maintenance Man. You need service?"

"Only if you can unstop this wet drain." She laughed.

As the door slowly opened, a nude and voluptuous figure stepped behind the door and waved him inside.

"It's been a long time, Malcolm," she said as the door closed behind him. "Now, get undressed!"

She walked toward the bedroom, grabbing a glass of champagne off the table on her way. She was completely naked except for the black Manolo Blahnik boots she was wearing and a diamond rope belly chain. She was in her mid-forties, but she had the body of a woman in her early twenties.

"Andrea, you haven't changed one bit, still straight to the point," Malcolm said while taking off his jacket. "Or should I call you Miss Smith?"

"You can call me anything you like," she yelled from the bedroom, "Just get that tight ass in this bed. I've been waiting for nearly a year to get some of that sweet meat!"

"Slow down, you'll get what you paid for!" He walked past her and into the bathroom and started to undress. "Speaking of tight asses, your ass is looking better than ever!"

"Pilates five days a week and thirty-thousand dollars in cosmetic surgery will tighten up anybody's ass," she laughed, walking up behind him. She admired herself in the mirror as she pressed her breasts against his back and began grabbing at his buttons. "I hope you're rested because I'm horny as hell."

Suddenly there was a knock at the door.

"You expecting company?" Andrea asked.

"It's probably just room service. I ordered sushi!"

When Malcolm opened the door, Marie was standing in the hallway wearing a lacy black bra and panties set and holding a tray with the sushi and wine on it.

"Surprise! How's this for room service?"

"How did you—?"

"You'd be surprised how far a nice set of legs can get you," she interrupted.

"Marie, I am busy right now, I can't—"

"I just wanted to show my appreciation." She barged past him to set the tray down on the table. "So, do you have two glasses so we can toast?"

"*I've* got three!" Andrea said as she walked out of the bedroom, still naked, holding three wine glasses and a bottle opener. She grabbed the bottle from Andrea's hand and started to open it. "Malcolm, when you said you were ordering sushi, I thought you meant raw fish!"

"Oh my God, I'm so embarrassed!" Marie said, looking stunned. "I had no idea."

"Relax my dear," Andrea said, just as she popped the cork. "I think we could all use a drink."

She calmly poured three glasses of wine and sat down on the sofa holding her glass.

"Well, I didn't fly all the way from New York for nothing." Andrea seductively opened her legs revealing her cleanly shaven vagina. "So if you're staying young lady, I'll need half."

"Half of what?" Marie asked

"Half of ten-thousand dollars. This man doesn't come cheap!"

"Malcolm, what is she talking about?"

"I think this may be a little out of your range!" Malcolm said sarcastically.

He grabbed her by the arm and ushered her toward the door. Just as he reached for the handle, Marie jerked loose and shoved him against the wall.

"I didn't say I wasn't interested!"

She playfully ran back into the room and sat next to Andrea on the sofa. She lifted her wine glass with one hand while caressing Andrea's inner thigh with the other. Then they kissed.

"So, how does this work?" she said as they tapped glasses. "Do you take credit cards, checks, or cash?"

"Cash only!" Malcolm said as he pulled off his pants. "Now, this is what I call a homecoming!"

CHAPTER 2

MAINTENANCE MAN II

Malcolm woke up the next day entangled in a beautiful ball of soft legs and arms. He quietly got out of bed and laid Maria's arm across Andrea's shoulder. He smiled as he slipped on his pants and shirt. Maria was only his fourth client since he broke up with Toni and he was starting to get back into the swing of things. Years out of the game had made him a little rusty. He didn't have his usual energy or stamina until last night. The clock on the nightstand read 1:45 p.m. but they had only been asleep since 9:30. He felt a sense of pride that he was the last one asleep and the first one awake. It was all ego—a man thing.

After he put on his shoes, he picked up the envelope filled with cash off the cocktail table and walked quietly out the door. "I'm back," he said as he walked down the hall. He used the hotel phone by the elevator to call the bellman to get his luggage out of the room he paid for but never made it to. Once he was in his car, he let the convertible top down and pulled onto Collins Avenue, headed south to his new home.

It was early October but it was 82 degrees and humid. He turned up the volume on the radio and pressed down hard on the accelerator, dodging in and out of traffic. A group of college-aged boys cheered as he sped past their BMW. They tried to race behind him but it was no use. He stepped on the accelerator and within seconds they were a blur in his rear view mirror. He made a left turn on Fifteenth and headed for his condo in a luxury high-rise on Ocean Drive. When he drove up to the valet, he saw a familiar face.

"Miguel, is that you?" Malcolm asked as he stepped out of his car.

"Hola, Mr. Tremell, it's been a while! How have you been?" They shook hands.

"I'm great! But what are you doing working here? I thought you would never leave that gig over at the Hard Rock Casino. Don't you miss cursing out all those rich pricks?" he laughed.

"No sir, Mr. Tremell. I don't miss it at all. The tips are much better here and there's less temptation…if you know what I mean," he said while lifting the luggage out of the trunk. "Besides, I get to take care of you again. Everybody is excited about you moving in."

"Everybody?" Malcolm asked with a curious look on his face. "Nobody's supposed to know I'm here!"

Just then, he felt a tap on his shoulder. When he turned around, there was a tall, brown-skinned woman standing behind him; she was holding a small white envelope.

"Well, a secret like that would be hard to keep, Mr. Tremell," she said.

Malcolm tried not to seem too impressed but it wasn't easy. She was stunning. She had light brown eyes, flawless skin, and high cheekbones. Her hair was jet black and it came halfway down her back. She was wearing a long white strapless dress that showed off her small but firm breasts.

"And you are?" he asked while extending his hand.

"Angelita—Angelita Hernandez," she announced proudly in a heavy Latin accent. "I'm the manager." She slowly released his hand while looking at him from head to toe. "You're taller than I expected."

"Well, you know what they say about expectations?" Malcolm slowly removed his sunglasses.

"No, I don't. But maybe you can fill me in some time."

"It would be my pleasure."

They both stood motionless, looking into each other's eyes. Miguel awkwardly waited for the moment to pass, then he cleared his throat to break the silence.

"Um, um! Mr. Tremell, would you like me to take these up to your suite?"

"Sure, but I'm coming up with you. It was a pleasure meeting you, Angelita."

"Likewise, Mr. Tremell." She handed him the envelope she was carrying. "Here are your keys and access passes to the elevator, fitness center, and spa. All of your furniture was delivered yesterday and your wardrobe was pressed and put away just as you instructed. And I must say, you have impeccable taste."

"Why, thank you. But please, call me Malcolm."

"Very well…Malcolm. If you need anything else, here's my card. Call me if there's anything that requires my immediate attention…day or night!"

Then she turned and strutted away. Malcolm put his shades back on and admired the view of her perfectly round ass.

"I think I'm going to like it here!" Malcolm smiled as he headed through the large glass doors. "There's no place like Miami."

"Mr. Tremell, do you mind if I ask you a personal question?" Miguel asked.

"Sure, what is it?"

"How do you do it? That woman hasn't spoken to anybody in the six months I've worked here!" he said while rushing behind Malcolm with his luggage. "You've been here less than five minutes and she's ready to have your children."

"Lesson number one, Miguel, the secret to attracting a beautiful woman is that there is no secret."

"I don't understand," Miguel said as he stepped onto the elevator.

"Men don't choose women, women choose men. A woman knows within five seconds if she's going to have sex with you. Everything that happens after that is usually the man talking himself out of her wanting to have sex!"

"So, what's lesson number two?" Miguel inquired frantically.

"I think that's enough lessons for one day; besides, the game is meant to be sold not told."

"Well, I've got fifty bucks." He started reaching for his pockets.

"I'm just fucking with you, Miguel," Malcolm laughed and slapped him on the back. "Class is over my friend. Now push the button and let's get this show on the road!"

"Yes, sir!" Miguel said as the elevator doors began to close. "But I was serious about that fifty bucks. I need professional help."

The elevator ascended to the 40th floor and opened into the living room of the lavish thirty-five-hundred-square-foot apartment. Malcolm tipped Miguel and then walked out onto the patio to admire the view. His unit had a one-hundred-and-eighty-degree view of the ocean and downtown Miami. He leaned over the railing and reflected on how long he had been away from the beach. The suburban lifestyle with Toni was quiet, too quiet. He was a Cancer, a water sign; he needed to be near water to survive. At that moment, a small plane was passing by over the ocean with a large banner trailing behind it that read: 2 FOR 1 DRINKS AT CLUB LIV. COME PARTY WITH THE MOST BEAUTIFUL PEOPLE ON SOUTH BEACH!

"Yep, I'm back home, alright," he laughed.

Just then his cell phone vibrated. It was a text from his friend Simon. It read: Reminder—Staff meeting at 3:00 p.m.

Malcolm checked the time as he rushed back into the apartment. It read 2:15 p.m.

"It's showtime!"

He felt an adrenaline rush as he flung open the doors to the walk-in closet. Rows of designer suits and tailored shirts filled the space to capacity. He pulled open the dresser drawer to make sure his neckties were organized the way he had instructed. He smiled when he saw they were in perfect order.

"Kudos, Miss Hernandez," he said to himself. He laid out his favorite black Armani suit, a crisp white shirt, and striped black and white tie. He scanned the rows of Italian and French leather shoes until he found the right pair. "Perfect," he said aloud as he pulled the black Ferragamo shoes off the shelf. While he got dressed, he looked over at the framed photo of him and Melvin that was taken when he first got into the gigolo game. It was sitting on the shelf next to the full-length mirror.

"Cool Breeze, a man can be the most sharply dressed one in the room," he said imitating Melvin's raspy voice, "but the first thing a woman's gonna look at is his shoes."

He put on his slacks, tucked in his shirt, and slid into his jacket. "You taught me well, Old Man," he said soberly. "I know you'll be with me tonight when the curtain goes up!"

CHAPTER 3

Simon looked down nervously at the clock on his phone. It was 2:50 and the neon sign for Melvin's Jazz Club was still not working.

"We're getting real close, Jack!" Simon yelled at the electrician while holding the tall ladder. "We can't have opening night in the dark!"

"Don't worry, Mr. Harris, I'll have this working in just a second!"

Just then, Malcolm's red Ferrari came speeding around the corner. He switched gear and did a donut, stopping only inches away from Simon.

"You crazy son of a bitch!" Simon yelled.

He let go of the ladder to go after Malcolm.

"Whoa!" Jack yelled as the ladder began to sway backwards.

Simon rushed back and grabbed it just before it tilted over. "You just wait until I get a free hand. I'm going to choke the shit outta you!"

Malcolm calmly stepped out of his car and slowly put on his suit jacket. "Calm down, partner. I can stop on a dime with this baby!"

"Your reflexes ain't what they used to be, you old dog!" Simon laughed.

"Is that right?"

Malcolm walked over to Jack's tool belt and pulled out three screwdrivers. He turned toward a piece of drywall that was leaning against the truck. He took a deep breath, closed his eyes, and tossed all three in the air. In three swift motions, he snatched them from mid-air and threw them at the drywall, each landing within inches on top of the other.

"What the—?" Jack gasped. "Where did you learn to do that?"

"Navy SEALs, class of '91. Hoorah!" Malcolm grunted. "Not bad for an old dog, huh?"

"Show off!"

Suddenly, the neon sign began to flicker. "I almost got it." Jack strained while reaching as far back behind the sign as he could. "One last connection…there we go!"

Malcolm walked backwards until he had a full view. He stood still and let it sink in that he was really back. It had been nearly two years since he walked through those doors. He closed the club shortly after Melvin's death. It just wasn't the same without him. But the passing of time and a failed attempt at living a normal lifestyle brought him back to the reality of who he was.

"You did it, Malcolm!" Simon said to him.

"No, we did it." Malcolm hugged Simon around the neck. "This wouldn't have been possible without you, partner. Thanks for leaving Atlanta to partner with me on this. You know how much it means to me to keep Melvin's dream alive."

"Hey, man, that's what friends are for," Simon said while walking toward the club. "Besides, after I found out Cynthia was still messing around with that sleazy pastor, it was time for a new start."

"What about the baby?"

"Man, please, that big-headed baby isn't mine," he laughed. "That's like mistaking Flava Flav for Denzel Washington."

"You're wrong for that! You know there's no such thing as an ugly baby!"

"Shee-iiit!" he laughed and they slapped five.

"Ok, maybe the baby's head was a little lopsided!" Malcolm added.

"Ok, that's enough about the past. It's time to step into the future. Come on, the staff is waiting and I've got a surprise for you."

"Now what?"

Malcolm followed Simon through the large glass doors into the newly designed building. The floor plan was basically the same as the original club; the stage was directly in the middle and the VIP area was elevated off to the left. But nothing else was familiar. The bar was completely new with mahogany counter-tops and a large bar mirror that stretched to the top of the ceiling. The carpet was new and so were all of the cocktail tables, chairs, and lighting. The most elaborate change was the stage. The old rotten wood platform was replaced with a set design right out of a late night TV show.

"Well, what do you think?" Simon asked.

"Un-fuckin' believable! I just hope you saved us enough money for booze. This must've cost you a fortune."

"It's not about what you know, it's about who you know. I begged, bartered, borrowed, and smooth-talked every contractor in Miami to get this done on time and under budget. You're not the only hustler from the south side of Chicago!"

"Well, alright then." He and Simon bumped fists.

"But that's not the surprise!" Simon told him. Then he pulled a small remote out of his pocket and pushed the button.

The satin stage curtains parted and a hidden door on the stage floor slowly retracted. "Check this out!" Simon said, walking toward the stage. A black Steinway piano and stool gradually came from beneath the stage. There was a bucket of ice and a bottle of champagne sitting on top of it.

"Is that what I think it is?" Malcolm's eyes lit up. He walked toward the stage almost in a trance.

"Yep, that's your baby!"

Malcolm sat down and ran his hand over the engraved initials on the face of the piano; it read M.T. It was the piano his dad had given him for his eighteenth birthday. He hadn't played it in nearly a year. He began pressing the keys, listening for the tone to see if it was right.

"She sounds as sweet as ever!" Malcolm said. Then he reached over and hugged Simon. "Thanks, man, I don't know what to say!"

"Just do me a favor and don't throw any more fuckin' screwdrivers around me," he laughed. "That Rambo shit is scary!"

"Deal!"

"Now, if you boys are finished bonding, we've got a club to open!" a woman's voice echoed from backstage.

"Ariel, is that you?"

"In the flesh!" Ariel stepped out onto the stage wearing a

long black cocktail dress. The top was cut low and wrapped around her neck showing off her cleavage. "I know you didn't think I was gonna let you boys have all the fun, did you?"

"What are you doing here?" Malcolm hugged her and lifted her off the ground.

"Put me down, boy!" she laughed. "You know a single woman can't afford to be out of work in this bad economy, and besides, where my boss goes, I go!"

"Wow, look at you! You've gotten a lot thicker since I last saw you in Atlanta. What in the world are they feeding you women in the south?" Ariel twirled around to show off her figure. "Damn, woman, I might have to give you a freebie!"

"Be careful, I might have to take you up on that offer. I'm so damned horny I burned out the motor on my vibrator and broke the ears off my rabbit."

"What's a rabbit?" Simon asked sounding clueless.

"Simon, you're the best club manager in the world, but you still don't know shit about women!"

"That may be true, but you're stuck with me for the rest of your life," he said while popping open a bottle of champagne. Ariel grabbed three long-stemmed glasses from the bar and rushed over to catch bubbles.

"To new beginnings, friendship, success, and—"

"And to Melvin," Malcolm cut in. "May your legacy live on with all of us."

They tapped glasses and took a long sip.

"Now, let's get this party started!" Malcolm said. "Doors open in a few hours! Let's make this a night this town will never forget!"

CHAPTER 4

MAINTENANCE MAN II

By seven o'clock the traffic on Biscayne Boulevard was bumper to bumper, creating a virtual parking lot. Parades of cars were at a standstill from the American Airlines Arena to the Intercontinental Hotel. Miami police officers were frantically waving their flashlights and yelling orders directing traffic into the parking lot of Melvin's Jazz Club, which was a half-mile south of the arena.

"Let's go!" one officer yelled as the light turned green. "Move it, move it, move it!"

The line to get in the club was two blocks long and getting longer. The VIPs drove up in their limos and exotic cars and were quickly ushered in by security, past the frantic paparazzi. Groupies lined the velvet rope on both sides trying to get a look at the celebrities and politicians who were rushing into the club. Ariel and Simon stood outside with the bouncers on opposite sides of the entrance instructing them on who to allow in and who to turn away. If someone met the standard they would discreetly nod their heads up and down; for those who didn't, they nodded side to side. It was a scene right out of Studio 54 in New York back in the '70s.

"Ariel, we're almost at capacity. You can let in another twenty or so women; after that, shut it down," Simon yelled to her. "I'm going inside to check on the bar!"

"Alright, boss," she yelled back. "This is exciting, isn't it?"

"It's exciting alright. Let's just make sure things don't get out of control!"

Simon rushed back inside the club and headed straight for the bar, but he didn't get five steps in the door before women began tugging at him asking about Malcolm.

"Excuse me, but where is Malcolm?" a beautiful Asian woman asked seductively.

"He'll be out shortly, ma'am, now if you will excuse me."

Simon maneuvered his way into the main lounge but was stopped again, this time by a blonde Caucasian woman wearing a tight red dress; she tapped him on the shoulder to get his attention. "I beg your pardon, but is Malcolm going to perform tonight? I flew all the way from London to see him?"

"I came in from Puerto Rico," another woman who was standing next to her added.

"Ladies, I promise you, Mr. Tremell will be out in just a minute," Simon told them while walking away. "Try to be patient.

I'm sure you understand it's a busy night for everybody."

"Eres un poco idiota," she shouted at him in Spanish.

Simon didn't even look back. He kept walking and disappeared into the thick crowd holding his head down hoping not to be recognized. It didn't help that his picture was on the brochure next to Malcolm's promoting opening night. Malcolm had insisted since Simon fronted most of the money to rehab the club.

Once Simon made it to the bar, the head bartender, Big Mike, was waiting on him. He was waving an empty bottle of Grey Goose in the air. At six-five, husky and dark-skinned, he easily stood out. It was clear from the expression on his face that he was having a good time with the crowd of gorgeous women who were flashing platinum credit cards and plenty of cleavage.

"How's it going, Big Mike?"

"Are you serious?" he responded sarcastically. "I feel like I've died and gone to plastic-surgery heaven. I've never seen so many big titties in my life. My dick is so hard I damn near knocked a case of Budweiser off the counter giving a woman her change."

"You need professional help," Simon laughed. "Just stay focused, it's going to be a long night."

"Stay focused? Come on, Mr. Harris, I haven't seen a bra size in here under double Ds. And these women aren't shy about showing them off, either. I mean, take a look at that white woman in the red dress sitting at the end of the bar," he discreetly pointed. "If Dolly Parton was sitting next to her, you would tap Dolly on the shoulder and say, 'Excuse me, flat-chested lady, but can you get your girlfriend's attention?'"

Simon burst out laughing so loud people stared at him. He put his hand over his mouth and tried to compose himself. But Big Mike didn't let up.

"All the while I'm pouring her drink, I'm thinking about how much I would love to wake up in the morning bouncing those beach balls off my face, ba ba ba ba!" he joked, shaking his head from side to side and poking out his lips.

"Ok, I've got to get away from you, Big Mike," Simon said, wiping the tears from his eyes. "I'll be back with another case of vodka. Do you need anything else?"

"How about a bottle of Viagra!"

"That's it, I'm outta here!" Simon said, lifting up the sleeve to get out of the bar area.

"Hey, Mr. Harris!" Mike yelled at him. "On a serious note, I appreciate you bringing me down here from Atlanta to work with you. I won't let you down."

"You're welcome, Mike," Simon replied. "But you earned it."

"I know, that's right!" he replied arrogantly, "Because I'm the best damn bartender there is!"

"Big Mike, you can't mix a drink worth shit," Simon told him. "But you're the funniest motherfucker I've ever met! Now get back to work before I call your wife and tell her you're down here flirting with white women."

"Yes, sir!"

The club was at capacity and the crowd was liquored up and getting restless. Simon directed one the waiters to grab another case of vodka for the bar, then rushed toward the back office to see if Malcolm was ready to start the show. He paused outside the office door and knocked.

"Hey, man, you decent?"

"Yeah, come on in!" Malcolm responded.

When Simon open the door, Malcolm had his shirt off and was doing pull ups on a device that was hooked onto the back of the bathroom door.

"Forty-three, forty-four, forty-five—" Malcolm counted out loud.

"What the hell are you doing?"

"I'm getting ready," Malcolm replied. "Forty-six, four-seven, forty-eight, forty-nine...fifty!" Then he dropped down to the floor. His upper body was sweaty from the workout. He toweled off his chest and walked into the bathroom that was connected to the office. Simon caught a glimpse of his Navy SEAL tattoo on his right arm as he walked by. It read U.S.M.C. on the top with a bulldog in the middle and at the bottom it read: Semper Fi.

"What does, Semper Fi mean, anyway?" Simon asked.

"It means, stop asking so many questions so I can get dressed," Malcolm joked.

"Very funny, smart ass!"

"It's Latin for always faithful."

"I guess that doesn't apply to relationships, huh?"

"What's that supposed to mean?"

"Never mind, we don't need to go there right now."

"No, let's just get this out the way," Malcolm said while putting on his shirt. "I knew it was only a matter of time before you brought it up."

"Ok, I thought you were all done with this gigolo thing. I don't mind being partners in the club business, but I was hoping that lifestyle was behind you."

"Simon, I have plans for this business, big plans! For the past two years I've been working on ideas on how to franchise the male escort business worldwide, and make my money legitimately," Malcolm told him. "You only see this business as being all about sex, but it's much more than that. It's about power, influence, and yes, money. Real money! But that's a part of my life I'm not always going to be able to share with you. You're just going to have to trust me on this one."

"And what about Toni? I thought you finally found *the one*!"

Malcolm slowly turned towards the two-way mirror that looked out into the club. He stood silent for a moment with his hand in his pocket, staring out onto the anxious crowd that was waiting on him.

"Toni was a pipe dream," he said in a somber tone. "She represented the normal life that I thought I was supposed to have. I expected her love to transform me, and so did she. But like every dream, you eventually have to wake up to reality. And the reality is, I am not a monogamous man. I never have been, and I never will be. And although she loved me enough to accept that part of me, I knew I would never change."

"Maybe you just didn't work at it hard enough, Malcolm. I've known you most of your life, and I know you loved that woman!"

"You're right, I did love her." He walked over to Simon and looked him straight in his eyes. "And the hardest thing for a man to do when he loves a good woman is to let her go!"

"Enough said!" Simon shook his hand and they embraced. "Now, let's get this show on the road. Knock em' dead, partner!"

"You got it!" Malcolm said while cracking his knuckles. "By the way, nice touch with these security cameras," Malcolm added, pointing at the seven large monitors on the office wall. "These cameras zoom in so tight I can read the numbers on a dollar bill sitting on any table in the house."

"When you've been ripped off as many times as I have in this business it's worth the investment. If anybody slips and falls on this property, their ass will be on candid camera," Simon laughed. "Now, give me about three minutes to get to the control room before you hit the stage. When the music stops, that's your cue to get into position."

"In the words of the great Marvin Gaye, let's get it on!"

Malcolm watched the monitors while he waited. The club was jam-packed with the most beautiful women in Miami, of every nationality, and the wealthiest. Every seat was taken in the VIP section. Waiters were swiping credit cards non-stop as celebrities dropped twenty-five-hundred dollars a bottle for Dom Perignon and Remy Martin. He glanced from one monitor to the next taking it all in. It's really happening, he thought. Melvin's was finally open again, and it was his now, his and Simon's. It was exciting and surreal.

Just as he was about to step out of the door that led backstage he caught a glimpse of a familiar face. But before he could make her out, the monitor flashed to another camera position. He paused for it to change back; when it did, he smiled. "Well, I'll be damned!" he said. "The night just got more interesting."

When the music stopped, Malcolm walked out of the backstage door and sat down on his piano stool and waited for Simon to introduce him. He took a deep breath, closed his eyes, and looked upwards. "This is for you. Old Man!"

"Ladies and gentleman, welcome to the grand reopening of the legendary Melvin's Jazz Club. It's been nearly two years since the doors closed, and the nightlife in Miami has never been the same. Well, we're back, bolder and better than ever. Now, put your hands together for the man who brought class and sophistication back to The Magic City, my partner and friend, Mr. Malcolm Tremell!"

The crowd erupted in applause as the lights dimmed. The sound of a thumping and rhythmic bass vibrated the large speakers as the stage curtains slowly opened. When the spotlight hit the stage, Malcolm ascended up from the stage floor and began playing. The applause grew even louder. Men and women began to chant, Malcolm! Malcolm! Malcolm! But Malcolm was in a zone. The applause quickly faded into the background. It was only him and his piano. He played with all his might, all his talent, all of his heart. It was the moment he had been waiting two years for and he was determined to take them on a ride…a musical journey they would never forget.

There was a three-piece band backing up Malcolm, a bass guitar, saxophone, and drums, but the energy made it sound bigger. They jammed non-stop for thirty minutes, playing contemporary jazz songs by artists like Grover Washington, Ronnie Laws, and Roy Ayers. He ended with a favorite of his by David Sanborn called "Chicago Song." The saxophone player, Eddie, took the lead and they brought the house down. After years of not performing in front of a live audience, Malcolm still had it. The audience gave him a standing ovation.

"Thank you, thank you very much!" Malcolm said, taking a bow. "It's great to be back here at Melvin's. It's been a long time since I've sat on this stage. I know Melvin is looking down on us from heaven, smiling from ear to ear and chewing on that old cigar! And if I know him, he's probably got two of the sexiest angels in heaven sitting on his lap," he laughed. "So, let's start this party where we ended it, with a toast."

One of the waiters rushed over and handed Malcolm three glasses of champagne.

"Simon, you and our beautiful manager, Ariel, join me on stage." He shielded his eyes from the stage lights and scanned the room. "Where's Ariel, anyway?"

"Here I am!" Ariel yelled as she walked toward the stage, making sure to strut slowly down the main aisle so that everybody could get a good look at the dress she had on. Once they were all in place, he lifted his glass.

"To Melvin, a man with a vision and the courage to go after it. We all miss you, Old Man."

"Here, here!" they all shouted.

"Malcolm, let's hear some John Coltrane!" a woman yelled out.

"Branford Marsalis!" a man shouted.

"I've got a better idea, how about we play a classic by one of

Melvin's favorite female vocalists, and I'll give you three guesses who it is."

"Ella Fitzgerald!" a voice shouted from the back of the room.

"Billie Holiday!" a woman standing by the bar yelled out.

"Sarah Vaughan!" Ariel added.

"No, no, and no!" Malcolm smiled as he sat back down at his piano. "It's Minnie Ripperton." He started pressing the keys. "Can I play a little Minnie for you?"

"Yeah!" the crowd shouted in unison.

"Ok, but I'll need a little help with the vocals, because you know I'm not going to try to touch that, right?" he laughed as he continued to play. "Now, what woman in here has the chops to sing a Minnie Ripperton song?"

Malcolm looked over in the direction of the woman he saw on the security monitor. He glanced in her direction at first, then he stared her directly in the eyes.

"Now, I know you're not going to leave me hanging!" Malcolm went on. "Don't make me come out there and get you and embarrass you in front of all these nice people...and you know I will do it!"

Suddenly, a tall bronze-skinned woman walked out of the shadows and made her way to the stage. Her hair was jet black and pinned up into a ball, which accentuated her long neck and high cheekbones. She was wearing a strapless champagne-colored Armani dress with a sweetheart neckline that showed off her full hips. Malcolm could hear chattering from both men and women as she walked onto the stage. She was stunning!

"Malcolm, I'm going to kill you when this is over!" she said to him as she inconspicuously snatched the microphone out of his hand.

"Ladies and Gentleman, may I introduce an old classmate of mine from Juilliard Academy, Ms. Alex Garcia."

"This was one of Melvin's favorites by Minnie and one of mine, too. It's called, 'Inside My Love.'"

As the band began to play the prelude, the lights dimmed and the packed room grew silent. Alex cleared her throat and stepped confidently to the front of the stage. Just as she was about to hit her first note, she closed her eyes.

"Two people, just meeting...barely touching each other," she sang. *"Two spirits...greeting, trying to carry it further. You are one, and I am another. We should be, one...inside each other."*

The expression on the faces of the audience was one of shock and appreciation. She sounded great and she was hitting every one of Minnie's high notes. Malcolm smiled as he glanced over at Simon. Simon nodded back and mouthed the word, "Wow!"

When the song was over, she received a standing ovation. She took a bow and then grabbed Malcolm by the arm and lead him backstage.

"Malcolm, how could you do that to me?" she said while pounding him on the arm and chest. "You know I don't sing anymore!"

"You sounded pretty damn good to me! And the crowd loved you."

"It's been ten years since I sang in front of a crowd! I didn't come here to perform!" she smiled and hit him again.

"Well, you must be getting a lot of practice in the shower because you sound better than ever!" he said, blocking her punches.

Suddenly, Simon and Ariel came rushing backstage. Simon was still clapping.

"Wow, that was incredible! When can we sign you up?" Simon said to Alex.

"See what you've started!" Alex said, then she hit Malcolm again. "Where is the ladies room?"

"Here, come with me," Ariel said to her. "You can use the one in the office."

She led Alex through the door that connected the backstage to the office. Simon and Malcolm stood there taking in what had just happened.

"Who is that?" Simon asked. "That was one of the best performances I've ever seen in my life! And she's fine, too! Can you talk her into signing a contract?"

"Easy, Cowboy! Calm down! That's never going to happen!"

"And why is that?"

"You really don't know who she is, do you?"

"You said she was an old classmate from your Juilliard days!"

"Damn, Simon, do you ever watch CNN, MSNBC, or C-Span?"

"No, I've been too busy busting my ass putting this club together; now stop playing 'Jeopardy!' and just tell me!"

"That's Senator Nelson's fiancée!"

"Senator who?"

"Senator Nelson, the one who is always on the news threatening to fire teachers and get rid of Medicare!"

"Get the fuck outta here!" Simon said, getting loud. "She's engaged to that jerk?"

"Well, it's not official, but that's the rumor."

"Hasn't that guy been married like a dozen times?"

"Three to be exact, but who's counting?"

"What a waste, she's a natural!"

"That's what I've been trying to tell her for years." Malcolm reached for the doorknob. "Now, do me a favor and don't say anything about her singing. She's still pissed off at me for putting her on the spot."

Alex was coming out of the bathroom just as Malcolm and Simon walked into the office.

"Well, Malcolm, thanks for humiliating me in front of all those people. That will be all over YouTube by tomorrow morning."

"That won't happen, Miss Garcia. We don't allow recording devices in Melvin's. No cell phones and no cameras are allowed. We've got the best security money can buy."

"What about all these monitors here on the wall, aren't they connected to cameras?"

"She's beautiful, not stupid!" Ariel said to Simon.

"Thank you, Ariel!"

"If it will make you feel better, I will erase this video right now!" Simon rewound the video and pressed delete. "There you go!"

"Thank you, Simon. I don't need the publicity."

"You mean, Senator Nelson doesn't need the publicity," Malcolm said to her.

"So, I see you read the newspapers."

"No, I watch the Miami Heat games on Sunday!" he laughed. "I see you two all hugged up in the floor seats."

"Same old Malcolm, always sticking your nose in someone else's business."

"Same old Alex, always choosing the wrong men!"

"Ok, on that note," Simon said and headed for the door. "We're going to leave you two classmates alone to scratch each other's eyes out! It was a pleasure meeting you, Alex."

"Likewise, Simon. You, too, Ariel. You guys have done an incredible job with this place, it's beautiful!"

"Thanks, Alex, hopefully, you'll come back and visit us soon. You've got an open invitation anytime you want to perform."

On the way out the door, he mouthed to Malcolm, "Get her to sign!" He was imitating signing a piece of paper. Malcolm waved him out and then took a seat on the edge of his desk.

"I can't believe you're going to marry that jerk! He's one of the sleaziest men in politics."

"He's not as bad as the media makes him out to be!" she said defensively. "And besides, he loves me and that's all that matters!"

"If he loves you so much, why aren't you singing instead of walking around like some kind of mindless trophy. You graduated valedictorian...not most likely to marry an asshole!" Malcolm said, getting in her face. "Why do you constantly choose men who want to control you?"

"Go to hell, Malcolm!" she shouted as she stormed towards the door. "I didn't come here for a lecture. I'm outta here!"

Malcolm went after her and grabbed her arm.

"I'm sorry, Alex," he said, holding her against his chest tightly until she stopped struggling. "I see we still love to hate each other!"

"I don't hate you, Malcolm! I just don't like reliving the past. Some of those memories are painful!"

"Not all of them!"

"Yeah, but the pain sometimes outweighs the good times."

"Alex, when are you gonna let that shit go?" Malcolm held her by the shoulders. "That guy should have gone to jail for what he did to you, and you let him get away with it!"

"What did you expect me to do, Malcolm, embarrass my entire family?" she shouted back. "I was young. I had been drinking and he was a star athlete headed for the pros. I was not going to take my parents through that."

"No, means no, Alex! Every time I see that hypocrite on a cereal box or a gym shoe commercial I want to punch a hole in the fucking TV!"

"I didn't tell you about the rape until months later for just that reason. I knew you would've killed him and I would've lost you. And I wasn't about to let that happen." she said, then leaned against his chest. "You were my best friend, Malcolm. And the sad thing about it is that you're still the only person I can trust."

She kissed him on the cheek.

"I've got to go now." She picked up her purse and headed for the door. "Thanks for the chance to live out one of my fantasies."

"Here, take my card! Call me if you need me, even if it's just to talk."

She took the card and put it inside of her bra.

"Will I see you again?" Malcolm asked.

"I'll try to stop by to check up on you from time to time. This is the only place I can go and not be followed or taped. Simon was right; you guys have the best security in the world! That's why I felt comfortable coming here alone tonight. Bye, Malcolm!"

As soon as the door closed behind her, Simon came rushing back into the room.

"So, did she agree to perform?"

"That woman has bigger problems than to worry about singing in this damn club." Malcolm's tone was serious.

"Ok, did I miss something? I thought you were just friends, but you guys argue like an old married couple."

"We're just friends, but we were close. I watched her make a lot of mistakes with guys."

"Guys like you?"

"No, guys worse than me! And this slick senator she's about to marry is at the top of the list of scumbags!"

"Hey, man, everybody has a right to throw their life away. You can't save the world."

"I know, but if she needs me I'll be there for her. And if he tries to fuck with her, it will be the worst mistake of his life!"

CHAPTER 5

At 10:45 a.m. Senator Nelson's jet landed at Ronald Reagan Washington National Airport in Washington, D.C., and taxied into a private hangar where a black Escalade and black stretch limousine were waiting. His security detail stepped out of the plane first, followed by the senator. He was a tall, white man of medium build in his late fifties. His hair was partially grey and his face was cleanly shaven.

As soon as he was inside the car, he pulled out his cell phone, dialed the number, and put the call on speaker. He gestured to his head of security, Vincent, who was sitting in the back seat across from him, to have the driver lift the glass partition.

"This is Senator Gary Nelson, put me through to Mr. Kross's office."

"Hello, Gary, how was your flight?" Mr. Kross asked.

"It was great. Thanks for sending your private jet to pick me up from Miami. It beats the hell out of first class."

"Well, the ultimate goal is to get you aboard Air Force One, right?"

"Yes, sir, that's the goal."

"No need to call me sir, Gary, we're all friends here. Call me Allan. By the way, all the other members are here with me. We're looking forward to your press conference when you make the big announcement."

"Gary, this is Randall Kross," another man's voice joined in. "We're ten votes short in the House and only one in the Senate. We've done everything in our power to stall the president on this HP 205 legislation, but it's only a matter of time before they get it passed, which will cost us billions! Now, we're prepared to back your campaign one-hundred percent, but we need to know that you're on board for the long haul. We have a lot riding on this next election."

"I understand. Don't worry, gentleman, you can count on me."

"That's what we need to hear," Mr. Kross replied. "Five-million dollars will be transferred to your campaign's bank account first thing tomorrow."

"Looking forward to doing business with you gentleman. Have a nice day."

Then he hung up.

"So, what's next?" Vincent asked while rubbing the deep scar on his right cheek.

"Now, we collect our money!" Senator Nelson said as he let down the partition. "Hey, driver, pull over so I can buy my fiancée some flowers."

"Are you serious?" Vincent whispered to him. "We're already thirty minutes late for the press conference."

"Look, if I'm going to run for the U.S. Senate I've got to marry this bitch soon," he whispered back with a sly grin. "She's beautiful…and she's half Puerto Rican. That should be good for at least half of the Latino vote."

CHAPTER 6

MAINTENANCE MAN II

Malcolm's alarm went off on his cell at 11:00 a.m. He sprang up out of bed and pushed the button on the remote to open his blinds. He stepped out onto the balcony and took a deep breath.

"Aaahh," he sighed. "There's nothing like waking up to the smell of the ocean!"

From his balcony he could see tanned bodies scattered on the beach from 8th Street all the way north to the W Hotel on 22nd. Thousands of people were tanning, biking, and jogging. That was all the motivation he needed. He quickly slid on a pair of running shorts, put on his gym shoes, and strapped his iPod onto his armband. "Time to get back in the mix!" he said as he pushed the elevator button, "No pain, no gain!"

Once he made it onto the beach, he stretched out for a few minutes then took off running. He sprinted for a quarter mile then jogged a mile. He repeated that routine for an hour. Once he was exhausted, he walked over to a water fountain that was across the street from the Betsy Hotel on 14th and Ocean Drive. Just as he started to take a sip, someone yelled out his name.

"Malcolm!"

When he turned around, he saw two men walking toward him. One was tall, blond, and tanned with a muscular build. He had on a pair of Ray-Ban sunglasses and was wearing a Dallas Cowboy T-shirt. The other one was short and stocky with short black hair. They were both pulling bicycles alongside of them.

"Adam and Jason, what's up fellahs?" Malcolm asked while embracing the tall one, Adam, and then Jason. "Long time no see!"

"Where the hell have you been, man?"

"Fuckin' Mayberry!" Malcolm laughed. "The land of minivans and soccer moms. And let me tell you, that shit was scary!"

"We heard you were back on the beach," Adam said to him. "We tried to get into Melvin's last night but it was jam-packed. Congratulations, by the way!"

"Thanks, bro! And I'll make sure you guys are on the VIP list from now on. Speaking of VIP, how's business? You guys still in the life?"

"What's left of it," Jason said sounding frustrated.

"What do you mean by that?"

"I mean, since you left the business, the level of class has dropped off the cliff!" he went on. "These new-school guys are putting their dicks in everything that's moving, and doing it for half the price."

"He's right, Malcolm," Adam added. "There are at least three new agencies that have opened in the past two years and all of them are cutting rates and hiring guys who don't know the difference between a la carte and a fucking grocery cart!"

"So, how have you guys been surviving?" Malcolm asked.

"I still have a couple of my high-end clients and I take a few modeling gigs here and there," Adam replied. "The pay is great but the work isn't consistent. This economy is no joke!"

"What about you, Jason?"

"I'm getting paid ten-k a month to walk poodles and chauffeur around this old Jewish broad. I'm her little Italian boy toy that she shows off to her rich friends. Personally, I think the bitch has been watching too much 'Jersey Shore,'" he laughed. "But you do what you gotta do!"

"Well, gentleman, I think I may have the solution to your problems," Malcolm told them. "I have an idea that will revolutionize the whole gigolo game. But it's gonna take hard work, dedication and, most importantly, loyalty."

"You know you can count on me, Malcolm," Adam said. "Let's take it back to the old school and show these amateurs how it's really done!"

"Count me in!" Jason added. "If I never see another goddamn dog it'll be too soon!"

"Meet me at the club tonight at eight sharp and be dressed to impress," Malcolm said. "And see if you can track down some of the experienced maintenance men from our old crew."

"What about interviewing some of the new guys on the scene?" Adam said to him, "There's a lot of rich young pussy on South Beach. Why leave money on the table?"

"He's right, Malcolm. The hip-hop crowd is taking over, they pay top dollar for private parties to keep their business on the low. Not to mention all these horny-ass married cougars...they will sign over their social security checks to get some of that young meat!"

"I'll consider it on a case-by-case basis," Malcolm rebutted, "but they've got to have at least three years of experience. I don't want to spend too much time breaking in newbies."

"Got it," Adam said. "Any other qualifications?"

"No, just the usual 3 B's!"

Adam and Malcolm slapped five.

"What the hell is that?" Jason asked, looking confused.

"Bilingual, bodybuilders, with big dicks!" Malcolm laughed. "Escorting is not about selling sex, but if the opportunity presents itself, they damn sure better be packing!"

CHAPTER 7

MAINTENANCE MAN II

Alex was sitting in her condo in Miami clicking her TV remote control back and forth from CNN, to FOX, to MSNBC. She was waiting impatiently for her fiancé, State Senator Gary Nelson, to make the announcement that he was running for the U.S. Senate. The news anchors on each network had announced several times that his press conference was being delayed. Finally, after a long commercial break, all the networks went live to the State Capital. Senator Nelson was wearing a dark blue suit and red tie. On his right lapel he wore an oversized American flag pin. Vincent, his head of security, was standing off to the right wearing dark sunglasses.

The room was filled with dozens of reporters pushing and shoving to get in close with their cameras and microphones. As Senator Nelson approached the podium, the room got quiet.

"Thank all of you for coming," Senator Nelson said. "Over the past few weeks there's been a lot of questions about whether or not I'm going to give up my seat as State Senator in Florida to run for the vacant U.S. Senate seat. Today I'm here to put an end to the speculation by announcing that I have accepted the Republican Party's endorsement to fill the Senate seat that was held by the recently deceased Democratic Senator Paul Rodriquez," he went on. "I'm looking forward to a spirited debate against my Democratic opponent, and may the best man win! Now, I'm sure you have a few questions, so let's start over here to my far right. Please state your name and your news organization."

"John Michaels with the BBC," a tall thin man stated. "If you win, you do realize that your vote could be the deciding factor in the passing or killing of a number of critical bills on environmental protection as well as health care reform?"

"Yes, I realize the implications of what my being elected could mean to getting work done on important legislation. Which is why I am announcing today that, if I am elected, I will work with the president on any ideas that will move this great country forward." Then he paused and looked straight into the camera. "As long as that doesn't mean raising taxes for the job creators or spending more of taxpayers' hard-earned money on programs that don't work."

"That just sounds like more of the same congressional grid-lock."

"Well, that will be something the president will have to explain to the voters, now isn't it?" Senator Nelson replied arrogantly. "Next question!"

"Frank Thomas with *The New York Times*," a short chubby

man wearing glasses announced. "It's estimated that the cost of running a U.S. Senatorial campaign could cost tens of millions of dollars. How do you expect to raise that much money?"

"Let's just say that I have enthusiastic donors who share my vision and they are willing to invest whatever it takes to make sure we get our country back!" He smiled as the room erupted with applause. "Okay, I only have time for one more question, then I've got to head back to Miami. As some of you may have heard, I'm getting married soon to a beautiful woman and we've got a lot of shopping to do and invitations to send out. Let's take one more question and we'll have to wrap this up."

He pointed at a young blonde female reporter. She took the handheld microphone that was being passed around and took a step toward the stage. She was standing directly in front of him when she spoke.

"My name is Carrie Simmons with OccupyWallStreet.org," she announced. "Isn't it true that you flew into Reagan Airport today on a private jet owned by the Kross brothers?"

His happy expression faded and his demeanor was less comfortable, but he kept smiling into the cameras.

"And what's your point?"

"My point, Senator Nelson, is that the Kross brothers own one of the largest pharmaceutical companies in the world and their coal mining corporation, Xetron, has one of the worst pollution records in the history of the industry."

"Look, young lady, I don't have time to listen to these unsubstantiated accusations," he said to her condescendingly. "The Kross brothers have donated over two-million dollars to cancer research, invested millions more into inner city after-school programs, and added over fifteen-thousand jobs into the economy this year. Now, those are facts, not fantasies!" he continued. "And when I am elected I will help my Republican colleagues create more real jobs and cut out the waste and government welfare. We need a leader with a plan, not a food stamp president!"

The conservative audience erupted with applause. "Nel-son, Nel-son, Nel-son!" they chanted while waving campaign signs.

"Thank you for coming and I'll see you on Election Day!" He stepped away from the podium and waved confidently into the cameras while rushing toward the nearest exit.

"Senator Nelson, are your corporate puppet-masters pulling your strings?" she yelled at him as Vincent ushered him out the side door. "You're a pathetic excuse for a politician!"

But no one could hear her. The hundreds of Tea Party supporters who had been bused in drowned out her comments. Alex sat back on the sofa stunned. For the first time, she began to question what she was getting herself into. Do I really know this man? she thought. She reached inside her purse that was sitting on the cocktail table in front of her and pulled out the flyer from Melvin's Jazz Club. There was a picture of Malcolm and Simon on the front of it. She leaned forward staring at it, reflecting back on the night before. She didn't want to admit it, but Malcolm was right, she belonged on stage. It was her passion, her gift, and her destiny. But how was she going to break the news to Gary? He was controlling and insecure. There was no way he was going to allow her to work, let alone be a nightclub singer.

She turned the television off and was headed toward the bedroom to get her cell phone to call Gary when there was a knock at the door.

"Who is it?" she yelled.

"I have a delivery for Miss Alex Garcia."

When she opened the door, she was greeted with a large wedding bouquet of red roses. There was a ribbon wrapped around that read: To my lovely fiancée!

"Sit them down on the table over there!" she directed him.

"Looks like someone's really trying to impress you!" he said. "By the way, congratulations on getting married."

"I'm not married—yet!" she blushed.

"Well, he's a lucky man whoever he is," he said while pulling out a pen. "Now, if you would just sign here I'll be on my way."

Alex scrolled down the page looking for a place to sign and noticed there was a discrepancy in the paperwork.

"It says here that there are two packages."

"I apologize, I got so caught up I almost forgot." He pulled a white envelope wrapped in a red bow from inside his jacket pocket, "This is for you."

"What is it?"

"I don't know, Ma'am, I'm just the messenger," he said while tearing away his copy of the form, then he headed for the door. "Have a nice day!"

Alex stood over the flowers and sniffed them while she anxiously cut at the corner with a letter opener. Once she saw what was inside of it, she slowly sat down to collect herself. It was a note from Gary and attached to it was a prenuptial agreement. The letter read:

These flowers are a token of my love and affection. I'm looking forward to us spending the rest of our lives together!

Love, Gary

P.S. Have your lawyer look over these papers and get them signed ASAP. I'll be back from Washington tomorrow night. Be dressed by five, we're going out to dinner to celebrate!

Alex set the letter down on the table and opened the pre-nuptial documents. She read all five pages and then signed them. "Flowers and a freakin' prenuptial," she said while shaking her head. "Malcolm was right, you are an asshole!"

CHAPTER 8

MAINTENANCE MAN II

Ariel was stocking the bar with liquor with the head bartender, Big Mike, when Malcolm walked into the club. He was wearing a karate uniform and carrying a garment bag over his shoulder.

"If it isn't Bruce Lee!" Ariel joked. "I didn't know it was Kung Fu Friday."

"Very funny. I have a six o'clock appointment and I didn't have time to change. And for your information, I study jujitsu, not kung fu."

"What's the difference? It's all about kicking and screaming." Ariel got into a karate stance. "Big Mike, hold up that empty Corona box. Watch this!" She lifted her right hand and swung as hard as she could. "Hi yah!" She split the cardboard in half.

Malcolm and Big Mike applauded.

"Not bad for a beginner." Malcolm laughed. "I'm going to start calling you Fist of Fury!"

"She's more like Five Fingernails of Death!" Big Mike laughed.

"Ok, smart aleck, can you do better?" Ariel had her hands on her hips.

"I don't want you to get hurt." Malcolm said to her. "Martial Arts is nothing to play around with."

"Come on, Malcolm, show us what you've got!" Big Mike said. He stepped from behind the bar and walked toward Malcolm. "I heard you Navy SEALs aren't all that tough!"

Malcolm looked down at his watch: it read 5:45.

"Ok, but let's make this lesson quick, I'm pressed for time."

Malcolm glanced around the room looking for something to work with. He saw a broken beer bottle in the trash can and pulled it out.

"Take this!" He handed it to Big Mike.

"Malcolm, I don't know about this, somebody could get hurt."

"You're right and it's gonna be your big ass!"

"Just so you know, I was a bouncer before I started bartending and I took boxing for ten years. I can take pretty good care of myself."

"If you took a class every day for the rest of your life you wouldn't last five minutes with someone from The Special Forces. Now shut up and try to cut me."

Big Mike and Malcolm were about the same height, but Mike was much bigger. His arms were the size of Ariel's legs and he was muscular, solid as a tree stump. Malcolm stood directly in front of him with his hands down by his side. When Mike wouldn't take a swing, Malcolm antagonized him.

"What you waiting on, Christmas?"

"Aren't you going to move, or duck, or something?"

"Let me worry about that, you worry about that fat gut of yours. You may be big but you're as slow as molasses!"

"I changed my mind, I don't want to do this!" Big Mike said, lowering the bottle.

But it was just a trick to take Malcolm by surprise. He swung with all of his might toward Malcolm's head. Malcolm grabbed him by the wrist and used Big Mike's momentum against him, tossing him over his shoulder and onto the floor. Once he was down, Malcolm twisted his wrist until he dropped the glass bottle.

"What the hell is going on?" Simon asked, rushing out from the back office.

"I'm just teaching twinkle toes here a little hand-to-hand combat." Malcolm said, still holding Big Mike by the wrist. Mike was trying to get up, but couldn't.

"Alright, let him up." Simon bent down to help Big Mike off the floor. "We're opening in an hour. I can't have a one-armed bartender."

"You know I went easy on you, right Malcolm?" Big Mike laughed while brushing himself off. "Next time, let's try wrestling."

"As big as you are it'll be more like Sumo wrestling." Malcolm laughed and patted Big Mike on the back.

"I can't believe I got my ass kicked by a piano player," Mike laughed as he limped back to the bar. "How in the hell did you go from music school to jumping out of planes and killing people, anyway."

"You can blame that on high unemployment and too many *Bourne Identity* movies," Malcolm chuckled. "I figured if I was going to serve, I might as well serve with the best."

"Speaking of serving, we're expecting another full house tonight," Simon said as they walked toward the office. "What do you have planned for tonight?"

"Let's just say it will be a night the ladies won't forget!"

"What's that supposed to mean?"

"Look, you handle the business and accounting and let me handle the entertainment. Deal?"

"Just don't have any donkeys and naked women on stage tonight. We don't have a license for that shit!" Simon laughed.

• • •

By 7:45 Melvin's Jazz Club had a standing-room-only crowd. While the four-piece band played classic jazz standards, the waitresses and bartenders were stuffing one hundred-dollar tips into their pockets trying to keep up with the orders.

"Two margaritas and a Grey Goose and cranberry," the waitress yelled at Big Mike!

"Got it!" he replied while pouring vodka with one hand and turning on the blender with the other.

"One Long Island Iced Tea and two shots of Patron," another waitress yelled from the other side of the bar.

"Silver or gold?"

"One silver, one gold," she replied, "and give me two limes and a salt shaker."

"Coming right up!"

The room was filled with wealthy men flashing their Bulgari and Rolex watches, each one checking out the other to see who could outspend the other and, most importantly, who had the most beautiful women at their table. Lavishly dressed women showed off their diamond necklaces, designer dresses, and Red Bottom shoes. Whether they were girlfriends, wives, or mistresses, they immersed themselves in their roles as kept women. Melvin's had a reputation for attracting the provocative, the affluent, and the eccentric. Nowhere else in Miami, or anywhere in the country, could you find such an eclectic mix of politicians, athletes, artists, moguls, and wannabes, all socializing under one roof. The atmosphere was electric!

A loud chatter subsided as the lights faded and the spotlight hit the stage. Malcolm stepped out from behind the curtain wearing a tan suit and a crisp white shirt. He sported a neatly folded handkerchief in his lapel pocket.

"Good evening, ladies and gentleman, and welcome to Melvin's. I'm your host, Malcolm Tremell. It's great to see so many familiar faces back with us. I hope to get reacquainted with you very soon." He smiled as he glanced around the room, looking into the eyes of some of his former clients. "For those of you who are new to Melvin's, enjoy the music, immerse yourself in all the beauty around you, drink up, and above all else, tip well. Enjoy the rest of your evening."

As he walked off the stage the band began to play a classic steppers song by Mike James called "Imagine This." The dance floor quickly filled with people bopping, hand dancing, two stepping, and swinging out.

"I'm surprised you're not out there," Simon said to Malcolm.

"Yeah, Mr. Smooth, show us what you got!" Ariel added.

"I'm not about to embarrass myself," Malcolm laughed, "besides, I have an important meeting in my office."

"With whom?" Simon asked.

"With them!" Malcolm said as he looked toward the club entrance.

At that moment, Adam and Jason walked into the club with five other gigolos following behind them. All tall, all tanned, all drop-dead gorgeous. They were dressed in dark suits and colorful ties. Two of them were twins. The club grew loud with chatter as they made their way down the center aisles.

"Who in the world is that?" Ariel asked while fixing her hair.

"That's step one of my master plan," Malcolm smirked. "Now, pick your tongue up off the floor and escort them back to the conference room."

"With pleasure," Ariel said while looking at her reflection in the bar mirror.

"Get going!" Malcolm said slapping her on the butt.

"Ok, ok, can't a girl get herself together first? Geesh!"

Simon watched the reaction of the women as the men made their way past the bar and down the hallway to the office.

"Oh my God!" one woman said aloud.

"Come to mama!" a drunken white woman shouted.

"Sweet Jesus!" a black woman sitting at the bar blurted out as she accidentally fell out of her seat!

Malcolm smiled as they paraded through the club. He looked over at Simon and put his hand on his shoulder.

"I told you to let me handle the entertainment, didn't I?" Malcolm pulled a cigar out of his jacket pocket and lit it.

"I've never seen mature women react like that before," Simon said, looking stunned. "It was like feeding time at the zoo!"

"Like I said, you're one of the best club owners in the business, but you don't know shit about women."

Malcolm laughed out loud as he made his way back to the offices. "Hold down the fort, partner!"

The conference room was quiet when Malcolm walked in. He took his time walking by each man, checking them out. He observed their shoes, suits, hair, and their cologne, calling out the fragrance by name, one by one, "Bulgari, Christian Dior, Serge Lutens Borneo, Clive Christian, and Kilian White Cristal." He paused at the last man, "Good choice!"

Before he sat down he peeked out of the window that overlooked the front of the club and the VIP parking lot. He deliberately reserved the parking spaces nearest to the club to observe the cars that each man was driving. From left to right there was a bright orange Lamborghini, two black Maseratis, a silver Audio R8, and a red 1969 Corvette Stingray.

Malcolm sat down at the head of the table and took a long drag off his cigar. "Please have a seat!" he said. "Let's make the introductions informal. I'm sure you all know who I am, as well as Jason and Adam since they invited you here. So let's find out who you are, starting from my left."

"Darius."

"Carlos."

"Juan."

"Ramon."

"And, I'm Blake."

"Well, gentleman, I know that you're all very busy so I won't waste time beating around the bush. In front of you are binders with contracts for exclusive rights to your escort services for one year, with a two-year option thereafter, and a detailed business plan on franchising the gigolo business worldwide! And here's the catch: we're going to do it one-hundred percent legit!"

"And how do you propose we do that?" Blake blurted. He was a light-skinned African-American man in his early thirties. He was about Malcolm's height, but much broader in the shoulders and chest. Everyone stared at him when he spoke out.

"If you shut up and let the man finish you might find out," Adam said to him. "Continue, Malcolm."

"As I was saying, the escort business is a multi-million-dollar industry but it's seen as a second-class street hustle. Why? Because it's associated almost exclusively with prostitution. I have created a formula whereby our clients can pay full rates and maintain their anonymity," Malcolm went on. "If we can standardize our rates, create protocol, and brand one name that everyone associates with the highest quality, we can own this industry!"

"But there are dozens, if not hundreds, of escort businesses all across the country, why would they choose us?" Carlos asked. He was a twenty-something Puerto Rican, and the youngest of the group.

"Because we'll offer them something they can't get anywhere else...diversity, class, a clean bill of health and, most importantly, privacy!" Malcolm said as he stood up from the table and pulled a screen down from the ceiling. "Hit the projector, Adam."

On the screen was a flow chart with dates at the bottom and other statistics along the right side.

"As you can see from this chart, the number of women earning six figures has doubled in the past ten years. In that same time period, the impotency rate for men also doubled."

"So, what's your point?" Blake asked in a sarcastic tone.

"My point is that successful women are not getting enough romance or sex. The more money they earn, the less likely they are to have a man or an orgasm. And these statistics will continue to rise," Malcolm continued. "Look at the number of female CEOs in the top Fortune five-hundred companies; it's tripled in the past ten years. Now, look at this graph of the percentage of men who are unemployed, incarcerated, in rehab, or have mental health issues. The ratio of single men to women is two to one. And in the Latino and African-American communities, it's ten to one. This is our time, it's the perfect storm...all we have to do is position ourselves to ride the wave. We can rake in millions!"

"And what's in it for you?" Blake asked abruptly.

Malcolm paused and took another pull off his cigar.

"Ownership of the brand...and thirty percent!"

"Thirty percent! That's a pretty large slice, isn't it Malcolm?" Carlos asked reluctantly. "I mean, what do we get for that kind of split?"

"First and foremost, protection. I have information on judges,

DAs, local and national politicians, and CEOs. And if I can't get to them, I'll put the pressure on someone close to them. Second is free legal representation, and stock options if we go public. Also, financial advice so you don't end up broke and on the streets, screening for clients so your dicks don't fall off, and the chance to be a part of something that's bigger than just fucking for money. When you've been in this business for as long as I have you learn that eighty percent of it has nothing to do with sex; it's about companionship, conversation, etiquette, and discretion."

"Get the fuck outta here!" Blake said as he stood up from the table. "I'm not giving up a third of my hard-earned money on this pipe dream!"

"That's your prerogative, there's the door!" Malcolm said, staring him dead in the eyes. "But before you go...let me ask you this, how much do you earn a year—on average? Fifty, sixty, maybe eighty-thousand dollars—if you're lucky."

"Man, I don't bank less than a hundred-k, and that's during a slow year." he said boastfully.

Adam and Jason laughed out loud.

Malcolm stood up from the table and walked toward him.

"Young blood, I earned that in a month, and that's during a slow year," he told him. "Stop thinking small and learn how to play this game at the highest level! You'll never last in this business leading with your dick!"

"Look, I don't need a seminar on how to be a gigolo. I'm a free agent and I'm going to stay that way!" he said to Malcolm while straightening out his suit. "Adam told me you were some kind of legend in this business...back in the day...but you're out of touch. Maybe you've been gone too long," he said, straightening out his tie. "It's a new day out here. Only the strong and sexy will survive."

"What's your name again, young buck?"

"The name is Blake."

Malcolm walked up to him and got in his face.

"Well, Blake, you may think the sun rises and sets on your smart ass but I've got news for you...the game never changes, only the players. I've seen your type come and go; you're just another young prick who rushes in and fucks every rotten apple lying on the ground. Whereas the professionals, like me, we take our time and pick from the top of the tree, where there are fewer worms and less competition from lazy dick swingers like you!"

"Are you finished?" Blake said smartly, putting on a pair of dark shades. "Because I've got a five-thousand-dollar date waiting."

"Man, get out of here before I throw your ass out!" Adam said to him.

"Thanks for the pep talk, Mr. Tremell," he said reaching for the doorknob. "By the way, nice place you got here!"

When the door closed behind him, everyone breathed a sigh of relief.

"What an asshole!" Jason said. "Who invited him anyway?"

"I did!" Malcolm said.

"What!?" Adam responded.

"That's right, I invited him. I heard about him through an old client of mine named Helen. She thought I could talk some sense into him. But he's a lost cause."

"He reminds me a lot of you in some ways, Malcolm," Adam said laughing.

"No, he's nothing like me. I always respected my elders and I never went out of my way to attract attention," Malcolm told them. "In a few seconds the engine is going to start on that bright orange Lambo."

A few seconds later, the ignition started on one of the cars that was parked in the VIP section. Adam leaped up from his chair and looked out the window.

"How did you know?"

"Because it's always the man with the biggest mouth who is the most insecure. That car is his way of screaming out for attention, and too much attention is dangerous in this business."

Malcolm took another long drag off his cigar and put it down in the ashtray.

"So, if there are no more interruptions, let's get back to business. We've got a lot to cover tonight!"

CHAPTER 9

MAINTENANCE MAN II

The sound of fists being smashed against flesh echoed through the abandoned warehouse in downtown Miami. Vincent, who was wearing a ski mask, stopped beating the Cuban man who was handcuffed to a chair. He sat down calmly in front of him and lit a cigarette.

"Have one?" he jokingly asked.

The man lifted his bloodied head and nodded—no.

"I don't blame you, these things will kill you!" he laughed.

He took a couple of long drags off the cigarette and then put it out on the man's forehead.

"Urrrgh!" he screamed out.

"That's for trying to register those fucking niggers and boat rowers to vote!"

Suddenly, the phone rang. Vincent looked down at the number; it was Senator Nelson.

"You mind if I take this?" he asked sarcastically.

He pressed the answer button and walked into an adjoining room, closed the door, and peeled off his mask.

"Yes, sir!"

"How's it going?"

"Everything is going like clockwork. Mr. Gomez and I were just discussing illegal immigration and conservative values."

"Well, I'm sure you'll make him see the light!" he laughed. "When you get done there's some business we need to handle over in Miami Gardens."

"What's the problem?"

"Some black preacher is getting his flock all fired up about voter suppression and civil rights."

"You want me to eliminate him or just scare him?"

"We don't need any martyrs this close to election. Just send him a message—are we clear?"

"Crystal, sir."

"There's only a month before the special election. We've got to turn this blue district red in a hurry. The only way we can lose is if the Black and Latino areas have a high voter turnout. Now that we have a law requiring voters to show a state ID, that should reduce the votes by fifteen or twenty percent. And I've got friends who can knock a few thousand democrats out of the database but that will not be enough if these voter registration drives continue to grow. My career, and yours, depends on a victory! The U.S. Senate today, the Presidency tomorrow!"

"Don't worry about it, Senator, I've got it all under control," Vincent said while pulling his nine-millimeter pistol out of the holster.

"And don't forget, we have a meeting with the Kross brothers in D.C. next week so let's make sure our poll numbers look good. In other words, get rid of all the troublemakers, starting with this goddamned preacher!"

"I'll be done here shortly and I'll be on my way."

"Do me a favor since you're coming back north, stop by Tom Jenkin's and pick up an order of barbecue."

"You want cole slaw with that?"

"No, just make sure you get plenty of hot sauce!"

"Hot sauce it is, sir!" he replied then hung up.

Vincent walked back into the empty warehouse with his gun by his side and the trigger cocked. When the Cuban man saw he wasn't wearing his mask he panicked, pulling and jerking on the handcuffs as hard as he could, trying to break loose of the metal chair.

"Looks like play time is over!" Vincent said without emotion while staring at his watch. "Tick Tock, Tick Tock!"

"No, please no!" he screamed. "I have a wife and kids!"

"You should've thought about that when I warned you the first time," Vincent said pointing the gun at his head. "You people just don't get it, do you? Democracy is an illusion; those who have the money have the power!" Then he pulled the trigger.

CHAPTER 10

MAINTENANCE MAN II

Malcolm was abruptly awakened by the loud noise of the garbage truck emptying the dumpsters behind the club. He had fallen asleep on the conference room table and was still wearing his suit from the night before. "What the—!" he said while shielding his eyes from the sunlight that was blaring through the blinds. The door was cracked open; he could hear footsteps coming down the hallway.

"I see you finally woke up," Simon said, barging into the room. He was holding a bran muffin and a cup of Starbucks coffee. "Here, drink this!"

"Man, what time is it?"

"Ten o'clock!"

"Where's everybody?"

"They left right after the club closed about four this morning. You were still banging away at your computer until a little after five, then you passed out. Great job on the logo by the way!" Simon pointed at the image that was being projected onto the screen. "It's simple, elegant, and intriguing—I like it!"

The background was completely black. The graphics were of two large platinum M's in bold lettering, in 3D. Below in italic letters were the words *Maintenance Men International*.

"Thanks. I think it will send off the right energy."

"There you go again with that Yin and Yang stuff."

"Whether you want to believe it or not, the universal laws apply to everything. Some people call it God, Buddha, Jehovah, or Allah, or just science. The bottom line is everything gives off a certain energy, and it attracts things to us."

"Right now, the only thing I'm trying to attract is this muffin into my mouth," Simon joked. "You want some?"

Malcolm looked at him and shook his head. "You're hopeless." Malcolm headed for the door. "I'll catch up with you later."

"Aren't you forgetting something?" Simon was holding the four binders that Malcolm used at the presentation.

"Is that what I think it is?"

"Yep, they all signed on the dotted line. Four out of five ain't bad!"

"Four out of five is all I need!" Malcolm put the folders underneath his arm. "I've got my logo, my crew, and a plan!"

"Just remember, Malcolm, no plan is foolproof. You're still breaking the law. If you slip up, you and the rest of those pretty boys will end up in jail, and I don't need to tell you how much they like pretty boys behind bars."

"I think Denzel said it best in the movie *Training Day*. This isn't checkers—it's chess. And I'm the best chess player in the business. There's a reason why I haven't spent a single night in jail after twenty-plus years in the game—I don't get greedy and I don't take unnecessary risks!" He turned and headed for the door. "Melvin always taught me never lay down with a woman who doesn't have more to lose than you do! I'm never going to jail. Don't even joke about it!" Then he walked out. "Catch you later, I need to get some rest!"

"It's not you I'm worried about," Simon yelled at him. "It's those horny rich women you're fooling around with! Sooner or later the odds will catch up with you. Women always bring drama; trust me, I know!"

Malcolm blew him off and kept walking.

As soon as he was inside his car, he let down the convertible top and tuned into Hot 105.1 on his radio. Just as he was about to pull off, his phone rang. The prefix read 305, the area code for Miami. He didn't recognize the number, but he picked up.

"Hello?"

"Malcolm, it's me, Alex."

"Alex? What a surprise!"

"I only have a minute, I just wanted to let you know you were right. I shouldn't have to give up my dream to get married! Tell Simon not to be surprised if I take him up on that offer."

"Now, that's what I want to hear! What brought you to your senses?"

"Let's just say I got a wake-up call, or more to the point, a wake-up delivery," she said reflecting on the flowers and pre-nuptial she received the day before.

"That's my girl! Why don't we get together and celebrate your regaining your sanity! I'm just leaving the club, you wanna grab a bite?"

"I don't think that's such a good idea."

"Why not?"

"I think Gary has someone following me. Ever since he announced he was running for U.S. Senator, he's been more para-noid than usual. I don't even trust the cell phone he gave me. I'm calling you from my girlfriend Marcia's iPhone. She lets me use it when I need privacy."

"Why doesn't that surprise me?" Malcolm replied sar-castically. "You better check your panties, too, while you're at it—he probably put a LoJack on them."

"Now, that's funny," Alex burst out laughing.

Her laughter quickly turned to silence. They both knew she was back in another bad relationship where she couldn't be herself and where she was being controlled. After a brief pause, Malcolm spoke up.

"Alex, I know you don't want to hear this, but—"

"Don't even say it, Malcolm," she cut him off. "I know it's pathetic! I'm pathetic! It's the same story over and over again. I know, ok? I know, I know!"

"Tell me where you are, I'm coming to get you! We need to talk. There's something I need to get off my chest!"

"I would, but—"

Alex stopped mid-sentence. She looked around to see if she was being watched. There was a man with a pair of binoculars across from her in the Bayside Mall looking in her direction, but he seemed harmless. The bay was directly behind her where the cruise ships docked and other people were taking pictures. Another bald man was sitting alone in the food court reading a newspaper. He paused occasionally to look her way, but she dismissed him as just another casual admirer.

"But what?" Malcolm said to her. "Alex, are you there?"

"Ok, we can meet. I'm at the Bayside Mall. But I don't want to take any chances. Meet me in the back of Marcia's Hair and Beauty Salon. She's the friend whose phone I'm using; she can let me out the back door. Just give me a couple of minutes so she can touch me up."

"Women!" Malcolm said. "I bet if you took a picture of yourself with that phone and texted it to me, you won't look any different after you get your hair done than you do before!"

"You know I'm technologically challenged. I tried to send an audio file attached to text and I accidentally emailed my mother a naked picture of myself," she laughed.

"Can I get a copy?"

"You're a mess. I'll see you in five minutes!"

Malcolm hit the clutch on his Ferrari and burned rubber out of the parking lot and sped off down Biscayne. The Bayside Mall was five blocks away. He knew Alex wanted to see him; she made it too convenient. She just needed him to insist. Maybe this would be the time he would tell her how sorry he was for not protecting her, he thought as he dodged through traffic. And maybe he'd tell her he always wanted to be with her. Not as friends, but as lovers.

As soon as Malcolm pulled up to the back door of Marcia's Hair Salon, the door sprung open and Alex dashed out wearing a short wig and dark round sunglasses. She leaped into the car and they sped off down the narrow corridor.

"So, where are we going?"

"Don't worry about that, you're in my hands now," Malcolm said confidently. "Just sit back and enjoy the ride!"

They merged onto the I-95 and headed south towards the Florida Keys. Malcolm had contacts there. People he knew he could trust to keep their mouths shut.

"This is going to be a long drive," Malcolm said. "What time do you have to be back home?"

"I am home," she said, reaching out to hold his hand. "Wherever we're going, I don't want to go back to that condo—that damned prison. Not tonight!"

"And what about Gary?"

"He's out of town raising money and counting votes. I won't be hearing from him until he needs me for another photo op!" she continued. "You see, Malcolm, I'm not as blind as you think I am. I know he's using me to look respectable and to influence the Latino vote. I even know about the other women. I've found makeup, condoms, and women's lingerie tucked away in his dresser drawers, but guess what? Two can play at that game!"

she went on. "I tried to love him but it's just about business for him—so I made it business, too. Now that I'm financially stable, I want to start living my dream! When you brought me on stage the other night, I realized that I had the courage to finally do it!"

"So are you going through with the wedding?"

"Why not, he's taking care of me and I'm making him look good; it's an arrangement that works for both of us. But once he's elected, I'm going to pursue my singing career—and start living my life on my terms."

"What's that supposed to mean?"

"It's means I want to live my life the way you do, Malcolm, no labels, no expectations, and no boundaries!" She pulled off her wig and threw it into the air. "Now shut up and step on the gas. I wanna have some fun!"

"In that case, strap on your seatbelt and hold on tight!" Malcolm hit the clutch on the Ferrari and it took off like a rocket. "This date is long overdue!"

CHAPTER 11

MAINTENANCE MAN II

Malcolm woke up the next morning just before sunrise. He could see Alex through the window lying on the balcony naked, smoking a joint. He grabbed his cell phone and poured a tall glass of wine and stepped out onto the balcony naked and joined her.

"I see you found my stash."

"It wasn't hard to find. You still keep it in the same place you did when we were at the music academy together," she replied while passing the joint to him.

"Old habits die hard!"

"Ain't that the truth!"

Alex took a long sip of wine and laid her head down in Malcolm's lap. They took turns taking pulls off the joint until it was gone, then Malcolm thumped it over the balcony into the sand twenty stories below.

"This is what I missed most," he said while stroking her hair, "waking up to nothing but the sound of the ocean!"

"You know what I miss?"

"What's that?"

"I miss waking up happy," she said to him. "Ever since Derrick raped me in college, I've been searching for love in all the wrong places. I was always attracted to powerful men because I thought they would protect me, but instead they ended up trying to control me. And I put up with it all these years because I was afraid they would either hurt me or leave me, but I'm not afraid anymore" she went on. "I envy you, Malcolm. You've always had the courage to do what you wanted to do. Me, I've spent my entire life trying to fit into other people's boxes."

"It doesn't work, does it?" Malcolm replied. He was thinking back on his relationship with Toni.

"No, it doesn't," she laughed sarcastically and then took another sip of wine. "It's taken me all these years to finally figure it out; we should fall in love with our friends and just date the men we think we love. That way you don't waste time and no one gets hurt!"

Alex sat up and turned toward Malcolm. They were face to face. She set the wine glass down and kissed him.

"What was that for?"

"That was for all the years of being my knight in shining armor, for forcing me to come on stage and, most of all, for last night," she said. "Thanks for making me feel beautiful and desired. Whatever you're charging for your services, it's worth every dime!"

"Is that an endorsement?" he smiled.

"No, silly, it's a compliment." She took his hand and placed it on her breast. "How much would tonight have cost me if I were a customer?"

"Trust me, you couldn't afford me, especially not on your

fiancé's salary," Malcolm laughed.

"Gary has a ton of money and it's definitely not coming from his government salary as a state senator. He drives a Bentley and a Porsche. I used to ask him where all the money was coming from, but after listening to all the ridiculous explanations I just stopped asking and went along for the ride!"

"He's dirty just like the rest of them. There's so much money being passed under the table it's ridiculous. Some of them have the balls to pay for strip clubs and prostitution services on their government credit cards."

"Are you serious?"

"I have the receipts, photos, and videos to prove it!"

"Ooh, can I see?" she said jumping up and down like a little kid. "Please, Malcolm, please!"

"Hell no, woman, are you crazy?" Malcolm laughed while trying to hold her down. "I am a professional. What happens with a Maintenance Man, stays with a Maintenance Man."

"Is that your motto?"

"No, I just made it up, but come to think of it, it would look good on a bumper sticker."

"Do you have any video of Gary?"

"No, but there have been rumors." Malcolm said. "All of these rich perverts have secrets and if any of them try to strong-arm me or my crew, I'll put on a show they'll never forget! All it takes is one click of a button and photos and videos of three-somes, bondage, and boy-on-boy sex will be all over the Internet!" he went on. "I've been in this game a long time. I know all their dirty little secrets."

"You make it sound so exciting!" Alex said while sitting on Malcolm's lap. "Can I be your assistant? It would be just like our music academy days. Remember how I used to set you up with my rich girlfriends back in school?"

"Ok, I think you've had enough to drink." Malcolm took the glass out of her hand. "This wine is starting to go to your head."

"Come on, Malcolm! I'm bored to death! I know dozens of wives at the country club and they are just as lonely and horny as I am—and their husbands are loaded!"

Malcolm knew he needed new clients. His new crew was going to expect to start making money right away. Alex was just what he needed, someone with affluent contacts, someone who knew the drill, and someone he could trust.

"Okay, I'll let you help under one condition."

"And what's that?"

"Never use my name, never use the word sex and money in the same sentence, and never give them a phone number," Malcolm said with his finger in her face. "Just tell them about the escort service and I'll take it from there."

"Yes, sir," Alex said, guiding his finger into her mouth. "Looks like Bonnie and Clyde ride again!"

"Speaking of riding, your break time is over."

Malcolm lifted her up and carried her back into the hotel room, then laid her down gently on the bed.

"There is one more condition I didn't mention!" he said while spreading her legs and then slowly licking her between her thighs.

"And what's that?"

"I want dinner...and dessert at least once a week."

She held him by the head and guided him down to her clit.

"Well, bon appetite!" she moaned and threw her head back. "Ahhhh!"

CHAPTER 12

One by one, the four black sedans with tinted windows drove into the underground garage of The Kross Brothers headquarters in Washington, D.C. Each driver stopped at the security gate to show his I.D. and then was directed to VIP parking at the back of the lot. Each car carried a passenger with great influence in industry and politics. As they emerged from their cars, their identities were revealed to each other for the first time.

In attendance were Bill Henry, President of the meat and dairy association; Mitch Sanders, the Senate majority leader; Robert Franklin, head lobbyist for the oil and gas industry; and Senator Nelson. He intentionally waited for the others to step out of their cars first; he was trying to make a statement. He was the missing piece of the puzzle and he wanted to make sure they all knew it. His head of security, Vincent, was doubling as his chauffeur.

"Well, this is it!" Senator Nelson said to Vincent. "There's no turning back now."

"Having second thoughts, sir?"

"Of course not!" he said, admiring himself in the rear view mirror and brushing back his hair. "I've always wanted to play in the big leagues, so let's go play ball!"

Vincent stepped out of the car and opened his door.

"Good evening, gentlemen," a husky man with piercing eyes said to them after they exited their vehicles. He was wearing a black suit and packing a nine-millimeter under his jacket. "Right this way."

He and another burly man patted them down, then directed them to step inside a private elevator. It was an express to the penthouse, no stops in between. During the ride to the fiftieth floor, no one said a word. Once the elevator stopped, they filed out and turned down a long corridor that led into a large conference room. The Kross brothers were sitting at opposite ends of the long black table smoking cigars.

"Welcome, gentleman!" They both rose from their seats. "Thanks for coming on such short notice. Please have a seat!" Allan Kross said to them.

"Would any of you like a cigar or a glass of cognac?" Randall Kross asked.

They all declined.

"Alright then, let's cut to the chase." Allan Kross stood up and began pacing around the table. "Everyone here stands to gain if we can win the next Presidential election. Our friends already control the House of Representatives and a victory by Mr. Nelson here will give us control of the Senate as well. According to the most recent polling, he's ahead by ten percent," he went on. "The minute he gets elected, I want to start putting pressure on the White House to start passing legislation that will allow us to get back to business as usual." Then he turned to a picture of the African-American president that was hanging on the wall. "This boy is causing too many problems! He's got to go!"

"May I make a suggestion?" Senator Nelson asked.

"By all means."

"All people care about are jobs. If we can make them believe that everything the president is doing is losing jobs, they will run him out of town next November. For example, when he starts talking about regulations on the food and oil industry, have our experts show statistics of how that will cost jobs."

"But there's no data to support that in the meat and dairy industry," Bill Henry said. "The only real cost is to top management and stock holders."

"Then create the data, dammit! Since when did the truth ever get in our way?" Senator Nelson shouted. "If you tell people a story long enough, they will believe it! Besides, it's not about the truth, it's about fear, and that's easy to sell when you can attach a black face to it!"

"He's got a point," Senator Sanders said. "We won a historic number of seats during the last election by putting doubt in people's mind that the president wasn't one of us. It would be easy to convince them that he's all for social programs but not for business."

"I agree with Senator Nelson," Robert Franklin argued. "I say we use our media contacts and those morons we're funding in the Tea Party and start a campaign to show job losses because of too much regulation. I'm sure my friends in the oil and gas industry will be willing to lay off a few thousand workers to make our point. And if we fire them right before Christmas, that will put more pressure on them to see things our way."

"All I know is something has to be done now!" Randall Kross added. "Ever since the White House announced this HP 205 legislation, our stock has been falling like a rock! We lost five-million dollars in revenue during the last quarter. The last thing we need is people getting free health care, more access to fitness centers, and cheap organic foods. The money is in the medicine, not making people well."

"I think we're all on the same page, gentleman!" Allan Kross said. "But first things first. Let's get Mr. Nelson elected in thirty days and get our filibuster-proof majority in the Senate and then let's start shaking things up! This time next year, I want that coon to be packing his bags!"

ACT II

MAINTENANCE MEN INTERNATIONAL

CHAPTER 13

Two weeks had passed since Malcolm agreed to allow Alex to work as his agent, and it was paying off—big time! Wealthy women from Miami Beach to Boca Raton were calling faster than he could fill the appointments. Some were booking for escorts, some for sex, and others for both. Each client was given a password and a user login to access the Maintenance Men International website to make their appointments anonymously. All the escorts had photo albums attached to their profiles and a month-to-month calendar showing their availability.

It was mid-October and every gigolo was booked solid through New Year's Eve. Malcolm and Adam had the most experience, so they handled the VIP clients, such as judges' and politicians' wives. Jason and the four new gigolos had their hands full with local celebrities, TV newscasters, rich businesswomen, and the wives of professional football and basketball players. By the end of the month, Maintenance Men International was making more money than Malcolm expected. To celebrate, he rented an eighty-foot yacht and invited his crew out to divvy up the money.

One by one they drove into the marina parking lot and valeted their exotic cars. They were all wearing white linen and carrying small backpacks flung over their shoulders as they were instructed to do. Each man was a different shape, size, color, and ethnicity. Adam was a blond-haired, blue-eyed white gentleman from California. He had a very distinguished look, but he still had the typical California surfer vibe. He retired from Wall Street after the crash and had been in the business ever since. Jason was an Italian from New Jersey. He was the shortest of the bunch, but he made up for it in confidence and his penis size. His clients nicknamed him Jason "The Situation" after the character on "Jersey Shore."

Darius was an African American from Atlanta and the intellectual in the group. An MIT graduate and part-time model, he was reluctant to get into the business initially, but he did what he had to do to feed his two children. Carlos was the youngest. Born in Puerto Rico, he was introduced to the lifestyle by his older sisters, who were both prostitutes. After his first big payday, he was hooked. The twins, Juan and Ramon, were both second-generation Cubans who were born in Miami. The gigolo business came natural to them; they loved women, worshipped money, and couldn't get enough sex. They specialized in the kinky side of the gigolo business, S&M, threesomes, and bondage—if the price was right. As they all approached the ship, Malcolm stepped out onto the dock to greet them.

"Permission to come aboard, captain," Adam joked to Malcolm.

"Permission granted," Malcolm replied. "Glad to see you boys brought a change of clothes. This is gonna be a celebration you won't forget!"

"Bring it on!" Carlos said, slapping him five as he came aboard.

"This yacht is hot! But where are the naked women at?" Jason asked. "These guys are sexy and all, but I don't want to look at their hard legs all day."

"Just come aboard." Malcolm popped him on the back of the head. "Pour yourself a glass of champagne and leave the entertainment to me!"

"So, Malcolm, where are we headed?" Darius asked while pulling a bottle of Coppertone out of his bag. "Wherever it is, I hope there's plenty of shade. Black people do get sunburn, you know."

"I thought this was going to be a relaxing cruise," Malcolm shouted to them, "but it's turning into comedy night at the Apollo."

Once all six men were aboard, Malcolm signaled the crew to untie the yacht from the dock. "Alright, Captain, let's shove off!"

The captain set course and carefully guided the large ship out of the marina. The weather was a perfect 80 degrees and sunny. The ocean waves were calm as the yacht cut through the royal blue waters. They came close to another yacht with a group of young women who were drinking and sunbathing nude on the deck. When Malcolm's yacht cruised by them, they flashed their breasts.

"Come to Papi!" Carlos yelled while holding his crotch.

"Bring it on fucker!" one of the ladies who appeared to be the most drunk yelled back. "I'll suck your dick till it falls off."

"Never mind!" Carlos yelled back. "I need my dick to stay on!"

They all laughed as the yacht picked up speed and headed out to sea. Once they were out of sight of the Miami skyline, Malcolm passed out Cuban cigars and directed the crew to bring out the bucket of champagne and seven glasses. After their glasses were filled, he moved to the center of the circle and raised his glass.

"I want to propose a toast…to the hardest-working Maintenance Men in the country. The city of Miami is on lock down! We own it! Next, we're taking the world by storm!"

"Here, here!" They all touched glasses and drank.

"Now, let's get down to business."

Malcolm reached inside his jacket pocket and pulled out six white envelopes and handed one to each of them.

"This is your reward for sticking to the plan, putting in the hard work and, most importantly, doing it with class!" Malcolm pulled out a cigar and lit it. "It's not crowded at the top, gentleman, it's crowded at the bottom. If we keep our standards high and our mouths shut, there's a fortune out there just waiting for us!"

"Goddamn!" Carlos shouted. "Twenty-thousand dollars!"

"That's chump change," Juan cut in, "read it and weep!"

"Thirty-two-thousand!" Carlos said, looking at Juan's check. "I need to put in more hours. I'll be damned if I'm going to let the Cuban outdo me."

"You can make the big bucks too if you let these freaky bitches tie you up and spank you!" Ramon added.

"They pay a lot more if you let them pee on you," his twin brother, Juan, added.

"Fuck that! Ain't nobody paddling my big black ass," Darius replied. "That's some freaky white boy shit! And I wish a bitch would try to pee on me!"

"Ok, soul brother," Juan said, "but it pays an extra grand an hour!"

Darius looked at Juan's check again.

"An extra grand, huh?" he put his hand on his chin. "So, how big is the paddle and just how much pee are we talking about, exactly?"

They all burst out laughing.

"How much did you make, Adam?" Jason asked.

"I'm a professional, I don't discuss my money like you youngsters."

"Ok, now that we got that out of the way!" Malcolm said as he walked into the cabin. When he came back out he was holding a small black box. When he opened it up, there were six keys, all labeled with each gigolo's name.

"What's that?" Jason asked.

"It's tonight's entertainment, smart ass. Now shut up and grab a key!" Malcolm told them. "Captain, how soon before we dock back in Miami?"

"About two hours, Mr. Tremell!" the captain yelled down to him.

"Well, you heard the man! You've got two hours to drink, smoke, screw, or pull out a reel and go fucking fishing, it's up to you. But there are twelve gorgeous and very skilled ladies downstairs waiting to do whatever your kinky imagination can come up with."

"Twelve, but there's only six of us," Jason said.

"That's two each, el idiota!" Carlos replied.

"You don't have to tell me twice." Darius snatched his key and took off below deck. "Lata!"

The rest of them scrambled to get their key and quickly disappeared into the cabins below, all except Adam. He followed Malcolm to the front of the yacht and stood beside him looking at the ocean and towards the horizon. Malcolm put his cigar in his mouth and was about to light it, but Adam quickly pulled out his lighter and beat him to it.

"Thanks, partner," Malcolm said to him. "We've been in this game a long time together, haven't we?"

"Yeah, maybe too long!"

"You wanna know what I've learned in all those years?"

"What's that?" Adam asked.

"You have to start planning your next move the day you start in this game. If you don't, you'll be trapped."

"So, what's your next move, then?"

"I'm headed to Paris tomorrow. I have a date with an old friend who can put me in touch with some good contacts in Europe. I want to put myself in a position where I don't have to go out on another fancy dinner date or see another piece of ass unless it's by choice—not out of necessity. The wise man is the one who figures out a way to get paid without being on someone else's schedule," he continued. "No matter how you look at it, being a gigolo is still a job. I don't know about you, but I didn't work this hard and for this long to be somebody's employee, not even to these rich assholes who throw money at us like we're trained monkeys in a zoo!"

Adam chuckled.

"What's so funny?" Malcolm asked.

"It's refreshing to hear someone in this business that actually gets it!" Adam put his hand on Malcolm's shoulder. "Did you know I have three degrees?"

"No, I didn't!"

"Yeah, two masters and a PhD," he paused. "And even with all those degrees, I earn more money drinking, eating, dancing, and screwing rich old hags than I could working on Wall Street or teaching at the best universities in the country. Is this world screwed up or what?"

Malcolm thumped the ashes from his cigar over side of the boat and then turned toward Adam and looked him dead in his eyes.

"Don't get it twisted, partner, we don't get paid for sex, we get paid so these rich hypocrites can hide," Malcolm said to him. "If you're worth millions you'll gladly pay a few thousand dollars to keep your secrets safe. But if you're worth billions, the sky's the limit! It's all a game, Adam, and I'm going to master it and play better than anyone else!"

CHAPTER 14

MAINTENANCE MAN II

Malcolm's Air France flight landed at the Roissy-Charles de Gaulle Airport in Paris at 1:15 in the afternoon. He slept comfortably in first class for most of the ten-hour flight, and was rested and ready to go. His meeting with Helen was at 2:30 and he needed to freshen up first. As he stepped off the plane, he could feel the nip in the air. The temperature was in the mid-50s and the skies were sunny. He walked at a quick pace toward baggage claim, anxious to retrieve his cashmere coat from his luggage. As he was coming down the escalator, he spotted a short, thin man holding a sign with his name on it.

"Bonjour!" Malcolm said to him. "Je suis Mister Tremell!"

"Bonjour, Monsieur Tremell. I am your driver, Alfonso," he replied. "I see you speak French."

"Il contribue à parler la langue."

"Yes, and it also helps to speak English!"

"Je suis, d'accord," Malcolm told him. "Yes, it does!"

"Madam Daniels is waiting for you at the Ritz Paris Hotel. As soon as we retrieve your bags we'll be on our way!"

"Merci."

Once the bags arrived, Malcolm pulled out his long coat and they headed out into the brisk Paris air. The driver loaded his luggage into an E Class Mercedes and they easily maneuvered through the light traffic.

"I haven't been to Paris in the fall in quite some time," Malcolm said.

"If you ask me, this is the best time of the year to come. No crazy tourists blocking traffic, you can get into the best restaurants with no wait, and the trees are filled with fiery orange and yellow leaves. There's no place like Paris!"

"You're right about that, Alfonso," Malcolm said, looking around at the historic statues and the Eiffel Tower in the distance. "It truly is the City of Love!"

The limo made it to within two blocks of the hotel and then came to an abrupt stop. The traffic was backed up and going nowhere.

"What's going on, Alfonso? I thought this was the slow season."

"It is off season for tourists, but not for the politicians!" he said. "The French President is entertaining the U.S. Secretary of State tonight at a formal dinner here at the Ritz. I thought you were here to attend."

"It looks like I am," he said as he took a deep breath. "So

much for advance notice."

After the Secret Service detail moved away from the front of the hotel, Alfonso drove up to the entrance and opened Malcolm's door.

"Enjoy your stay, Monsieur Tremell. Tell Madam Daniels I appreciate the business. Au revoir!"

The valet carried Malcolm's bag into the lobby and stopped short of the front desk. Two large men in black suits approached him and flashed their French Intelligence badges.

"Nous devons examiner l'intérieur vos sacs," one of the men said.

"No problem, go ahead and look inside my bag, there's nothing there but clothes and a shaving kit."

"You are American?"

"C'est exact!"

Suddenly another man stepped in. He was a tall black man, medium build, with a bald head and no facial hair. As soon as he walked up, the other two agents backed away.

"We'll take it from here," he said to them. "Sorry for the inconvenience, Mr.— "

"Tremell, Malcolm Tremell."

Malcolm extended his hand and they shook.

"As you know, we have a number of VIPs in the building and we have to take every precaution. I'm sure you understand. I'm Agent Harris with the U.S. Secret Service." He flashed his badge. "Do you mind if we run your bag through the scanners?"

"Be my guest."

He handed the bag over to another agent, who rolled it over to a holding area. In the meantime, they made small talk. Malcolm knew that was just another opportunity to be interrogated.

"You mind if I take a look at your passport?"

"Here you go."

"So, Mr. Tremell, what brings you to Paris?" the agent said while looking at Malcolm's passport with a concerned expression.

"I'm here on business."

"What kind of business, if you don't mind my asking?"

"I'm in the entertainment business."

"Can you be more specific?"

"I'm—"

Before he could finish his sentence, Helen spotted him and rushed over, talking loudly, and making a scene.

"Malcolm, darling! I've been looking all over for you!"

"Ma'am, do you know this man?" Agent Harris asked her.

"Of course, I know this man, why else would I rush over here and put my arms around him?" she said snobbishly. "And don't call me ma'am, young man, I am a youthful forty-five."

Malcolm tried not to laugh; he knew she was pushing sixty, but Helen looked good for her age. A recent breast lift and en-largement, coupled with a personal trainer and a vegan diet, made it easy for her to pass for her late-forties.

"Alright, after you get your bags, you can go." He handed Malcolm his passport back. "Enjoy your stay, Mr. Tremell."

After Malcolm retrieved his luggage, Helen escorted him upstairs to her suite on the twenty-fifth floor. It had a huge bal-cony that overlooked the park and the Eiffel Tower. Once Helen tipped the bellman, she wasted no time in trying to get him into bed.

"Oh, how I missed you, Malcolm. Come to mama!" she said, tugging at the buttons on his shirt.

"Helen, we need to talk."

"Well, go ahead and talk," she said while dropping down to her knees and unzipping his pants. "I'll be down here saying hello to my little friend!"

"Helen, slow down for just a second!" He grabbed her by

her shoulders and lifted her up. "We have to talk; there's some information I need to get from you."

"Damn you, Malcolm! I didn't fly you halfway around the world to talk. I want to have sex, intercourse—fuck!" she pouted and then poured a glass of wine. It nearly overflowed. "I've been watching porno and masturbating for two straight days! If I don't get some sex soon I'm gonna explode!"

"I just need your contacts at the top escort services in the states, Europe, and Asia, if you have them."

"What makes you think I use escort services in those places?" she asked with a guilty expression on her face.

"Look, you old cougar. I've been out of the business for almost two years and I know you're not going without!"

Helen drank the entire glass of wine and stepped out onto the balcony. Malcolm followed her out and continued to press her.

"And don't tell me you met that gigolo Blake you recommended to me in Miami at a church function. You've got an insatiable appetite and the money to satisfy it!"

"Blake was a one-time thing. I thought you could teach him the ropes," she said looking out onto the city. "And who are you calling a cougar? I'm just a sexual, confident woman in her prime!"

"Whatever you say, Helen. Now, will you help me out?"

"What's in it for me?"

Malcolm started unbuckling his pants and taking off his shirt. Once he was completely naked, he lifted up her dress and went down on her.

"That's not fair!" she moaned.

"Is that a yes?"

"You know I can't say no when you eat me like that!"

Malcolm abruptly stopped and guided her by the hand back into the room.

"Why did you stop?"

"I'm not stopping, I'm changing locations. I've been on a plane for ten hours, I need a shower."

He went into the bathroom and turned on the water.

"So how much time do we have before the banquet tonight?" Malcolm asked while peeling off her clothes.

"It's not until six o'clock. And you're going to need every minute of it to satisfy me. Now get your fine ass in the shower. I plan on getting my money's worth!"

CHAPTER 15

As the sun set on Paris, the piercing sound of police sirens broke the silence of the night. A small army of French soldiers and Secret Service agents began putting up barricades around the Ritz Paris Hotel in preparation of the formal banquet that was about to take place. A parade of food and beverage trucks lined up to make their deliveries at the back of the hotel. Paris policemen stopped each one at a checkpoint to inspect the cargo, then flagged them through to the dock near the kitchen. Malcolm was on the floor doing inclined push ups when he heard the commotion outside. He put on his robe and stepped out onto the balcony.

The procession of limousines and luxury cars was more than two blocks long. The service entrance was just as packed with caterers and other deliveries. He watched as the police at the checkpoint processed one truck after the other; it reminded him of his tour in Afghanistan when his SEAL team had to protect the Army barracks from terrorist attacks. We never let one bomb through, we never lost one man, he thought. It wasn't long before the chilly 48-degree Paris air snapped him back to reality, but just as he was about to go back inside, he noticed how casual one officer was with his inspection. While one officer, who was tall and burly, checked the papers of the drivers, the other officer was supposed to check the contents of the truck. But instead, he pointed his flashlight at the boxes, pulled the door shut and gave them the all clear. He did the same thing with the next truck.

"That's some shitty police work!"

"What did you say, darling?"

Malcolm rushed back inside the room and pulled a pair of small binoculars out of his luggage.

"Helen, my driver told me the U.S. Secretary of State and the French President are attending this event tonight."

"That's right, along with the Israeli ambassador and a dozen other dignitaries," Helen said while powdering her face. "That's why I needed my best man here tonight. I hope you're brushing up on your foreign affairs."

Malcolm went back out onto the balcony and zoomed in on the shorter officer who was doing the inspection of the contents of the trucks. A pastry caterer was the next in line. It was a small white truck with the name of the restaurant, Le Grenier a' Pain, on the side of it. Malcolm noticed that this time the inspector went all the way inside the truck with his flashlight and did not emerge for at least two minutes. When he stepped down, he twisted has ankle and fell to the ground. When Malcolm zoomed in closer he could make out a large tattoo on his wrist, but his uniform jacket was covering part of it.

"Now, that's interesting."

"What's interesting?" She joined him on the balcony wearing her fitted black gown and diamond necklace. "So, how do I look?" She twirled around to show off her figure.

Malcolm ignored her. He was still looking through the binoculars at the policemen twenty stories below.

"Malcolm! Put that damned magnifying glass down and tell me how beautiful I am!"

"You look ravishing, Helen!" he said still looking through the binoculars.

"Ok, that's it!" she snatched them out of his hands and threw them over the balcony.

"What the—!"

"Look, Malcolm, I gave you the information that you wanted, the least you can do is give me your undivided attention for another twenty-four hours!"

"You're right, Helen, maybe I am being a little paranoid. Old habits die hard; once you're in Special Ops you see everything as a potential threat."

"The only threat you need to worry about tonight is me," she said while guiding him back inside. "Now get dressed, I want to show you off to my snobbish girlfriends." She stopped in front of the mirror and admired their reflection. "Wait until those bitches see what I've got!"

CHAPTER 16

<u>MAINTENANCE MAN II</u>

It was 6:30 when Malcolm and Helen made it down to the lobby. Security was tight. Every purse was checked and no one was allowed entry into the main ballroom without walking through the metal detector.

"Now that's more like it," Malcolm said as he walked through the device.

"What did you say, darling?"

"Oh, nothing," Malcolm said while scanning the room for any signs of trouble.

His antenna was still up after seeing the Paris cops' shabby police work. It didn't make sense to him that they would let two trucks go by without even so much as a peek, but inspected the remaining trucks meticulously. He tried to relax and focus on what he was getting paid to do. Helen was an important client with lots of important contacts and she was a longtime friend. He tried to put his military training in check so he could focus on doing his job.

While they waited in line to be seated in the ballroom, a waiter walked by them with a tray of champagne. Malcolm took two off the tray without breaking the waiter's stride. He handed one to Helen.

"Here's to the most stunning woman in Paris," Malcolm said as they crossed wrists and took a sip. "Vous êtes mon beau angel."

"Thank you, Malcolm, that's the sweetest thing you've ever said to me."

As they made their way to the front of the line, Helen pulled the invitations out of her purse along with their passports and handed them to the hostess who was checking names off the list.

"Bon soir, I am Ms. Daniels. J'ai une réserve pour deux!" Helen announced.

"Bon soir, Ms. Daniels. Un instant et je vous assis."

The hostess scrolled down the list until she found Helen's name.

"J'ai trouvé vous, Mademoiselle" she said. "Follow me, please!"

As they were passing through the crowded entrance, Malcolm noticed a stunning Egyptian woman walking toward him. She had huge light brown eyes and a flawless brown complexion. She smiled at him. He smiled back. His attention was diverted just long enough to separate him from Helen. When he turned around to get his bearings, he crashed right into Agent Harris and wasted his drink on him.

"Oh, my goodness, I apologize, Agent—"

"Harris!"

"Yes, Agent Harris," Malcolm said, wiping him off with his pocket handkerchief.

"Next time, watch where you're going!"

"Ditto, Agent Man. I believe we were both a little distracted."

There was a slight pause, then Agent Harris smiled. He knew they were both looking at the same woman.

"You have a good night, Mr. Entertainer," Agent Harris said to him. "By the way, you never did tell me what you did for a living."

"I'm in real estate and I also own a club down in Miami called Melvin's, maybe you've heard of it."

"Sounds familiar, do they play live music?"

"The best in town. I play the piano myself. What about you, Agent Harris, you musically inclined?"

"Does playing the flute in high school count?"

"I don't think so!"

They finished brushing themselves off and Agent Harris got a call in his earpiece.

"Duty calls, you have a good night, Mr. Tremell."

"I'm impressed, you remembered my name."

"I've got a photographic memory," he said, rushing off. "I remember everything!"

By the time Malcolm caught up with Helen, she was surrounded by several of her wealthy girlfriends and was eager to show off her boy toy. For the next hour, Malcolm charmed his way through the entire room, taking photographs, speaking on politics in French, Latin, German, and Chinese, and he danced with as many beautiful women as he could get to. Helen sat back and watched with admiration as he worked the room in a way only Malcolm could. And at every opportunity, she let every woman know that Malcolm was with her and, most importantly, he was leaving with her.

The program for the evening was scheduled to end with a performance by an American jazz band, in recognition of the U.S. Secretary of State, and a group photograph with all the dignitaries. Malcolm was dancing with the Egyptian woman he admired earlier when the music faded and the announcer came to the stage to introduce the band.

"Bonne soirée mesdames et messieurs et notre estime guests," he said, then he repeated it in English. "Good evening, ladies and gentleman and our esteemed guests. I'm sorry to inform you that tonight's performance of the American jazz band has been canceled due to illness of the maestro," he went on. "Now, if you will indulge me, please let's move on to the end of the program and prepare for the photograph."

The crowd began to fill with chatter of disappointment. It was a highly anticipated performance. American jazz was extremely popular in Paris. Malcolm was standing next to the stage while he was trying to calm the crowd down. He raised his hand to get the announcer's attention.

"Excusez-moi, Monsieur," Malcolm said to him. "I am a jazz pianist. There's no need to cancel. I can play with them—if it's okay with Monsieur Président and Madam Secretary."

The French President nodded his head in agreement and the crowd erupted with applause. As the band took the stage, Malcolm kissed the hand of the Egyptian woman he was dancing with and the host escorted her off the floor. The lights dimmed and the performance began with the classic song, "Anthology," the rendition by jazz pianist Bud Powell, the guitarist took the lead for a Pat Metheny Group song called "Take Me There" and they concluded with a upbeat selection by Ramsey Lewis, "The 'In' Crowd." Malcolm followed the band for a while, then took off. Every head in the room was bobbing and fingers were snapping to the beat. After the set was over, Malcolm and the band took a bow.

"Merci, merci beaucoup," Malcolm said as he blew kisses at the audience and one directly at Helen.

Agent Harris even clapped a time or two. Malcolm could see him standing near the entrance occasionally adjusting his earpiece. Malcolm was sweating and looking around for a towel and a waiter.

"Excusez-moi, de l'eau veuillez," he shouted to a nervous-looking waiter who was standing at a bar nearby.

The waiter, who was limping, rushed to the bar to get him a bottle of water. When he reached up to hand it to Malcolm on the stage, he lost his balance and slipped, revealing a large black swastika tattoo. That's when everything started to come together. The applause of the audience faded into a deafening silence. Malcolm calmly took the bottle out of the waiter's hand and slowly walked off the stage toward Agent Harris, all the while shaking hands and smiling. He had to remain calm; he couldn't flinch. How many are there? What's their plan? he was thinking. Is it too late?

By the time he reached Agent Harris, the host was already organizing the dignitaries to line up for the photo.

"Great Job, Mr. Tremell!" Agent Harris said. "You really do know how to play!"

"I need you to listen to what I'm about to say, it's going to sound crazy, but whatever you do, don't make any sudden change of facial expression," Malcolm said, still smiling.

"What the hell are you talking about?"

"I'm a former Navy SEAL, Team Six, counterterrorism. I know you understand what that means so let me tell you the situation. The waiter near the bar was dressed as a cop about an hour ago inspecting catering vehicles that entered the dock area. He allowed at least two trucks to go by uninspected; they could be carrying guns, bombs, who knows!"

"You're serious, aren't you?" Agent Harris said. He glanced around the room casually and noticed how anxious the waiter was looking. "How do I know you're not a part of this?"

"A jazz-piano-playing terrorist, I don't think so!" Malcolm stared at him with an urgent expression. "Goddammit, man, this is the real thing. We don't have much time! Just contact your guys and tell them to check the docks by the kitchen; that's where the truck came in!"

"Unit one," he called out on the radio. There was no answer.

"Unit one, come in!" Still no answer.

"Where were those men stationed?" Malcolm asked him.

He paused as reality set in.

"They were stationed by the docks!"

"You'd better switch frequencies, your team has been compromised."

He switched over to the emergency channel and tried to reach his second team.

"Unit two!" he urgently called out, trying not to change his facial expression.

"Unit two here!"

"Unit one is down, I say again, unit one is down. This is a priority one situation; get the president and secretary out! Do it quickly and quietly, and secure all the exits."

"Ten-four!"

Malcolm began walking toward the kitchen.

"Hey wait a second, where do you think you're going?"

"I'm going to take a piss!"

"What?"

"Trust me, I know what I'm doing. You just keep an eye on that waiter!"

Agent Harris got word to the host to stall the photograph session; he figured that had to be the opportunity they were waiting for to make their move. Malcolm exited the front entrance and headed for the docks at the back of the hotel. There were two men dressed as Paris cops standing next to a police vehicle. One of them was the tall, burly man Malcolm saw earlier inspecting trucks with the waiter. As he moved in closer, he could hear him talking into his radio.

"Nous sommes en place! Les agents américains sont morts!"

It was just as he had suspected; both agents were dead. He crept up through the heavy brush that lined the side of the building and rushed them. He grabbed the shorter man by the neck and smashed his head into the trunk of the car, punched him in the forehead with two rapid punches, then flipped him backwards violently against the pavement, fracturing his skull. The burly man rushed him from behind and lifted Malcolm into the air. He tried to drive him into the nearby wall, but Malcolm lifted his legs and pushed off the wall, sending both men to the ground. He reached for his gun. Malcolm kicked it out of his hand and punched him in the jaw. When the big man tried to punch back, Malcolm ducked and then kicked him in the shin snapping his knee, causing it to bend backwards.

"Urghh!" he screamed out.

Malcolm quickly moved behind him and covered his mouth and choked him until he stopped breathing.

"That's for killing those two agents, motherfucker!"

Malcolm dragged both of their bodies into the bushes and eased his way down the dark corridor to the dock area, staying as close to the building as possible. He could see one man standing on the dock dressed in a valet uniform holding a gun. There were several trucks parked at the dock close to where he was standing. If he could make his way behind one of the trucks without being detected, he could catch the man by surprise and take him down without giving him a chance to warn his comrades.

The corridor was dark and damp. Several street lamps were out, creating shadowy areas between him and the dock. As he drew closer, he could hear footsteps coming up behind him. He had to think fast. He looked around for something to defend himself with, but there was nothing but a stack of cardboard boxes next to a dumpster. He had one chance. He whipped out his dick, leaned against the wall, and started to urinate. A bald man with a swastika tattooed on his forehead stepped out of the shadows pointing a sniper's rifle at him; it had a silencer on it.

"Hey, vous, Que faites-vous?"

"I no speaka French," Malcolm slurred.

"What are you doing? You're not supposed to be back here!"

The closer he came to Malcolm the more he lowered the gun. The ruckus got the attention of the cook who was smoking on the docks. The cook drew his pistol and began walking toward him.

"I'll be done in just a second. This French wine goes right through you, doesn't it?"

"Get going you drunken American dog!"

Malcolm waited until he was another step closer, then punched him in the throat crushing his Adam's apple instantly. He snatched the rifle out of his hand as the man fell to the ground and in one motion turned and shot the other man before he could get a shot off. Malcolm searched through the clothes of the man with the rifle and found a photo of the Israeli ambassador. He took the pistol off the man that he shot and stuffed it into his waist. He lifted the dumpster lid and was about to toss the rifle inside of it when he saw the dead bodies of the two secret service agents; both had been shot in the head. Just then, several agents came bursting through the back door with their guns drawn.

"Drop it!" they yelled

"It's me, don't shoot," Malcolm yelled back. He immediately dropped to his knees and put his hands behind his head. "You got two men down, but I got the shooter."

"I'll take care of this one," Agent Harris told them as he walked over and handcuffed Malcolm.

He walked him back into an interrogation room they had set up in the adjacent ballroom. He excused the other agents then unlocked his handcuffs.

"Ok, you're free to go."

"But don't you want to know what happened?"

"I already do."

He pulled open a set of drapes and there, sitting handcuffed to a chair, was the waiter with the limp. He had been beaten to a bloody pulp.

"We apprehended him right after the president and secretary were out of danger. He told us everything!" Then he pulled out a small box filled with several smoke bombs and flares. "The plan was to cause a panic and force the VIPs out the back, where the sniper was waiting. The real target was—"

"The Israeli ambassador," Malcolm interrupted. "The shooter had this on him." He pulled the photo out of his pocket that he had taken off the sniper.

"Not bad for a piano player. If you ever need a real job, let me know. I'll personally vouch for you," Agent Harris joked while handing Malcolm his card. "We could use another good man in our anti-terrorism unit."

"No offense, but you guys don't get paid enough—and the hours are shitty! Not to mention I would look terrible in that *Men in Black* outfit." He popped the collar of his tailor-made tuxedo. "Tell the president I said you guys need a makeover!"

CHAPTER 17

"You look gorgeous in that dress!" Mrs. Hilton, the owner of an exclusive bridal boutique in Coral Gables, said to Alex.

"I don't know," Alex replied while modeling the long white gown in the full-length mirror. "Marcia, what do you think?"

"Girl, with that body of yours, you would look good in a potato sack," Marcia laughed while adjusting the sleeves. "Besides, by the time I get through working my magic on your hair, nobody's gonna be looking at this raggedy dress."

Marcia began feeling around the hem of the dress searching for the price tag. When she finally found it, she flipped it over.

"Damn!" she shouted. "Twenty-five-thousand dollars?"

"Quality costs!" Mrs. Hilton said to her.

"Ok, I'll take it!" Alex blurted out.

"But you haven't tried on any of the other ones yet!"

"A dress is a dress! Just charge it to Senator Nelson's account. I'm sure he won't have a problem with the price."

"Very well. I'll have my seamstress alter the waist and sleeves."

"Don't forget to have her tighten the front around my chest. I want my breasts to be standing at attention!"

"Right away, Miss Garcia. I'll go set up the appointment now," Mrs. Hilton said and then walked out of the fitting area.

"I may as well look good even if this is not a real wedding," Alex said under her breath.

While she went into the dressing room to take off the dress, Marcia began taking pictures of some of the designer dresses with her cell phone.

"I can't wait to download these pictures on my computer at the shop. They're gonna be so jealous!"

She grabbed a size four dress off the rack and held it in front of her size fourteen body.

"I hope I can afford an expensive dress like this when it's my turn to walk down the aisle. Hell, I hope I can fit into one of these dresses when it's my time. I need to lose some weight," Marcia said while looking at her stomach in the mirror. "How does it feel to spend that kind of money on a dress?"

"It's not my money," Alex replied nonchalantly.

"You know what I mean."

"The dress doesn't make the wedding, Marcia."

"Maybe not, but it damn sure doesn't hurt!"

"I would trade in this overpriced dress for that potato sack you talked about for some consistently good sex!"

"Alex!"

"I'm serious, girl. All the money in the world can't replace a man that knows how to put it down properly. I mean the kind of loving that makes your legs wobble when you stand up." They both burst out laughing. "Have you ever been sitting in your car or at home watching TV and had a flashback of some good dick—and it made you shiver?"

"Girl, you're a mess," Marcia said while wiping the tears from her eyes.

Alex came out of the stall holding the dress. She paused and looked at her reflection in the full-length mirror.

"It's a damn shame that I have to go through all this trouble just to put on a show so Gary can look respectable."

"Then don't go through with it! We both know you don't love him anyway."

"I used to love him, but then I realized the relationship was all about fitting into that wholesome all-American family image. Next thing you know, he'll start asking me to have kids. And that sure as hell isn't going to happen!"

"If that's the case, what's the point of going through with it?"

"The point is, I made a deal."

"With who?"

"With myself! Once this election is over, I can start working my way out of the relationship. He and I both know it's all about the Christian and Latino vote anyway, so once the election is over, the charade is over! We both get what we want."

"You told me he had you to sign a prenuptial agreement? So what exactly are you getting out of it?"

"I never wanted his money, but I did use this opportunity to save mine, and I put another degree under my belt. Not to mention all the great contacts I've made since we've been together. But the most valuable thing I'm taking away from this relationship is a lesson! Never again will I allow myself to get involved with another controlling and insecure man," she went on. "You know…it's funny…women think it's the blue-collar guys who have the biggest issues with educated and ambitious women, but in reality it's the guys with money who end up trippin'. They're so accustomed to buying their way through life that when they run into a woman who can't be bought, they don't know how to handle it. Next thing you know, they're going through your phone, following you around, and sniffing your panties."

"That's deep, Alex, I didn't know it was that serious."

"Yes, it's pretty messed up," Alex said, getting upset. "I'm tired of looking for that knight in shining armor only to end up disappointed and with my self-esteem all jacked up—fuck love! I just want to be happy!"

"Yeah—fuck love!" Marcia screamed back and gave Alex a high five. "And fuck these expensive dresses that my big ass will never be able to afford or fit into."

They embraced and held each other tightly while rocking back and forth playfully.

"You know what I'm going to do the day after that damn election?" Alex asked.

"What?"

"I'm going down to Melvin's Jazz Club and I'm gonna sing like I've never sung before!"

"Now, that's the woman I want to hear! Let's get out of here! We've got a bachelorette party to go to. I hired a stripper and I brought this new DVD called *Do Women Know What They Want?* It's by that radio jock and author, Michael Baisden."

"Hell, he should have interviewed me for that one. I know what women want: a man who is honest, respectful, responsible, with good communication skills, and who's not intimidated by a sexually confident woman."

"Well, damn, I guess I can return it and get my money back!"

"No, let's watch it anyway. I might learn something new. Besides, I'm not in a hurry to get back home to that insecure little dick bastard anyway!"

CHAPTER 18

MAINTENANCE MAN II

Malcolm's plane landed at Miami International Airport early Sunday afternoon. He picked up his bags at baggage claim and met his limo at curbside. Once he was inside the car, he pulled out his phone and checked his messages. There were two new texts, one from Simon that read: Welcome Home, Partner. The other was from Alex. It was from her girlfriend Marcia's 305 area code. It read: Wedding at 2:00pm, St. Francis Cathedral, I need you to be there! Don't be late! And don't do anything crazy! He checked the time on his phone: it read 12:33.

"Oh shit!" Malcolm said out loud. "Step on it, driver!"

The drive to his condo usually took fifteen minutes, but there was an accident on the causeway and traffic was backed up, which added another twenty minutes to the trip. Malcolm scrolled through his list of clients hoping to find one who would be willing to pose as his date. When he couldn't reach anyone, he called the only other single woman he knew. As the phone rang, he anxiously kept checking the time on his watch.

"Hello!"

"Hey, Ariel, this is Malcolm."

"Hey, Malcolm, what's going on? Is something wrong at the club?"

"No, what made you ask that?"

"Because that's the only time I ever hear from you, that's why!" she said with attitude.

"What are you talking about? We talk all the time."

"Okay, then tell me, when was the last time you called me—other than work?"

There was a long, uncomfortable pause. Malcolm knew he never called Ariel unless it was work-related and even then, Simon usually made the call.

"Okay, so maybe it's been a while. Look, I need a personal favor."

"Uh hum!" she said sarcastically. "I'm listening."

"My friend Alex, who you met at the club, is getting married in about an hour. I need you to be my date."

"Are you serious?"

"Yes, I'm serious! This is an emergency!"

"Malcolm, I still have rollers in my hair and I already have a date!"

"I'll pay you!"

"Are you gonna pay to find me another man, too, because it's taken me a year to meet this one!"

"I'm sure he'll understand, just tell him it's related to work."

"There is no way I'm canceling! Steven is a plastic surgeon with no kids and he's introducing me to his mother today!"

Malcolm knew that was the nail in the coffin. He buried his head in his hands and shook his head.

"Thanks for nothing, Ariel."

"You're welcome, Mr. Tremell—bye."

As he was finishing up his call, his car pulled into the driveway of his condo. Miguel hurried to open his door.

"Welcome back, Mr. Tremell."

"Miguel, get my luggage and bring the Ferrari around—and leave the engine running! I'm in a hurry!"

"Yes, sir, Mr. Tremell!"

Malcolm rushed into the lobby and onto the elevator. Once he made it into his apartment, he began peeling out of his clothes, leaving a trail from the elevator to the bathroom. He showered as fast as he could, put on deodorant, and slid into the first suit in his closet. He grabbed his phone and invitation off the counter and made a dash back onto the elevator, which was still waiting on his floor.

"Come on! Come on!" he said, impatiently waiting for the elevator to descend to the lobby.

When the elevator doors finally opened, he rushed out and crashed into the building manager, Angelita, who was holding a stack of folders. Papers flew everywhere.

"Oh mi dios!" she screamed.

"I'm sorry, I didn't see you." He bent down to help her pick up the papers.

"Malcolm, you scared me to death!"

While he helped collect the documents, his wheels were already turning. Angelita was attractive, professional and, as far he knew, single. As usual she was impeccably dressed, so her attire wasn't an issue. Just as she was about to walk onto the elevator, he made his move.

"So, Angelita, what are you doing this afternoon," he said while holding the elevator door open.

"Nothing special, why?" she blushed.

"I have an event and I need a date."

"Really? What time?"

"Now!" he said bluntly.

She looked down at her watch and then glanced around the lobby. When she spotted her assistant at the front desk, she rushed over and handed her the files. Then she rushed back to Malcolm while fondling her hair.

"Do I have time to get my purse?"

"No!" Malcolm said as he grabbed her by the hand and led her outside and into the passenger seat of his car.

"Put on your seat belt and hold on tight!"

"This is exciting," she said, buckling herself in. "I like to go fast!"

"Not this fast!"

Malcolm burned rubber out of the driveway and sped into traffic barely missing a group of bikers. He switched gears and raced down Collins Avenue and onto the MacArthur Causeway. He looked at the clock on the dashboard: it read 1:30. He dodged between cars and drove on the shoulder to avoid the slow drivers when he couldn't maneuver past them.

"These people in Miami can't drive worth shit!" he said while blowing his horn and then accelerating past a Domino's pizza delivery truck.

"This must be an important event!" Angelita said while holding onto her hair, which was blowing wildly in the wind.

"It's important alright, once in a lifetime," Malcolm said with a sly grin. "Because it's definitely not going to happen again!"

• • •

Malcolm arrived at St. Francis Cathedral at 2:15. He parked his car and rushed inside with Angelita trailing behind him. As he entered the church, he could see Alex and Gary already at the altar reciting their vows. He eased his way down to the front and positioned himself directly over Gary's right shoulder hoping Alex would see him. She glanced in his direction and smiled to acknowledge him. He smiled back and nodded. By then the preacher was near the end of the vows.

"If any person here can show cause why these two people should not be joined in holy matrimony, speak now or forever hold your peace."

Malcolm sarcastically cleared his throat. Alex stared at him and squinted her eyes. He laughed as the preacher went on.

"So, with the power vested in me by God and the state of Florida, I now pronounce you man and wife. You may kiss the bride."

The church applauded as Alex and Gary embraced. Camera bulbs flashed as they walked down the aisle being showered with flower pedals.

"That was beautiful!" Angelita said. "Are you a friend of the bride or the groom?"

"The bride."

"She looks beautiful."

"Yes, she does, doesn't she?"

Alex and Gary exited the front of the church and made their way out onto the front lawn where the reception was to take place. Small children were running around wildly and Christina Aguilera music was blaring from the DJ booth.

"That's my cue! It's time to go!" Malcolm took Angelita by the hand and headed toward his car.

"But aren't we staying for the reception?"

"Nope!" he quickened his pace. "I can tolerate weddings, but I definitely don't do receptions."

Alex was posing for pictures and spotted Malcolm and waved at him! He waved back!

"Thank you!" she mouthed to him.

"You're welcome!" he mouthed back.

Once Malcolm was back in the car, he untied his tie and let the top down. He sat there speechless for a moment, just smiling.

"Hum," he moaned.

"What's on your mind?"

"Many of those people in that church were married, and so were most of the wedding party."

"And?"

"And many of them are former and current clients of mine. It just makes you wonder why people go through all the trouble of getting married when their lifestyles haven't changed one bit!"

"Are you against marriage?"

"No, I'm against hypocrisy!" Malcolm said, turning on the ignition. "Both men and women are out there playing a dangerous game, and eventually somebody gets burned!"

"Some would say you're playing the most deadly game of them all."

"The difference between them and me is that I'm honest about who and what I am. I'm just smart enough to get paid for it!"

"Touché', Señor Tremell. Point well made."

Angelita let down her hair and unbuttoned the top two buttons on her blouse. "So now what?"

"Now—I'm going to drop you off so you can get back to work and I'm going to bed." Malcolm said scanning the playlist on his iPod. "I've been on a flight from Paris for ten hours, I'm exhausted."

"Do you mind if I join you?"

"Look, Angelita, there are two things you learn day one in this business. Number one, don't shit where you eat. And two, don't ever lay down with a woman who doesn't have more to lose than you do. No offense, but having sex with a condo manager is not a smart career move."

"You're being very presumptuous, Mr. Tremell."

"So, you're saying you don't want to have sex?"

"Oh yes, I've been dying to fuck your brains out ever since I laid eyes on you," she said while reaching over and grabbing his penis. "I'm talking about presuming I'm just some lowly condo manager. Did you even bother reading the name on your condo docs? My family owns that building and several other high-rises and hotels on South Beach—and around the world," she continued while tightening her grip. "So, as you can see, Mr. Tremell, I have plenty to lose. Now, what do you have to say to that!"

"You're lucky I've been traveling for ten hours and we're sitting in the parking lot at my friend's wedding, otherwise I would let you fuck my brains out right now!" he joked and then sped off headed toward South Beach.

CHAPTER 19

It was 7:05 p.m. on Election night, and the polls had just closed. Senator Nelson was trailing by fifteen percent against his Democratic opponent. The campaign headquarters was buzzing with activity as staffers frantically worked the phones talking to pollsters to get the latest numbers. The two largest counties, Miami Dade and Broward, which were mostly Hispanic, African American, and Caribbean, had yet to be counted. Senator Nelson sat in his office sipping coffee and flicking back and forth to FOX, CNN, and MSNBC. His head of security, Vincent, was standing by the door talking on his cell phone. After he hung up, he gave the senator a thumbs up.

"We're all set," Vincent said confidently. "You want me to break out the champagne, sir?"

"Not yet, let's make them sweat a little longer. I don't want to appear overconfident. We'll wait until FOX makes it official. Call our people over there and let them know they'll have an exclusive interview after the announcement. We Republicans have to stick together, right?"

"Yes, sir."

"Where's Alex? We'll need her on stage for the victory speech."

"I'm right here, Gary," Alex said, coming out of the back restroom that was connected to his office. "I had to powder my nose."

"We're about ten or fifteen minutes away from going live, stay close."

"Are you guys sure you're not counting your chickens before they hatch?" She was looking at the monitor, which was tuned into CNN. "You're still down by fifteen percent."

"What makes you say that?" Gary asked her.

"I heard what you guys said about breaking out the champagne. That's a little cocky, isn't it?"

"You've got great ears, honey!" Gary said nervously while looking over at Vincent. "We'll have to soundproof that restroom now, won't we?"

"I think we need to get set, Senator; it's almost time."

"Well, this is what we worked hard for, right?" He stood up and began fixing his hair. "Let's give these Democrats hell!"

The clock on the wall read 7:15, when the FOX news anchor came on the air to announce the winner.

"It looks like the Republicans are going to chalk up another win during this special election in Florida. We're projecting that the former state senator Gary Nelson will win the vacated Senate seat in Florida. In what can only be described as a miraculous late finish, he comes back from fifteen percentage points down to stun his Democratic opponent. Let's go live to Miami to Nelson headquarters."

The stage was littered with American flags. A group of African-American and Latino children were bused in from a foster home and positioned directly behind the senator. Alex was just to the right of her husband to make sure she was in the camera shot. When the on-air camera light flashed, Gary walked onto the stage to thunderous applause and stepped up to the podium.

"We did it! The people have spoken!" he yelled. "I want to thank my incredible staff, my lovely wife, Alex, and, of course, all of the voters who sent a message to the Democrats and the Republicans—we need jobs! Now that we have a majority in the House of Representatives and a super majority in the Senate, there's only one thing standing in our way of real change and that is the Presidency! No more taxes and no more social welfare—we want our country back!"

The crowd chanted in unison, "We want our country back, we want our country back!"

"It's time to put these abortion doctors in prison and bring prayer back into our schools," he went on. "And when I get to the United States Senate, we're going to get rid of these discriminatory Civil Rights laws and destroy the labor unions that are driving up the cost of doing business in this country. And, finally, we must rid our country of Muslim extremism! Not only by fighting the battle in Afghanistan, but right here at home by investigating any Muslim organization that engages in anti-American rhetoric. We don't need more mosques, we need more Christian churches—and we need to bring prayer back into schools. We want our country back!"

The crowd chanted again in unison, "We want our country back! We want our country back!"

"Now, let's get to work and make this the country that our forefathers meant for it to be! God bless you, and God Bless the United States of America!"

The crowd of over two-thousand supporters applauded passionately as he exited the stage waving and holding hands with Alex. He paused to take pictures, then went backstage to begin his interviews with all the national news networks.

"You can go now, I'm done with you," he said to Alex, abruptly letting go of her hand. "I'll meet you back at the condo later tonight. The driver is waiting out back."

She stood there stunned as Vincent escorted Gary to the back room where the press was assembled. Now that the acceptance speech was over, it was as if she were invisible. Even the part-time staffers didn't acknowledge her as she walked back to the main office to get her purse. Once she was inside, she closed the door and pulled her cell phone out and called Malcolm.

"Hello?" he answered apprehensively.

"Malcolm it's me, Alex!"

"Hey, Alex, sorry I didn't recognize the number. Who's phone are you calling from this time?"

"It's my personal number. I finally got my own iPhone. Now that the charade is over, there's no sense hiding."

"I hope you learned how to attach a photo to text message," he laughed. "I'm still waiting on that naked picture you accidentally sent to your mother!"

"I'll do you one better. I'll send you a voice memo of the song I wrote just for you!"

"I'm impressed, you've turned into a regular geek."

She put him on speaker while she tried to figure out how to attach a file.

"Damn, I accidentally sent it to Marcia. That's what I get for having two friends whose names start with M. Let me try it again!"

"That can wait, let's talk about how good you looked on TV tonight. I just saw you on MSNBC; you were rocking that blue dress. And I've gotta hand it to Gary, he really knows how to pander to that Tea Party crowd. Do me a favor and ask him what the hell he means by we want our country back? Does he mean back from that nigga president? Why don't they just come out and say it?"

"Malcolm, you're such a militant! You sure your last name isn't X?" she laughed.

"Enough about those crooks, what's going on with you? Are you still coming by the club tomorrow night?"

"Of course, I'll be there. I've already got the perfect dress picked out and I'm performing one of your favorite songs," she said while walking into the bathroom. She put her purse down on the floor and sat down on the toilet.

"Simon is so excited he ordered a brand-new microphone just for you."

"How sweet! Tell him I won't let him down." She laughed as she began to pee.

"Is that sound what I think it is?"

"Hey, those Pellegrinos go right through you," she laughed.

"You're getting way too comfortable in this relationship, Mrs. Nelson."

Just then she heard someone coming into the office.

"Let me call you tomorrow." she whispered. "Someone just came in!"

Malcolm hung up, but the memo window was still open on her iPhone. When she put it down on the sink to reach for the toilet paper, she accidentally hit the record button.

"Mr. Kross and Mr. Kross, the senator will be up shortly," she heard a man's voice say. "Can I offer you gentleman anything to drink?"

"No, thank you, we won't be here long."

Alex was about to flush the toilet when she heard Gary come into the office.

"Gentleman!" Gary said. "Glad you could make it!"

"Let's cut the bullshit and get down to business," Randall Kross said. "We want you in Washington first thing tomorrow morning to start pushing through our prescription drug legislation Senate Bill HP 1189. We have a man inside the FDA who will make sure we get fast approval."

"I was told the president threatened to veto it."

"You let us worry about that. We have new data that shows that our new drugs are safe."

"You mean the drugs that cause cervical cancer and eventually kill people five or ten years later?" Gary said. "And according to the confidential reports I read, your company is also manufacturing the drugs to treat the side effects that your drugs will cause. As you can see, I've been doing my homework."

There was an extended pause. Then Alex heard one of the men clear his throat.

"Since when did the truth ever get in our way?" Allan Kross asked. "That's what you said at our last meeting, remember?"

"Yes, sir, I do."

"There'll be lots of money in it for you. It takes a lot of cash to run for president."

"Understood. I'll be on a flight first thing tomorrow. Let me check with my staff on what's available."

"Why wait for tomorrow? We have a jet fueled and ready to go tonight. Let's meet at the West Palm Beach Airport. We've got a few things to pick up at our Boca Raton estate before we go. Our driver will pick you up. How does midnight sound?"

"Sounds perfect!" Gary said while standing up from his seat. "Let me have Vincent see you gentleman out. I still have a few more interviews and then I'll be on my way."

"Thank you, United States Senator Nelson," Randall said, shaking hands with him. "By the way, thanks for the invite to your wedding last week. Sorry we couldn't make it to the ceremony. Too many cameras."

"No problem, I understand."

"Where's that lovely wife of yours, anyway?" Allan Kross asked.

"She should be halfway home by now! I didn't want to keep her out too late."

"Be sure to give her our best."

"I'll do that, Allan!" Gary tapped on the thick glass to get Vincent's attention. He was standing outside the office guarding the door. "Vincent, make sure they get safely to their cars, then meet me back here in ten minutes. I have another interview."

"Right this way, gentleman."

"Vincent, if you don't mind my asking, where did you get that awful scar?" Randall Kross asked.

"I cut myself shaving!" his said in a serious tone.

"That must have been one helluva razor!"

"Yes, sir, it was. Let me get that door for you."

Then Alex heard the door close behind them.

She was trembling as she pulled up her panties. The conversation she overheard could get her killed and she knew it. She peeked around the door, grabbed her phone, and then sprinted out of the bathroom and out of the office. She tried to keep her composure, intentionally avoiding making eye contact... she didn't want to be noticed...she didn't want to be stopped. Once she made it outside, she rushed inside the limo without waiting for the driver to open her door. The driver got behind the wheel and drove off, but he came to an abrupt stop. The exit was blocked by a group of Occupy Wall Street protestors who were picketing in front of the senator's office. They were holding up signs that read: *Corporate Welfare But No Child Welfare* and chanting, "We are the ninety-nine percent! We are the ninety-nine percent!" The driver got out of the car and attempted to get them to unblock the way. Alex was desperate to leave and was about to get out of the car to go after the driver when out of nowhere Vincent knocked on the glass; he used a hand gesture to direct her to lower her window. She kept her hands hidden in the shadows so he couldn't see them shaking. She took a deep breath and tried to put on a smile.

"Good evening, Mrs. Nelson, you still here?" Vincent said looking at her suspiciously.

"Yes, as you can see our way has been blocked by these protestors. Can you assist the driver in getting them out of our way? I really want to go home and get some rest."

"No problem," he said to her. He started toward the crowd, then suddenly, he stopped. "Do you mind holding this for me?" He handed her her purse. "You left this inside the bathroom in the office."

"Why, thank you, Vincent. I was wondering where that was." She kept smiling trying not to give herself away. "Have a good night, Vincent."

"Good night, and try not to sleep in too late, time is so precious," he said while rubbing the jagged scar on the right side of his face. "Tick Tock, Tick Tock!" His smile was sinister.

She quickly rolled up the window and slumped into the seat. Once she was a block away from the office, she turned off her phone. What if they know? What if they check my phone records and see that I was talking to Malcolm, she thought. What will they do to us if they thought we knew?

She opened a miniature bottle of rum that was in the limo and drank it down.

"Oh, my God, what have I gotten myself into?"

CHAPTER 20

"**R**ight there, Malcolm, that's my spot!" Rachel moaned. "Don't move. I'm cumming, I'm…ah…ah...oh!" she screamed out!

Malcolm unwrapped her legs from around his waist, put on his boxers, and drew back the curtains in the pitch-black room. The sunlight blared in.

"Malcolm, baby, close those blinds and bring that sweet meat back to bed. It's eight o'clock in the morning. I don't do anything before noon."

"I usually don't either, but I couldn't resist your invitation, or your offer. Ten-thousand dollars is a lot of money."

"There's a lot more where that came from," the other woman Maria said as she walked up behind him and pressed her erect nipples against his back. "I haven't cum that hard in ages."

"Me either," said the black woman who was still lying on the bed.

At that moment, Malcolm's phone rang.

"Excuse me, ladies, I have to take this call. It's important business."

"So is this," the other woman, who was Cuban, said to him. "And don't even think about leaving. We're paid for six hours and you're still on the clock!"

Malcolm pulled back the sliding glass doors and walked out onto the pool deck to have some privacy.

"What's up, Simon?"

"Nothing's up. I just wanted to make sure everything was set for tonight with Alex. People are still talking about her performance on opening night."

"I told you...she'll be there! We talked last night after the election. Now stop blowing up my phone. Man, you're worse than a telemarketer."

"Okay, okay! I just want tonight to be perfect. The house is sold out and we're hosting the Miami Heat after-game party. Ariel set it up. And you know how much money those ballplayers throw around. Not to mention all the groupies!"

"The Miami Heat, huh, who are they playing tonight?"

"The New York Knicks!"

"Aw shit, it's gonna be a battle tonight. The Heat hate the Knicks."

"I know, but there's damn near more Knick fans in the stadium than Heat fans."

"Hell, half the city of Miami is from New York!"

"Tru dat!" Simon laughed.

While Malcolm was talking, Rachel and Maria came out onto the pool deck and joined him. They were both naked.

"Hold on for a second, Simon," he said, muting his phone. "Come on, ladies, just give me another five minutes and I'm all yours."

"In five minutes my pussy will explode!" Rachel said. "I need you inside of me now!"

"Is this a sex-for-money exchange or date rape?" Malcolm laughed.

Rachel guided Malcolm down onto the pool chairs and pulled his boxers down.

"Grab his dick while I suck his balls," she said to Rachel. "Let's see how long he can concentrate on his phone call then."

"Ladies, you are messing with the wrong man. I have nerves—and balls—of steel!"

Malcolm unmuted his phone and continued his call with Simon while Rachel and Maria did their best to distract him.

"As I was saying, Simon, I'll see you at the club tonight and I'll let you know if I hear from Alex. She's got a pet peeve about being prompt, so I wouldn't worry!"

"Cool," Simon replied. "And I'll let you know if Ariel can get you a pair of comp tickets for the game; her cousin is a sports agent."

"Heat and Knicks ticket and a sold-out club. Now that's the beginning of a great evening!" Malcolm told him. "I'll check back with you later." Then he hung up.

Malcolm reclined all the way back in the pool chair while Rachel and Maria went to town giving him a blow job. But he was emotionless, totally detached. The way he was trained to be. He looked around the luxurious estate he was laying in the middle of and dreamt about a place like that being all his one day. After the Paris trip, he was getting closer to his dream. Just a few more moves—one more contact—and everything would change, he thought. He was so close. So close he could taste it!

"Are you ladies finished?" He tapped them both on the head. "I've got to be going."

He pulled up his boxers and went back inside the house and started collecting his things. Rachel and Maria followed behind him determined to get more sex.

"Malcolm, if you're not going to stay until noon like you agreed, we want part of our money back," Maria said with her hands on her hips.

"No problem. I'll credit your account when I get back to the office."

"I don't want a refund, I want my nipples bitten and my ass slapped. And I want to cum hard again, goddammit!" Rachel said slamming the patio door shut and pouting.

"Maria, isn't your father going to be home soon anyway?" Malcolm asked while putting on his shirt.

"No, he's in Orlando playing golf with the governor and then he's probably going to smoke some weed with his judge buddies. They're all a bunch of pot heads."

"Well, don't you ladies have something to do? I mean, you're only twenty-six years old and you don't have jobs. Why don't you go to the mall and spend your rich daddy's money?"

"I'd rather spend it on you, Malcolm. Do you have any idea how hard it is to find a straight man in Miami who's not strung out on drugs, or just can handle a threesome?" Maria put her finger in her mouth and sucked on it. "You have me spoiled. I'm addicted to that pene negro grande!"

"Addicted or not I've got to get going." Malcolm put on his shoes and headed for the door.

"Would you stay if I got you courtside seats to the Heat-Knicks game?"

Malcolm stopped dead in his tracks.

"Keep talking!" he said.

"My father has two courtside season tickets and you can have them if you fuck me until I'm sore!"

"For two courtside seats, I'll send both your asses to the emergency room!" Malcolm started to undress. "But there are only two seats and three of us. How do we decide who goes and who doesn't?"

"I've got an idea!" Rachel ran to the closet and came back with a Twister board game.

"You're kidding me, right?" Malcolm asked. "You want to play butt-neckid Twister?"

"Come on, this will be fun!"

"Let me see the tickets first before I make a fool of myself."

Maria rushed out of the room and a few seconds later she was back with the tickets. Malcolm folded them up and put them inside his pants pocket while they laid down the game mat.

The things you do for a fuckin' basketball game, he said to himself.

Rachel and Maria were standing on the game board ready to go. Malcolm took off his boxers and joined them.

"Ok, let's get this party started. I've got a game to go to tonight," he said, then he picked up the spinner and thumbed it with his finger. "Right hand, red!"

CHAPTER 21

MAINTENANCE MAN II

Senator Nelson raised his right hand and was sworn in as a United States Senator. Afterward, he shook hands with the vice president and posed for a photo. He tried to keep a straight face while the camera bulbs flashed.

"Congratulations, and welcome to the United States Congress, Senator Nelson."

"Thank you, sir, it's an honor to serve the American people."

Once the photographers were gone and the door was shut, the façade came down and the real conversation began.

"I hope we can work together to move the country forward," the vice president said to him.

"That depends, Mr. Vice President. Now that we have a super majority, the president can't pass a jaywalking bill without our approval. He's going to have to make some concessions on regulations and taxes if he wants to get anything done."

"I see those Tea Party folks have already gotten their claws into you. How long do you think you will last blocking every piece of legislation the president brings up for a vote?"

"Well, let's see, we've won a majority in the House of Representatives and now the Senate. Looks like we have the perfect recipe for your man to lose next November."

"You know, I've been in the game a long time. I've seen guys like you come and go. You rape the system, pocket the special-interest money, and then stand in front of the camera waving the American flag! Where is your commitment to the people?"

"Spare me the patriotic speech. We're all a part of the same hypocrisy," Senator Nelson said as he stood up from his chair. "The game has changed today and everybody seems to realize it but you and the president. Tell him for me, I'll be coming for his job next!"

He walked over to the door and opened it.

"Of course, that's strictly off the record!" he said with a devious grin.

"Get the hell out of my office!"

The politics in Washington were more divided than ever. The public opinion polls about the president were at an all time low, as well as the polling numbers on Congress. But as long as they were dragging the president down, the Republicans were willing to take the whole country down with him. They were willing to destroy millions of jobs just to get one man's job. And Senator Nelson was the missing piece of their puzzle. He was young, new to Washington, strong with the Latino vote, and ruthless. He was to be the Republicans' best chance in the next election. And he was going to take advantage of all the perks that came with that reality.

As he walked down the halls of the Senate with his staffers, his phone rang.

"It's me!" Vincent said.

"Hold on."

"I'll meet you guys at the office," he told his staff. "Get everything set up and we'll meet at two o'clock for a briefing."

Once the coast was clear, he found the nearest exit and went outside to talk.

"Go ahead!"

"We may have a problem, sir! Alex may have overheard your conversation with the Kross Brothers last night."

"How is that possible?"

"After the meeting, I saw her coming out of the office. When I went to secure the room, I found her purse in the restroom."

"So, what? Just because she went back to get her purse doesn't mean she knows anything!"

"That's what I thought, too, but why was she still in the building in the first place? We were on those interviews for at least five to seven minutes after you told her to leave," he continued. "And why did I see her coming out of the office—but not going in? I was standing near the exit with you and she didn't come by us. So, where did she come from?"

"Holy shit!"

"What do you want me to do?"

"Check all her phone calls and texts and have your man send me everything he has on where she's been and who she's been with over the past thirty days. We've been paying this guy a fortune to watch her every move and we haven't checked in with him in months. I've been too damned trusting of that bitch!" he said while muffling his hand over the phone. "It's time to find out what the hell is going on. Let's hope he's as good as you say he is!"

"And what happens if we find out she knows something?"

"What do you mean, what happens? We do what we always

do; we tighten up all the loose ends. I'm not throwing away my chance at the White House over a piece of ass! And if you find out she been talking to someone, take them out, too!"

"If you want me to do this thing right, we're going to need some cover—some kind of angle to make this look legit."

"Don't worry, I'll take care of that. You just be ready to pull the trigger. If this gets back to the Kross brothers, we're both as good as dead!"

"I'm on it, sir!" Vincent said. "One last thing, do you want this done quietly or do you want it public?"

Senator Nelson paused for a second and thought about it.

"Let's go public. The more media attention we get, the better! Besides, the sympathy vote for a widowed senator can be just what we need in an election year."

CHAPTER 22

"**L**et's go Heat! Let's go Heat!" the fans chanted as they poured out of the American Airlines Arena.

The Miami Heat has just defeated the New York Knicks in overtime and the crowd was still hyped. Malcolm hurried to his car hoping to beat the traffic, but it was hopeless. The stadium was jam-packed and people were celebrating and moving slowly.

Instead of screaming "let's go Heat," how about "let's go traffic?" Malcolm said to himself as he maneuvered through the chaotic traffic. "Damn! These people in Miami can't drive worth shit!"

The traffic got worse as he drew closer to Melvin's Jazz Club; most of the high rollers from the game were headed there for the after-party. Maseratis, Lamborghinis, and Porsches lined the streets waiting to pull into the parking garage and up to the valet. Malcolm sped by the long line of cars and swerved into his reserve parking spot in front of the club. He jumped out of his car and made his way through the thick crowd into the club.

"Hey, asshole, you can't cut the line!" he heard a man yell at him.

Malcolm didn't even bother to turn his head; he was focused on getting inside and making sure the entertainment was set. That was his department. The standing-room-only crowd was expecting a great show. It's what Melvin's was known for—that and the upscale and eclectic clientele. But this night was special. Not only because of the VIPs from the NBA who were attending the after-party, but Alex was opening the show for the first time. It had been years since she performed in front of a live audience. Malcolm surprised her on opening night when he brought her on stage; she didn't have time to think about it. He knew she would be nervous opening the show as headliner and he wanted to be there for her.

The second he walked in the door he could feel the energy of the crowd. It was even more intense than opening night, and there were more people—and more egos. People with money have a way of pushing people around. They're used to getting what they want, when they want it. Malcolm could see the stress on the faces of his staff as he moved toward the bar.

"Where's Simon?" he shouted at Big Mike, the head bartender. "And is Alex ready to go on stage?"

"He's in the back office!" he shouted back. Then he handed the customer in front of him her drink and moved in closer to Malcolm. "You better get back there, boss, she's not looking too good," he whispered to him.

Malcom tried to look calm as he made his way through the aisles of loud and intoxicated people. He didn't want anyone reading his expressions, but he was panicking. When he got to the back office, Alex was sitting on the sofa biting her nails. Simon was sitting next to her, trying to comfort her.

"What's going on?"

"I don't know, man. She was a little uneasy when she came in, but she got even worse when she saw him."

"Who?"

Simon walked over to the wall of security monitors and pushed the control for the camera in the VIP section. Sitting in the front row, surrounded by his bodyguards, was Derrick Mayes. He was a retired Hall of Fame forward, a national celebrity—and the man who raped Alex back in college. Malcolm's face turned stone-cold.

"I don't get it," Simon said sounding clueless. "Did they have a thing or something?"

Just then Ariel came rushing in.

"Oh my goodness, Derrick Mayes is here!" She sounded like a high school girl with a crush. "He's my favorite player of all time! Don't you just love his Wheat Grams cereal commercial?"

"Both of you—out!" Malcolm demanded.

"Was it something I said?" Ariel said while glancing around the room at all the long faces. "So, I guess it's not okay if I ask him for his auto—"

"That's enough, Ariel!" Simon said, cutting her off. "Why don't you go make sure we have enough champagne?"

After Simon and Ariel were out of the office, Malcolm and Alex sat there in silence. The music and the loud chatter of the crowd faded into the background. Malcolm knew an old wound had been reopened. But he didn't know there were new wounds, more deadly ones. After a few minutes of neither of them speaking, Malcolm walked over to the one-way glass that looked out into the club and leaned against it.

"I'm not about to give you a intervention speech telling you to get over it. I've never been in your position, so I'm not going to try to tell you I know what you're going through. But a few weeks ago you said something that made me very proud of you. You said you're not afraid anymore, remember?"

Malcolm walked back over to the monitors and zoomed in on Derrick, who was being swarmed by his fans.

"Don't let this asshole ruin your night. You've waited a long time to get to this point!"

"Malcolm, I don't give a damn about Derrick Mayes!" Alex blurted out. "Dealing with flashbacks about being raped in college is the least of my worries." She stood up and began to pace. "Seeing him was just a trigger!"

"Then what the hell is going on?"

"Last night, after we got off the phone, I overhead something I wasn't supposed to hear." She began to bite her nails. "Gary was talking to some men about how they were going to pay him lots of money to help pass legislation that would benefit this big drug company, and how he knew the drugs caused cancer, but Gary agreed to push it through anyway."

"Did you hear them mention which drug company?"

"All I remember was the last name Kross and him calling one of the men Randall!"

"That's not good," Malcolm said sounding concerned. "You eavesdropped on the Kross brothers! Those are two of the most ruthless bastards in corporate America. If they can't sue you, they'll buy you, and if they can't buy you—well, let's just say they usually get what they want."

"So what's that supposed to mean?"

"It means that if they perceive you as a threat, they will find a way to neutralize or eliminate you. The question is, do they know?"

"I can't be sure. Vincent found my purse in the bathroom and brought it to me as I was trying to leave."

"Who's Vincent?"

"He's Gary's personal bodyguard. He's about your size, with spooky eyes, and he has this nasty scar on the right side of his face, like someone tried to cut his face off." She brushed her hand across her face to describe the mark. "I could tell he was probing—trying to see if I knew something. But I kept it together—I think!"

"You already have one thing going in your favor."

"And what's that?"

"You're still alive!"

Alex closed her eyes, took a deep breath, and exhaled. Then she grabbed her small bag and carried it into the office bathroom.

"So, I guess this means you're performing tonight?"

"I'm at a point where I just don't care anymore. I'm tired of being afraid and I'm tired of letting people control me. Whatever happens, happens! I just don't want anything to happen to you! I would never be able to forgive myself for dragging you into this."

Malcolm walked over to Alex and embraced her.

"Don't worry about me, I can take care of myself, but if they decide to take this to the next level, trust me, I will turn this into a war they'll never forget!"

"Listen to you sounding all dangerous—and James Bond-ish!"

"I thought you knew, my nickname is triple-O-nine. And the nine is for—" he put his hand on his crotch.

"You're such a freak, Malcolm," she laughed and punched him in the shoulder. "But thank you for making me laugh and, most of all, thank you for making me feel safe. No matter how strong and independent a woman is, she wants a man who makes her feel secure."

"I'll always protect you, Alex," he said, looking into her eyes.

"I know you will, Malcolm. You've always been my knight in shining armor and I love you for that!" They kissed passionately and held each other tight. She let go and grabbed her bag walking backwards toward the bathroom.

"So, are you going to sing that song you wrote for me tonight? You never did text it to me."

"I accidentally erased it when I downloaded my wedding pictures onto Marcia's computer. But don't worry, I've got a much better song for you. It's one of your favorites."

She slowly closed the bathroom door in his face.

"Now let me go so I can get ready! I don't want you to see me until I'm on stage so—get lost!"

As Malcolm was preparing to walk out the door, he took one last glimpse of the security camera of Derrick Mayes sitting in the VIP section. He was surrounded by three huge bodyguards and was autographing a woman's breast.

"What a jerk!"

At that moment, Adam arrived with the other five gigolos. Malcolm had reserved a table for them all so they could sit together for the show. Just as they were passing Derrick's table, Carlos spilled his drink on Derrick's suit. The bodyguards bolted from their seats and grabbed him.

"Damn! Any other time but tonight!" Malcolm said as he ran out the door.

By the time he made it over to the VIP section, his security was already breaking things up. Carlos, who was about six-two and one-hundred-and-ninety pounds, seemed dwarfed standing next to the two six-foot-five, two-hundred-and-eighty-pound bodyguards. And Derrick was even taller than them, standing six-nine. He wore a thin goatee and his hair was short and wavy. After years of being out of the league he was still in great shape. When Malcolm stepped in the middle of the scuffle, it didn't take long before it turned personal.

"Everybody calm down!" Malcolm said, getting between them. "Adam, get Carlos and the rest the guys outta here!"

"That's right, you better get those bitches outta my face!" one of the bodyguards said.

Darius, the African-American gigolo, and nearly as tall as Derrick, rushed back over trying to get at him. "Back off, I said!" Malcolm yelled. "And Derrick, you better control these gorillas before I have all of you kicked out!"

"Alright, calm down man, don't get yourself all worked up!" He signaled to his bodyguards to sit down. "Have a seat fellahs, I wouldn't want to miss the show!"

"Is everything alright over here?" Simon asked.

"Everything is cool," Malcolm told him.

"That's right, everything is everything!" Derrick said nonchalantly. "Piano Boy here was just taking our drink orders!" He took a sip of his drink. "I bet you didn't think I remembered you? You were that faggot friend of Alex's who used to play piano back in New York when we were dating."

"Be careful, Derrick."

"That's right, you're a bad ass now. Didn't you join the Coast Guard or Boy Scouts right afterwards?"

"It was the Special Forces, you arrogant asshole. And if you say another word I'm going to have an Iraq flashback and put my foot up your wise ass and then put these two gorillas in a coma."

Malcolm said it with such calmness and conviction that it sent chills down Simon's spine. He had never seen Malcolm this way. He knew about his background in the service, but for the first time he saw the look in the eyes of a man who had killed before—and could kill again.

"Malcolm, he's not worth it," Simon said while holding on to his arm.

"My lips are sealed!" Derrick said smugly. "Now where's my waiter? I need another bottle of champagne!" He took a long sip of his drink and banged it on the table. "As a matter of fact, I want to buy a drink for the little Puerto Rican fellah," he said, gesturing toward Carlos.

"Save your charity for the Red Cross, Puta!" Carlos said.

"Adam, for the last time, get them out of here," Malcolm said. "And let's get the show started."

"Now, that's what we're all here for, right? To see my sexy college sweetheart sing," Derrick slurred. "I can tell you from personal experience she knows how to use those vocal chords!" he laughed.

Malcolm knew he wasn't just referring to having sex with her, but the rape itself. He quickly composed himself. There was no way he was going to fight Derrick without killing him. He had that much rage built up. Besides, he wanted him to see that he hadn't broken Alex's spirit. That would be the best revenge of all.

"You gentleman have a good evening and enjoy the show," Malcolm said calmly as he and Simon walked away.

"Hey, Piano Boy!" Derrick yelled as he pulled out a stack of one-hundred-dollar bills, "don't forget your tip. You can go buy a box of my cereal." Then he flicked one at him.

"Let it go, Malcolm," Simon said to him. "Just concentrate on Alex."

"That's what I've been trying to do. That's the only thing keeping me from whipping his ass!"

CHAPTER 23

MAINTENANCE MAN II

The curtain went up at eleven o'clock sharp, right on schedule. Malcolm was tense; he wanted Alex to have a great performance. She needed it. With all that she had been through, she deserved it, he thought. As the lights dimmed, he swallowed hard and prayed. "Lord, let this be her night!" He had no idea what song she was going to sing; even the band wouldn't give it away. She made them swear a vow of secrecy. As the spotlight hit the stage and the band started to play the first beat, he broke into a wide grin. The song was "Smooth Operator" by Sade. It was his favorite song by his favorite artist, and Alex knew it.

She appeared on stage through a thick mist wearing a long fitted red dress with her tight abs exposed. Her hair was pulled back in a long ponytail that came down to the middle of her back. In a classic smooth Sade style, she strutted up to center stage and stood there with her head down while the saxophone prelude played. Then she lifted her head, cupped the microphone in her hand—and killed it!

Diamond life, lover boy.
He moved in space with minimum waste
and maximum joy.
City lights and business nights.
When you require street-car desire for higher heights.

No place for beginners or sensitive hearts
When sentiment is left to chance.
No place to be ending but somewhere to start.

No need to ask.
He's a smooth operator.
Smooth operator[1].

The crowd sprung to their feet and applauded. They sang along to the lyrics and swayed from side to side. Malcolm was overwhelmed by how flawlessly she sang and how strikingly beautiful she was. At that moment, it all began to make sense. He realized why the men in her life wanted to possess her—to control her. She was stunning and powerful. She would expose the weakness in any man who was insecure. Men know when a woman possesses a strength they cannot match, intellectually or sexually. Instead, men try to break women down so that they don't have to step up. It assures that she won't leave him for a

1 Smooth Operator | Sade | Copyright 1985

better man—or just leave, period, Malcolm thought. He watched Derrick's expression while she sang with confidence and poise. The song was as much for him, and Gary, as it was for Malcolm. When she sang the lyrics, *His eyes like angels, his heart is cold*, she looked right at Malcolm. They were all smooth operators, but he was the one who was secure enough to allow Alex to be herself.

When the song was over, the crowd was completely enamored with her. Several men ran up to the stage placing flowers and one-hundred-dollar bills at her feet. Alex graciously took a bow and exited backstage. That song was the only one she planned to sing that night. She had closure with the men in her life and to herself. She was free; no one to answer to and no one to define her. Malcolm rushed back to the office to congratulate her. When he walked in the door, she rushed into his arms.

"I did it Malcolm, I did it!"

"That's an understatement!"

"How about this outfit?" she stepped back to model it. "Is this Sade enough for you?"

"Sade, who?" he laughed. "You made that song your own tonight. I'm proud of you!"

"Thank you, Malcolm. Now, I have one request."

"What's that?"

She walked over to him and put her arms around his neck.

"Take me home with you tonight?"

"Alex, I—"

"Shssh," she put her hand over his mouth. "I already know what you're going to say. Don't—not tonight!"

"But I—"

She kissed him before he could speak. She pressed her hips against his hard dick and then let go.

"Don't tell me this is only business between us, Malcolm.

Don't tell me about the rules of the game. I already know them," she said. "I'm not trying to obligate you. For once in my life I just want to be loved by someone who really knows me."

"Are you done?"

"Yes," she said fighting back the tears.

"Then pack your bag and let's get the hell outta here!" He kissed her on the forehead. "When we first agreed to work together I promised you dinner and dessert. Well, tonight you're going to get both!"

"Can I wear this dress?"

"Oh, no—that might be a little too fancy for where I'm taking you. Put your jeans on."

"Jeans?"

"Just trust me, woman!" he said. "Now, get going!" He slapped her on the butt.

"Ouch, okay already!"

Malcolm sat in his office chair watching the monitors while he waited. People were still buzzing over Alex's performance. The bar was crowded with beautifully tanned women and colorfully dressed men flashing one-hundred-dollar bills trying to get the bartenders' attention and the attention of the gold diggers who were looking for a sponsor for the night. He could see Simon and Ariel on camera at the club entrance trying to manage the hundreds of people still trying to get in. He laughed as he watched Simon trying not to look uncomfortable with the six-foot transvestite who had just come in. Malcolm could tell by his expression that he was trying to figure out if he was a she.

"Poor Simon, you don't know shit about women or transvestites!" he laughed.

Malcolm put his feet up on the desk while he checked his phone messages. There was a text from Helen: It read: The meeting was a big success. They accepted your proposal to franchise Maintenance Men Intl. in Germany, London, Japan, and Italy. I'll forward the contact information later; the rest is up to you. Good Luck, Darling. P.S. I want a year's worth of freebies for this one. lol

"That's my girl!"

He was about to tell Alex the good news when he saw Carlos and Adam on the security monitors drinking beers and walking into the men's room. Derrick and his three bodyguards were trailing behind them. One of them stood outside blocking the door and the other three went in.

"Oh shit!" Malcolm said as he sprang from his chair and then rushed out of the office.

The crowd was so dense he could hardly move. "Get out of the way!" he yelled as he pushed people aside. The dance floor was packed. The DJ was mixing "Freaks Come Out at Night" by Whodini, and the volume was cranked up. Everyone was laughing and having a good time. No one was able to hear him screaming directions. A few times he stopped to scuffle with some of the men he was knocking over. As he approached the bathroom, the bodyguard saw him coming. He tried to throw a haymaker, but Malcolm dunked underneath it and punched him in the groin and then gave him a fierce uppercut that broke his jaw and shattered two of his teeth. He quickly pushed him aside and entered the bathroom. By then Carlos and Adam were being held against the wall and had been beaten nearly unconscious. Derrick was sitting back watching and laughing.

"Well, well, well, if it isn't Piano Boy," he said while sipping on his drink. "I told you to control these bitches, didn't I?"

"And I told your arrogant ass that I would put your boys in a coma," Malcolm said, taking off his jacket. "But you—you I'm saving for last. I've waited a long time to get my hands on you!"

"Well come on with it, you pretty motherfucker!"

Malcolm methodically walked toward the closest man, grabbed him by the back of the head, and rammed his head into his nose. His nose snapped like a walnut and blood spewed everywhere. While he was down, Malcolm kneed him in the forehead cracking his skull wide open and knocking him unconscious.

The other bodyguard let go of Adam and tried to use his size to bull-rush him. Malcolm stepped aside and used his momentum against him and rammed his face into the commode. The sound of his head hitting the metal rang out. "Urggh!" he screamed. Malcolm swept his legs from underneath him, sending him crashing to the floor. While his back was turned, Derrick ripped the paper towel holder off the wall and tried to hit him over the head. Malcolm saw him coming in the reflection of the bathroom mirror and drop-kicked him in the stomach, sending him flying back into the wall.

By then the bodyguard who was on the floor grabbed Malcolm from behind in a chokehold and pushed him into the stall. He shoved his face into the toilet trying to drown him. Malcolm was struggling to get out and was running out of air. He reached up and hit the flush button and got some oxygen as the water went down. Once he recovered, he kicked the bodyguard's knees, causing him to lose his balance. Malcolm elbowed him in the face, breaking his eye socket. Once he was up, Malcolm swung on the stall door frame and kicked him with both his feet, sending him crashing into the sink and mirror. He cut the back of his bald-headed scalp and fell to the floor bleeding and out cold.

"Fuck this GI Joe shit!" Derrick picked up the beer bottles Adam and Carlos had with them and smashed them against the wall.

Malcolm stood up straight and caught his breath. He stood still with his hands down by his side as Derrick walked up on him.

"I'm gonna cut up that pretty face of yours," he said, lifting the sharp edges up toward Malcolm's face. "Now what you got to say to that Piano Boy?"

"Thank you!"

"Thank me for what?"

"Thank you for giving me a reason to kill you!"

Just as Derrick was trying to stab Malcolm, Simon and the security guards rushed in. But it was too late. Malcolm grabbed Derrick's right arm and twisted it over his right shoulder and snapped it in half. When Derrick swung the bottle in his left hand, Malcolm grabbed it just before it pierced his stomach.

"This is for Alex!"

"No, Malcolm!" Simon yelled.

Then he twisted the bottle out of his hand and stabbed Derrick under the arms with so much force it lifted him off the ground. Derrick fell to the floor shaking. He was going into shock.

Malcolm turned to the small crowd of people who had rushed in to the see the fight. He was emotionless—cold. He was ready to kill. He picked his jacket up off the floor. It was covered with glass and bloodied one-hundred-dollar bills from Derrick's pocket. He bent down to get closer to Derrick's ear.

"You better be glad they walked in on us, you lucky bastard. If I see you again, I'll kill you." Malcolm stood up and headed for the door, then he stopped and peeled one of the bills off his suit jacket. "And by the way, I hate Wheat Grams. I eat Cheerios, motherfucker!" He flicked the money back at him.

"Call the paramedics for Adam and Carlos." Malcolm said as he coolly put on his jacket. "And have the janitors come clean up this mess. We've got a business to run."

Malcolm went back to the office and went straight to the bathroom to clean the cuts on his hands. He had some bruising around his neck and his hair was damp and slightly out of place, but other than that he looked normal. Alex was waiting on the sofa with her bag packed. She didn't notice anything was wrong with him until she followed him into the bathroom and saw the blood in the sink as he washed the cuts.

"Oh my God, what happened?"

"Nothing. Just hand me the peroxide from under the sink and one of those Ace bandages."

"How did you cut your hand?" she asked while looking closer at his face. "And how did you get those bruises?"

"Stop asking so many questions? Just get ready to go!"

"Why won't you tell me what happened, I can—"

"Look, dammit!" he cut her off. "Are you going with me or not?" he yelled at her.

"Not like this!"

She looked at the security monitors and saw the paramedics rushing into the club.

"Malcolm, what did you do to Derrick?"

"Don't worry, he's still alive!"

"I told you I don't care about what happened with him!"

"This wasn't about you," he said coming out of the bathroom with his hand wrapped. "Carlos and Adam nearly got beaten to death by those goons. There was no way I was going to let him get away with that. He got what he had coming to him, and that's the end of it!"

She continued to watch the monitors and saw Adam and Carlos being carried out of the restroom. They were beaten badly. Adam was barely conscious and his lip was split wide open. And Carlos's face was swollen and both his eyes were black from all the punches he took. Alex's sympathy for Derrick quickly faded.

"I'm sorry, Malcolm, I didn't know."

"Maybe you'll trust me next time. Now hand me your car keys!" he said while shuffling through Simon's drawer. "I'm not taking any chances. If Gary suspects that you know something he's definitely going to have someone following you."

Malcolm put both their keys in the drawer, took out Simon's car keys and put them in his pocket.

"Let's go!"

He took Alex by the hand and they went out the back door of the club that led into the alley. Simon's purple minivan was parked next to a catering truck.

"You're kidding me, right?" Alex said to him.

"Simon is going through a transitional phase of his life," Malcolm said, trying not to laugh. "And besides, if we want to be inconspicuous, this is it! Now get in!"

"So, where are you taking me in this?"

"Somewhere that nobody would expect to find us."

"And where's that?"

"Denny's!"

ACT III

MONEY CAN'T BUY EVERYTHING

CHAPTER 24

"**H**ousekeeping!" a woman yelled as she pounded on the door. Malcolm awoke from his sleep and bolted from the bed. His head was still spinning from the medications he had taken.

"We'll be leaving in just a second!" Malcolm yelled back.

The channel on the television was still set on MSNBC from the night before. Rachel Maddow was interviewing a Republican senator who was trying to explain why they were trying to change the voting laws. Malcolm looked around the room and there was no sign of Alex. Her purse and luggage were gone. He shuffled through the Walgreens bag filled with Tylenol, peroxide, and ibuprofen trying to find his phone. He remembered putting it there when he and Alex were checking into the Holiday Inn. He checked the time on the clock sitting on the nightstand; it read 2:15. He went to the bathroom and splashed cold water on his face. That's when he saw the letter from Alex. It was written on Holiday Inn stationery and was propped up between the faucet and mirror.

I'm sorry, Malcolm, but I have to work this out myself! I told you, I could never forgive myself if anything happened to you. I'm meeting with Gary tonight before his event. That's the only way I'll know for sure if I'm safe. I can't live in fear for the rest of my life.

Love, Alex

P.S. Guess what? I woke up happy today for the first time since college. Thanks to you!

Malcolm rushed over to his cell phone and called Simon.

"Malcolm, where the hell are you?" Simon said sounding frantic. "The police are looking for you?"

"I'm not worried about that right now, where's Alex?"

"She showed up in a taxi last night right before the club closed and picked up her car."

"Did she say anything about where she was going?"

"No, she didn't," Simon said. "And I didn't ask."

"Goddammit!"

"Wait a minute, she did ask to use the office phone to make a call. I overheard her talking to someone named Marcia. Why, what's wrong?"

"I can't get into that right now. Just do me a favor and put my leather garment bag in the trunk of the Ferrari. And I'll need my black gym bag, too! It's in the back of the closet."

"What are you gonna do about the police?"

"Nothing!" Malcolm said boldly. "By the time they get through taking statements from Adam and Carlos, they'll be looking for Derrick and his boys, not me! Now, let me get out of here and find Alex before she does something stupid!"

"Hey, don't forget to bring my minivan back in one piece!"

"You don't have to worry about that. I'll be dropping this

Barney mobile off at your place in twenty minutes," Malcolm said jokingly. "There's no way I'd be caught dead driving around in this piece of shit!" Then he hung up.

While he put on his clothes, he watched the news. Senator Nelson's election was still the top story on all the networks. As Malcolm slipped on his shoes, there was a special newsbreak. The anchor reported that Senator Nelson had received death threats; they went live to a news conference that he had set up in Miami. Gary was standing at the podium wearing a conservative blue suit and red tie.

"As all of you know, I have always been a staunch critic of how the president handled the Iraq War. It's my belief that we withdrew our troops too soon. And I've always spoken out publicly against the mosque being rebuilt in downtown Manhattan. In my opinion, it was just another slap in the face for the families who lost loved ones in the 9/11 attack." He deliberately paused to allow for applause and then he continued. "But I guess freedom of speech has its cost because immediately after my victory speech two nights ago, my office received a flood of threatening phone calls. And today there was a bomb threat made at my campaign headquarters here in Miami." There was a gasp in the crowd. "The Department of Homeland Security has already begun an investigation and the Secret Service has assigned agents to insure my safety as well as the safety of my staff. I will not be deterred and I will not be intimidated! My Republican fundraiser will still go on tonight as scheduled at the Gleason Theatre at six o'clock sharp. God bless you and God bless America!" he said and then exited the stage.

As the reporter began to talk, recapping the story, the video feed of Gary walking off stage was still showing. Malcolm couldn't believe his eyes when he saw the Secret Service agent who was walking behind him. His head was bald and he wore dark sunglasses. It was Agent Harris, the Secret Service agent he met in Paris. "Now, that's some karma for your ass!" he said while reaching for Agent Harris's card. He still had it in his wallet; for some reason, he never threw it away. "Maybe this will come in handy after all."

There was another man walking right next to Gary. He had an athletic build. Gary was talking to him discreetly in his ear as they walked down the stairs. The Secret Service agents were at least three steps back. Malcolm wondered if that was Vincent, the man Alex said confronted her after Gary's meeting with the Kross brothers. As Gary made his way through the crowd, the TV cameras zoomed in as the reporter tried to get an interview. That's when Malcolm noticed the scar on the man's cheek. He knew then that Alex was in serious trouble. Vincent moved like a killer and he had those killer's eyes.

"Alex, this guy will cut your throat without thinking twice about it!" he said to himself.

Then he grabbed his keys and rushed out the door.

CHAPTER 25

It was late afternoon by the time Malcolm changed cars and put on fresh clothes. He drove up to the Bayside Mall looking for Alex's friend Marcia. He tried calling her cell number, but there was no answer and the number to the salon was constantly busy. He parked his car and walked toward Marcia's Hair Salon. As he approached the entrance he noticed vintage concert posters of Gloria Estefan, Bob Marley, and Aretha Franklin displayed in the window. It was a reflection of the diverse Miami culture and the clientele of the salon. Women of diverse ethnicities filled the seats at the stylist's booths, talking and reading magazines. The room was buzzing with chatter as the radio played reggae music loudly in the background. Malcolm walked up to the receptionist, a black woman wearing long braids. She was preoccupied answering calls and didn't see him coming. Malcolm waited for her to get off the phone and then he cleared his throat to get her attention.

"Excuse me, is Marcia in today?"

"Do you have an appointment?" she asked while writing in a large journal. Her head was still down.

"Do you know if she's coming in today?"

"Nope!" she said rudely, still not looking up at him.

"No, she's not coming in, or no you don't know?"

"Look, Mister—"

She stopped mid-sentence when she looked up and noticed Malcolm's muscular six-foot-five-inch frame and handsome face. He had on beige linen pants and a short-sleeve shirt, exposing his ripped arms.

"I apologize, Mister—?"

"My name is Malcolm. Malcolm Tremell!"

"So you're Malcolm?" she said sounding excited. "Alex talks a lot about you. You guys must be really close!" she winked.

Malcolm discreetly pulled two-hundred dollars out of his wallet and partially covered it with her appointment book, then he leaned in close to her.

"I need to ask Marcia some questions. I've been dialing this number all day and I can't reach her." He showed her Marcia's phone number on his cell phone. "Can you please help me? I think Alex might be in trouble and maybe Marcia, too!"

Her flirtatious demeanor quickly changed to one of concern.

"I haven't heard from Marcia today—nobody has. It's not like her not to call, especially on a busy day like today."

"Is there anyone who can go by her place to see if she's okay?"

"We tried that already, but nobody answers. Like I said, it's not like Marcia to be late. Even on her worst day, she's here by noon and it's after four. I'm starting to really get worried."

"What about the police?"

"What about them?" she said sounding aggravated. "You know they won't do anything until a person has been missing for at least twenty-four hours."

"If you give me her address, I'll go check to make sure she's okay and I promise you a locked door won't stop me."

She discreetly wrote down Marcia's address.

"Marcia and Alex are like two peas in a pod. They were just in here the other day downloading Alex's songs and some pictures off her cell phone onto her computer. They were like two teenagers. I'm sure if you find one you'll find the other. Here!" she handed her card to him. "I put my number on there just in case you find out anything."

"Thank you—"

"My name is Tanya." She shook his hand and slid him his money back. "I'm Marcia's sister."

"Tanya, if she calls, give her my number and have her call me right away." He handed her his card. "And don't worry, I'm sure she's alright."

She had a hopeful but pitiful expression on her face. She knew something was wrong, and so did Malcolm but he tried not to show it. He put the address in his pocket and made his way through the thick crowd back to his car. While rushing through the parking lot he glanced down at his phone, checking his e-mails and text messages hoping for any kind of communication from Alex, but there was nothing. He knew he was running out of time, or maybe he already had.

As he sped toward the address scribbled on the paper his mind began racing about how far Gary and Vincent would go. Would they go after Simon, Ariel, or maybe someone else close to him? If he found Marcia alive then he could calm down and recalculate his strategy. That was if she was still alive! Malcolm shifted gears and merged onto I-95 north driving over one-hundred miles per hour toward the city of Aventura. There was less than two hours before Senator Nelson's event at the Gleason Theatre. He knew time wasn't on his side.

• • •

Malcolm arrived at Marcia's subdivision at a quarter to five. Her house was inside a gated community and Malcolm wasn't about to take a chance of driving a bright red Ferrari into a middle-class neighborhood. He would stick out like a sore thumb, he thought. And it might be a set-up. He drove down two blocks to a strip mall and pulled out the black gym bag he asked Simon to pack. Inside the bag was a jogging suit, a pair of gyms shoes, a Chicago Bulls cap, and a nine-millimeter Beretta. He changed into the jogging suit, put the cap on, and stuffed the gun inside his jacket pocket. He knew most gated communities have second-rate security. They rarely stopped unauthorized cars from following each other in and they almost never stop people from biking or jogging in. As he approached the gate, he tilted his hat down, made a friendly gesture, and jogged right by them. One guard was busy watching ESPN and the other was eating a Subway sandwich. Malcolm sighed in relief and picked up his pace as he glanced at the street sign to make sure he was headed in the right direction.

As he approached Marcia's house, he slowed down and looked around to see who might be watching. Her home was at the end of the block. It was covered by lots of palm trees and high bushes that made it easy for a killer to get in and out undetected. He knocked on the door and rang the bell, but there was no answer. He crept around to the backyard and peeked into the patio window. Nothing in the house was out of place. There were no shattered windows or any other signs of forced entry. Malcolm knew that meant nothing. If they sent a pro to kill Marcia he didn't expect to see any signs of foul play—at least not from the outside. He leaped over a high fence that separated the yard from the side door of the garage and that's when it hit him. It was the unmistakable odor of carbon monoxide. He put his ear next to the door. He could hear the sound of a car engine idling. Malcolm took off his Chicago Bulls cap and covered the glass as he smashed the window with the butt of his gun. The carbon-monoxide fumes gushed through the small crack. Malcolm covered his nose and mouth with his jacket and reached through the small crack to unlock the door.

He coughed violently as he searched for the button in the garage to open the door. Once he found it, he pressed the button with his fist to let the door up. As the main door opened, Malcolm saw Marcia's body slumped over the steering wheel of her white Lexus. He used the sleeve of his jacket to turn the key off in the ignition. He didn't even bother looking for any marks on her body; he already knew they set it up perfectly to look like an accident, or suicide, or whatever story the police wanted to come up with. Marcia was also overweight; there are plenty of drugs that can imitate the symptoms of a heart attack, Malcolm thought. There was no time for remorse; he had to find a clue, something the killer overlooked in his rush to get away.

Marcia's phone was on the floor next to the gas pedal, but all of the text messages and phone numbers had been deleted. He popped the trunk and found a suitcase full of Alex's clothes, which meant Marcia was probably on her way to meet her to drop them off. The clothes had been rummaged through. He wasn't surprised that nothing helpful had been left behind. Think, Malcolm—think, he said to himself while looking down at his watch. It was five o'clock and he was running out of time. He had only one chance. He used his sleeve to turn the ignition back on, then he activated the navigation system. "Bingo!" he said. Marcia had already locked in her destination. Palladium Hotel, 2nd and Ocean Drive.

Malcolm took off running out of the garage, then he

suddenly stopped and ran back. He realized he was leaving himself open to be framed. He had to put everything back the way it was. He closed the garage door, swept up the broken glass and duct-taped the window with cardboard. He closed the trunk and slumped Marcia's body back over the steering wheel. Then he wiped everything down and turned the ignition to her car back on.

"Sorry, Marcia," he said as he closed the door shut. "You paid one helluva price for friendship."

Malcolm ran back to his car and burned rubber out of the strip mall parking lot. He thought about dialing 9-1-1 but realized he couldn't report anything to the police without implicating himself. Marcia was already dead and he didn't know if Alex was alive or not. As he sped toward Miami Beach, his military training had him thinking three moves ahead. How do I find Vincent before he finds me? Even if Alex is alive, how do I protect her and everyone else I care about? And how will I get away with killing a United States Senator—because if she's dead, he's dead!

CHAPTER 26

MAINTENANCE MAN II

It was just after five when Alex arrived at the Palladium Hotel. It was an upscale boutique hotel near the end of Ocean Boulevard, a block away from Nikki Beach. She handed the keys to her Porsche over to the valet and walked into the lobby. Gary was sitting at the bar surrounded by his staff, bodyguards, and a group of young women who were trying to get his autograph. There was a bald black man with him that she hadn't seen before.

"Well, well, well, if it isn't my beautiful wife!" Gary said as he walked toward Alex and kissed her on the cheek. "I'm glad to see the terrorists didn't get you!"

"Yes, I'm fine, Gary, and I can see you're just as popular as ever!"

"What can I say, I'm the flavor of the month," he laughed. "Hey, everyone, this is my lovely wife, Alex. Alex, this is everyone!"

"Hello!" they all said in unison.

"I'm familiar with most of your staff, but who's this gentleman," Alex said, gesturing to the bald man. "I don't believe we've met."

"I'm Special Agent Harris from the Secret Service, ma'am," he said while shaking her hand. "I've been assigned to your husband temporarily because of the bombs threats."

"Yes, I heard about that, it's all over the news. Is my husband going to be safe?"

"Yes, ma'am, that's what I'm here to make sure of."

"Okay, that's enough about bombs and terrorists," Gary said while guiding Alex toward the elevator. "Let me get my wife settled into her suite, then we can head over to the fundraiser. Agent Harris, you can wait for me down here in the lobby. My guys will escort me upstairs."

"Okay, Senator. And it was a pleasure to finally meet you, Mrs. Nelson."

"Likewise, Agent Harris."

The second the elevator doors closed, his demeanor changed. He let go of her hand and his voice became stern.

"So, where have you been all day?"

"I was out shopping for this dress so I could look my best for you," she said convincingly.

"And what about last night?"

"Don't you think we should talk about this in private," she said making reference to the two bodyguards who were on the elevator with them.

"You know what, you're right. Let's talk when we're in private."

The way he said it made Alex uneasy, but she kept her poise as the elevator climbed to the tenth floor. Once the doors opened, the bodyguards waited outside the suite while they went inside.

The minute the door closed he turned Alex around and slapped her in the face.

"Now that we're in private, let me ask you again, where were you last night?"

"I went out to a club with my friend Marcia," Alex said, holding the side of her face.

"And then what?"

"And then nothing, I went home!"

"Wrong answer!" he smacked her again sending her flying across the room. "Now, let me ask you for the last time, where were you last night?"

"I told you I was with Marcia. We went to get something to eat after the party and then she drove me back to my car."

"You're lying to me bitch!" he balled up his fist and punched her in the face, blood gushed from her nose.

"Oh God!" she screamed.

"God can't help you now!" he said. "I blocked out every room on this floor and the room below us. You scream all you want, nobody's gonna hear you through this hurricane-proof glass." He tapped on it with the ring on his finger.

There was a knock at the door. Vincent walked in pushing a room service tray. It had Pellegrino water and a sandwich on top of it.

"I had an idea that you might be working up an appetite, sir."

"Why, thank you, Vincent," he said calmly. Then he straightened out his suit and took a bite of the sandwich. "You want some, honey?" he pointed the sandwich at Alex.

"She's probably full after eating that Western omelet at Denny's last night!" Vincent laughed.

Alex's eyes filled with tears. Gary knew about the Holiday Inn, he knew about Malcolm, he knew everything!

"It's almost time to go, sir. Your car will be here in five

minutes," Vincent said looking down at his watch. "What do you want me to do with her?"

"Wait until nightfall, then have one of the guys take her home. I think she's learned her lesson, right honey?" He took another bite of the sandwich and set it down on the tray.

"Someone will be right outside the room to make sure you stay put," Vincent said to Alex while going into her purse and pulling out her cell phone. "I also put a block on the hotel phone so you can forget about calling the cavalry."

"Sounds like we're all set." Gary walked over to Alex and bent down next to her. "Just so you know, your girlfriend is dead, and your little fuck buddy will be joining her as soon as I find out how much he knows. And you—" he grabbed her by the hair. "You better have some goddamn answers by the time I get back, otherwise we're going to pick this conversation up where we left off, and next time I won't be so gentle." Then he punched her in the face again. "Let's get out of here. I've got millions of dollars waiting to be collected."

"Help yourself to some sparkling water and the rest of that club sandwich," Vincent said to her. "It tastes great with a little mayonnaise and mustard."

After Gary and Vincent walked out the door, Vincent put a device underneath the door and attached it to the wall with adhesive and screws.

"That oughta keep our little Señora in her place!"

They both walked calmly onto the elevator as if nothing happened. Vincent kept looking down at his watch, double-checking the time against his cell phone.

"You, stay outside the room until I call you," Vincent told one of the bodyguards. "And make sure your cell phone is on. Trust me, you don't want to be late for this call. Tick Tock, Tick Tock!"

CHAPTER 27

"**M**ove out of the way, dammit!" Malcolm screamed as he fought his way through traffic. He looked at the clock on the console; it read 5:54. He was only ten blocks away from the Palladium Hotel, but the traffic on 5th Street was bumper to bumper. He cut in and out of traffic, drove on the shoulder, and ran red lights. By the time he made it to Jefferson Avenue he gave up and pulled into a Shell gas station. He grabbed his nine-millimeter off the passenger seat and jumped out of his car and started running. *Gary needs an alibi. He wouldn't harm Alex until he was in front of people—in front of those damned cameras*, Malcolm thought. The fundraiser at the Gleason Theatre was just what he needed to cover his tracks. Malcolm ran with all his might, jumping over cars and knocking people down along the way. He ran south across Meridian Avenue, then across Euclid. He ran through a red light barely avoiding getting hit by a UPS truck. He passed Washington Avenue and then Collins. He finally made it to 5th and Ocean Drive and headed south. That's when the anxiety hit him. His watch read 5:57.

"Dammit, Alex, don't you die on me!"

Malcolm was running so fast no one noticed the gun he was carrying. He was a blur as he flew by them. The closer he got, the faster he ran, past 4th then 3rd. He cocked the chamber on the gun when he got to 2nd Avenue. He rushed into the hotel lobby and headed straight for the front desk.

"What room is the senator in?"

"I don't know."

He shot off a round over the front desk clerk's head.

"I'm only gonna ask you one more time, what room is Senator Nelson in?"

"I swear to God, I don't know!" the female clerk screamed. "He reserved all the rooms on the 10th floor. But he's not here! He left fifteen minutes ago!"

"Was his wife with him?"

"No, she didn't come down!"

"Call the police right now!" he screamed. "I said now, god-dammit!"

Malcolm pushed the button for the elevator, but the small hotel only had one and it was already on its way up. Malcolm made a dash for the stairs and ran up the ten flights of concrete stairs four and five steps at a time. When he came to the tenth floor, the door was locked. He looked through the small glass window and saw a large man wearing a black suit entering the elevator. He shouted to get his attention.

"Hey, hey!!!! Open the door!" he yelled at him.

When the man ducked his head out of the elevator to see what the commotion was, Malcolm knew it was one of Vincent's men and his reaction let Malcolm know he knew who he was, too. The man quickly hit the button on the elevator and the doors shut. Malcolm stepped back and shot the lock off the door and ran into the hallway screaming Alex's name.

"Alex! Alex!!" he yelled.

The hotel had twenty rooms per floor. He started at the back of the hall and went from one room to the next slamming his fist against the door and calling out Alex's name.

"Alex! Alex!!" he yelled.

He paused at each door and put his ear up to it so see if he heard anything. When he made it halfway down the hall, he could hear her calling out.

"Malcolm! Malcolm! I'm in here!"

"Where?"

"Here! I'm in here!"

Malcolm looked down at his watch as he ran as fast as he could toward the sound of her voice; it read 6:00. Seemingly in slow motion, he took one step after another getting closer. He could see the device that was holding the door shut. He could see her bruised face sticking halfway out the door. She had loosened the bracket by pulling on it and was almost out. She reached her arm out toward him, as she frantically tried to open the door the rest of the way.

"Malcolm! You came for me!" she said with a smile on her face. He smiled back. And then—*Boom*!!! The catering cart that Vincent brought into her room had a bomb underneath it. Malcolm was blown down the hallway and back into the stairwell. Alex's room was obliterated. A ball of fire shot fifty feet straight into the air; glass flew everywhere. The fire alarm went off and the sprinkler system kicked in. The last thing Malcolm remembered was her bruised face trying to squeeze through the door to escape and her arms reaching out to him thinking she was saved. Then everything faded to black.

CHAPTER 28

MAINTENANCE MAN II

"Is he conscious?" Malcolm heard a man's voice ask. "You think he can hear us?"

"I don't give a shit if he can hear us or not!" another man said. "When he gets out of this hospital we're going to take care of him, right after I find out what she told him—and if he has any files."

"Why not just do it now, Vincent? Don't you still have the stuff we used in Aventura on the fat bitch?"

"Man, there are so many ways I can think of to kill this bastard I don't even know where to begin."

"Let me do it," the first man said. Malcolm felt his arm being lifted. "He saw my face at the hotel before the bomb went off!"

"So what?" He felt his arm drop back to his side. "He's just a fucking prostitute! I don't give a damn if he's prior military or not. I used to eat those fuckin' Navy SEALs for lunch!" Malcolm felt a piece of sharp cold steel run across his face. "You're time is running out, pretty boy! Tick Tock, Tick Tock." Then he passed out again.

CHAPTER 29
MAINTENANCE MAN II

When Malcolm awoke the next day he was still in the hospital. There was a nurse holding a clipboard and checking his IV. He glanced around the room trying to focus his eyes. The sun was blaring through the blinds and ricocheted off a metal bedpan sitting on the table across the room.

"How long have I been here? Where's the remote for the TV?" Malcolm said sounding groggy while covering his eyes. "And can you please close the damn blinds?"

"Siete molto bossy," she said in Italian.

"I'm sorry, I don't mean to be bossy," he responded. "I'm just trying to figure out what's going on."

"You speak Italian, I see."

"Sì, e lei è molto bella," he said to her.

"So, you think I'm beautiful, huh?" she smiled. "Grazie!"

"Di niente!"

She walked over and closed the blinds and then turned on the television. She sat the remote in the bed next to him and put a plate on his lap.

"Now eat this; it will make you feel better. I'll be back to check on you later to take you upstairs for your CAT scan. Once we get the results, you can go. Addio!"

Malcolm took one look at the plate of food and set it aside on the table next to him. He flipped the channel on the remote checking to see if the news was covering the story about the bombing. But none of the major networks mentioned the bomb and the local channels reported it as a gas line explosion.

"This is all bullshit!" he said, throwing the remote at the TV. "They're not going to get away with this!" He tried to get up out of bed but his feet were shackled.

"What the—"

"It was for your own safety!" a man's voice said out of nowhere.

Malcolm turned his head and there standing in the doorway was a husky, bald black man. It was Agent Harris.

"Why am I in handcuffs? Where's Alex? And what is the garbage on the news about a gas line explosion?"

Agent Harris closed the door and drew the blinds shut on the door to have some privacy. He took off his holster and set it down on the chair. Then he walked over to the foot of Malcolm's bed.

"I'll explain what I can, but you have to promise me you'll stay calm," he said while pulling out his handcuff key. "I'm only doing this because you killed those bastards who took down my men in Paris—don't make me regret it. Deal?

"Deal!"

Malcolm ripped the IV tubes out of his arms and stood up from his bed. He was still a little wobbly. Agent Harris caught him and stood him up until he was steady.

"You alright?"

"I will be," Malcolm said. "I just need a minute to get my bearings. What the hell did they put in that IV?"

"Just a little something to keep you sedated. It'll wear off in a few minutes."

"Now, tell me what in the hell is going on," Malcolm said. "And is Alex still alive?"

"If you mean the senator's wife, the answer is no. She's dead."

Malcolm leaned against the window and put his head down against his arm.

"Were there any remains?"

"No, at least not any pieces large enough to put in a shoe box, let alone a casket. It was pretty messy."

"I saw her face right before it happened. I was so close!" Malcolm took a deep breath and collected himself. "Was anyone arrested?"

"No, but we're looking."

"Have you tried questioning the senator?"

"Why?"

"Because he's the one who did it. Him and his bodyguard, Vincent."

"Can you prove it?"

"Hell, I was looking right at one of his men when he took off down the elevator right before the explosion!"

"That's not proof! He told the police he was getting a bottle of water for Mrs. Nelson."

"And you believed him?"

"Look, we have our best men on this bombing. Whoever is involved is going to pay."

"Maybe you need to be asking the right questions, Agent Harris."

"Such as?"

"Why was she in the room in the first place? And why was her door bolted shut from the outside?"

"Can you prove that?"

"Have your guys go through the debris and see if they can find a long thin metal device that was either screwed or nailed to the door frame from the outside. Let's see if the bodyguard can explain that. In the meantime, I'm going to pay a visit to Vincent."

"Hold on, you're not going anywhere near Vincent or the senator. Let me handle this!"

"I know you think you know these guys, but you don't. They won't stop until they've killed anybody who stands in their way."

"Stand in their way of what?"

Malcolm started putting on his clothes trying to avoid the question.

"Where's my piece?"

"It's at the Miami Beach Police station along with your Ferrari. Nice interior, by the way, and comfortable, too."

"What did you do, take it for a joy ride?"

"I thought about it. There's no way I'll ever be able to afford a fancy car like that on my salary."

"Maybe I'll let you take it for a spin one of these days."

"That's a deal! I'll take a picture and forward it to my old crew back in Brooklyn!"

"Is that where you're from, Agent Harris?"

"Yep, do or die Bed-Stuy! And what about you?"

"Chi-town," Malcolm said proudly. "The South side."

"Well, from one big city boy to another, don't go after the senator while I'm on duty. I'm sworn to protect him from enemies foreign and domestic." He walked up to Malcolm and got in his face. "That means even from you, Malcolm."

"But he's dirty!"

"Hell, they're all dirty!" he said raising his voice. "And unlike you I don't get to pick and choose who to work for. Now, I know you want revenge but that's not going to bring her back, is it? Now let me handle this my way, otherwise it's going to get real complicated between you and me."

"It's already complicated! I just watched someone I care about get blown to bits right in front of me and I know that son of a bitch is responsible. It's no wonder that no one pressed charges; they want me back on the streets so they can get to me. Or they'll try to get to someone else I care about. This thing is just getting started," Malcolm said while putting on his shoes. "And lying to the media about a gas line explosion just to cover up another lie about a terrorist attack is not going to stop these guys! The senator planned this whole thing, starting with the fake bomb threat just to cover up killing his own wife. Now, what do you think they're going to do to me if I sit back and wait for them to make the first move?"

Malcolm walked toward the door and opened it.

"Let me ask you a question, Agent Harris, from one big city boy to another. What would you do if you were me?"

He paused and wiped his hand over his bald head.

"I would let the law handle it."

"No, I said what would you do if you were me—not you?" Then he walked out the door.

• • •

Malcolm picked up his gun and his Ferrari from the Miami Beach Police station and then drove by the Palladium Hotel. He wanted to see the damage that the bomb left behind and the last place he saw Alex alive. He drove as close to the hotel as he could get. The streets were roped off two blocks in every direction.

There were dozens of trucks, dumpsters, and other heavy equipment lining the streets from 1st to 3rd avenues. An army of construction workers was clearing the debris while federal agents sifted through for evidence. Malcolm turned down 1st Avenue and picked up the phone to call Simon.

"Simon, meet me at the club right away and call Ariel, she needs to be there, too!"

"Why, what's wrong?"

"I'll tell you all about I when I see you!"

"Alright, I'm on my way." Simon paused. "And Malcolm, I heard about the gas line explosion. I'm sorry about Alex."

"It wasn't a gas line explosion. It was a bomb!"

"A bomb?"

"There's a lot more to it. Just get to the club as soon as possible! Don't stop for anything or anybody!"

CHAPTER 30

S imon arrived at Melvin's Jazz Club and parked in his usual space in the back. As he entered the club, he could hear the faint sounds of piano keys playing from inside the main lounge. When he walked into the room, Malcolm was on stage playing along to George's Benson's song, "This Masquerade." He was drinking and singing along with the lyrics while the CD played.

Are we really happy here
With this lonely game we play
Looking for words to say
Searching but not finding
understanding anywhere
We're lost in a masquerade[1]

1 This Masquerade | George Benson | Copyright 1976

Simon sat quietly and watched—and listened. He hadn't heard Malcolm play the piano with such passion since Melvin died. Something was wrong—very wrong. Ariel came in shortly afterward and sat down next to him. They admired Malcolm's extraordinary talent as he stroked the keys flawlessly and let out the pain of what he was dealing with. He was sharing an intimate part of himself; it was personal and it reflected in his music. When he finished playing, he took a long sip of his cognac and rested the glass on the piano. Neither of them said a word until Malcolm spoke and broke the uneasy silence.

"You ever listen to the lyrics of that song? I mean, really listen?" he said sounding intoxicated. "It's trying to tell us something."

"And what's that?" Simon asked.

"It's trying to tell us that we're all living a lie. We're all hiding behind something—from something!"

"And what are we hiding from, Malcolm?" Ariel asked him.

He paused and took another sip.

"We're hiding from the one thing we can never get away from—ourselves. It's all a masquerade." He pushed his stool back from the piano and stood up. "This whole damn thing is a masquerade, it's not real!"

"What does this have to do with Alex?" Simon asked. "You said that she wasn't killed by a gas explosion—so what happened?"

"That's what I've been trying to tell you, it's all one big lie! The terrorist bomb threats, the gas line explosion, all of it! Alex was murdered!"

"What?" Ariel shouted.

"That's right, she was killed. But I can't prove it! But I was there, I saw her face right before—," he stopped and took another sip of his drink.

"Killed by who?"

"I can't tell you that—not yet! The less you know the better!"

He lifted his empty glass off the piano and walked over to the bar and was about to pour himself another drink. Simon went and grabbed the bottle out of his hand.

"Okay, partner, that's enough! Why don't you go lay down on the sofa in the office and sleep it off?"

"There's no time to sleep, they're coming. Maybe not today or tomorrow, but they're coming. They can't leave any loose ends. And I'm a loose end and so are you!"

"Malcolm, stop talking in codes, you're scaring me!" Ariel said looking upset.

"Good, you should be scared because this isn't just about Alex, it's about you, it's about Simon, it's about all of—this!" he said, spreading his arms out.

"So what does Alex being killed have to do with us?" Simon asked.

"Alex told me about a conversation she overheard that she wasn't supposed to hear and now that she's out of the way they may be coming after me and anyone who they think I spoke to. The only chance either of you have of surviving is not to know what that is. And for them to believe you don't know."

"Why don't you just go to the police?"

"Because they own the police! This thing goes up to the highest levels. Even my contacts with the judges can't help us!"

"Why not?" Ariel asked.

"Because we're not just dealing with a crooked politician, we're dealing with killers—real killers!"

"Killers like you?" Simon said out of nowhere.

Suddenly the room got quiet. Ariel and Simon both saw the recording of what Malcolm did to Derrick and his bodyguards. Simon had cameras everywhere in the club. What they saw was not a fistfight, but an execution. They didn't recognize Malcolm on the video. That Malcolm was cold, calculating, and dangerous.

"Yes, I was a killer, but they're worse than me," Malcolm said to them. "They kill without conscience. They kill because they enjoy it!"

"And you?"

"I was trained to kill to protect my country—to protect what I care about and to survive."

"So, you're trying to tell me that a group of assassins might be coming after you—and us?" Simon yelled. "I thought dealing with a cheating wife and a crooked preacher was a pain in the ass, but this is some real *Bourne Identity* shit!"

"So what do you want us to do?" Ariel asked Malcolm. "We can't barricade ourselves inside this club twenty-four/seven."

"So far, they haven't come after me—yet! You both should be safe. There's no reason for them to hurt you unless—"

"Unless what?"

"There's something I'm missing," Malcolm put his hand over his face. "I just need time to figure some things out."

He began walking toward the offices.

"Just be careful and don't do anything or go anywhere out of the ordinary. I've got to get my head together. I've got to figure this thing out!" He slammed the office door behind him.

Simon walked Ariel outside to her car. He was looking around nervously to see if anyone was watching them.

"What are you looking at?" Ariel asked him.

"I guess all this talk about murder and assassins has me a little jumpy."

"Do you think we're in any real danger?"

"I don't know, Ariel. Malcolm is a lot of things but he's not delusional."

"But he's been through a lot. He lost Alex and nearly got himself killed. Did you see his face? He doesn't look good."

"Let me talk to him alone for a while. I'll see you back here at the club tomorrow. Call me when you get home to let me know you got home safe." Ariel got inside her car and closed the door, then she let down the window.

"You be careful, boss. I wouldn't want to lose you. The job market is terrible out here!" she laughed then drove off.

Simon watched her car as it turned the corner. He went back inside the club locking the door behind him. When he walked into the office Malcolm was sitting at his desk watching television. Senator Nelson was about to speak at a press conference about the explosion on CNN. Malcolm had an angry expression on his face like he wanted to punch a hole in the TV. Simon sat down and watched with him as Senator Nelson approached the microphones. His eyes were red as if he had been crying and he was holding a tissue in his hand.

"Let me begin by thanking everyone for their prayers and well wishes. As you can imagine, this has been an overwhelming and traumatizing experience. Last night, my wife, Alex Nelson, was killed in a gas line explosion at the Palladium Hotel in Miami Beach. The authorities are conducting a thorough investigation to determine if there were any signs of foul play. All I know is, I lost the love of my life." he said, choking up.

"Give me a fucking break!" Malcolm shouted at the TV.

"Shhh," Simon said. "Let's hear what he has to say."

Malcolm turned up the volume and moved in closer to the TV. He wanted to see every detail of Senator Nelson's facial expressions.

"The funeral will be held this Sunday afternoon. The services will be for the family and close friends only, so I would appreciate it if the members of the media would respect our privacy," he went on. "But let me add this before I go. If there is any proof whatsoever that this was a terrorist attack on me because of my position on Iraq and Afghanistan, I will hunt you down like a dog and kill you. I'm a Christian man, but I believe in the Old Testament, too—an eye for an eye!"

The crowd applauded wildly as he stepped away from the cameras. Malcolm could see Vincent and Agent Harris in the background escorting him backstage.

"This is like a bad fucking dream!" Malcolm said. "He's actually getting away with murder! And the people are applauding him like a hero! This can't be happening!"

"Malcolm, look at it from the public's point of view. There's not a shred of evidence that what you say happened, happened!"

"Are you saying you don't believe me?"

"What kind of dumb ass question is that? Of course, I believe you. But I'm not the judge and jury! And the reality, whether you want to accept it or not, is that Alex is dead and there's nothing you can do to bring her back! Besides, if they feel that they've gotten away with it, why would he need to come after you?"

"Because of what I know!"

"Which is what?"

"I told you, the less you know the better. If anything ever happened to you or Ariel I would kill him in cold blood and call it a day!"

"Look, partner, why don't you chill out and think about how far you want to take this. We've got a pretty good thing going here. The club is doing great, your escort business is taking off, and as of right now, you're still alive. Now I know what I'm about to say is going to sound cold, but maybe Alex just got in over her head with some bad people. It's like you always told me, if you want to run with the big dogs you have to be willing to pay the price."

"But she was killed, Simon, it wasn't an accident!"

"I told you, I believe you, but should you have to give up your life for a life you can't get back? Just think about it."

Simon got up and walked over to the security monitor controls.

"Look, I was saving this for a special occasion, but I think tonight is the perfect time to show you this." He handed Malcolm a photo of Alex taken from her first night at the club, then he pressed the button on the DVD player. It was the recording of Alex, the night Malcolm embarrassed her by bringing her up on stage.

"You told her you deleted that."

"I lied," he laughed. "And Malcolm, I miss her, too. I was her biggest fan, remember? But you're like a brother to me and I love you. Don't do anything that's going to take away all the hard work we put into getting to this point. Just ask yourself, is it worth it?" he said to him and then he turned off the lights. "Enjoy!"

As the video began to play Malcolm looked at the photo of Alex and flashed back to when she reached out to him in the doorway at the hotel. He could hear her shouting, "Malcolm, you came for me!" Her voice played back in his head like a broken record over and over again. When he closed his eyes he saw her bruised face smiling back at him through the cracked door; she looked so happy that he was there to rescue her. He was so close. Then, suddenly, she was gone.

As Alex began to sing the Minnie Ripperton song, "Inside My Love," Malcolm buried his head in his hands. He didn't want to accept that Alex had been murdered and they were getting away with it. He was torn between his feelings of getting revenge on Vincent and Gary and his friendship and obligations to Simon. He tried to put the violence of what happened out of his mind as the video continued to play. Malcolm remembered how much fun he and Alex had together and how compatible they were.

He laughed out loud when he thought about how she

jumped up and down on him at the hotel in the Keys. How they sat naked on the balcony and shared a joint and how great the sex was. But his laughter was quickly replaced with pain. She was gone because he didn't protect her and he would have to live with that for the rest of his life. What hurt most was accepting that Simon was right. Like so many other women, Alex traded off her happiness for what she thought was security and she played the game with a dangerous and powerful man. She was gone and he had to get on with his life. For the first time since Melvin died, he let his guard down emotionally and let a tear fall. It was his way of saying good-bye to Alex.

CHAPTER 31

MAINTENANCE MAN II

It was 6:30 when Senator Nelson's limousine drove onto the Kross Estate in Boca Raton. The long driveway was lined with large bushes and well-manicured palm trees. A small army of landscapers were scattered across the posh ten-acre property. Vincent let down the window just as they were approaching the front door.

"So, do you know what this meeting is about?" Vincent asked the senator.

The driver gave him a look of annoyance through the rear view mirror.

"Just keep your mouth shut," Senator Nelson told him. "We'll find out soon enough. "

Once the car was stopped, they were met at the door by the butler. He was an older white man who looked to be in his 70s.

"Right this way, gentleman. They're waiting for you in the library."

"Wait here, Vincent. I'll be right back."

"The brothers want to see both of you. Right this way!"

The limousine driver followed them inside. He was a big man, six-eight, with broad shoulders and hands the size of baseball mitts. The senator had an uneasy expression on his face. Vincent just shrugged his shoulders and walked in unfazed by the giant who was walking behind him. When they entered the library, Allan Kross was looking out of the window at some young men who were lying by the pool. Randall Kross was sitting in a leather chair reading a book. Neither brother acknowledged them when they came in. The butler directed them to sit in two chairs near the back of the room and then he walked out, closing the door behind him. The limousine driver posted himself in front of the door and crossed his arms behind his back. The room was so quiet you could hear a pin drop.

"Senator Nelson, have you ever read *The Art of War*, by Sun Tzu?" Randall Kross said, breaking the silence.

"No, Randall, I—"

"I prefer that you refer to me as Mr. Kross," he said, cutting him off. "Allan is the civil one, I am not!"

Senator Nelson swallowed uncomfortably and responded.

"No, Mr. Kross, I haven't."

"You should read it sometime. You could learn a lot about warfare and power. Do you know what power is, senator?" His voice was stern. "Real power is putting yourself in a position where you don't have to use it!"

"I'm not sure I understand your point."

"The point is you're making too much noise! Why do you think we haven't been on camera or photographed for years? People pay attention to the things they see and hear. True power moves in silence; it does not seek to draw attention. And you, sir, are attracting too much damned attention!"

"As I said, I don't under—"

"Don't play games with us!" he shouted. He quickly composed himself. "Don't make the mistake of believing we're as naïve as those sheep who come to your rallies or the spoon-fed media. We own them—and we own you!"

"We know the explosion at the hotel was no accident! We have people inside the Miami Beach Police Department and the FBI," Allan Kross said, still looking out the window. "Do you want to tell us what's going on or do we have to find out for ourselves? The latter could be a problem."

"I don't know where you gentlemen are getting your information, but I was told that it was a gas line explosion."

"Okay, if you want to play this game it's fine with us," Randall said. "But if this in any way affects our business, we won't be happy."

"I assure you I have everything under control."

"Do you now?"

Allan walked over to where Senator Nelson was sitting and pulled up a chair across from him.

"Look, Gary, my brother and I have a lot invested in you. Why don't you tell us what's going on and let us put someone on it. We're all in this together—we're all family."

Vincent gave Senator Nelson a look as if he was contemplating telling them the truth about the bombing and everything else, but Gary knew the Kross brothers all too well. They had a reputation for being king makers, but they also had the reputation of making more people disappear than organized crime. He wasn't about to let them know that he suspected that their conversation about payoffs and bad drugs was overheard—or worse. Gary sat up in his chair and leaned forward toward Allan.

"Like I said, we've got everything under control."

Allan shook his head in disappointment and stood up from his seat.

"Okay, you're on your own. Tony, take them back to Miami," he directed the limo driver.

"It was great seeing you gentleman again," Senator Nelson said as he stood up and straightened out his suit.

As they were leaving the library, Randall Kross spoke up.

"Senator Nelson!"

"Yes, Mr. Kross."

"You've got to make up your mind if you want to play president or play gangster. You can't do both. Your methods are crude and so are your man's. Whatever you need to get done, do it. But do it quietly."

"That's good advice, Mr. Kross. In fact, I'm going to put that advice into action right away." Then he walked out.

CHAPTER 32

MAINTENANCE MAN II

The wind was blowing and it was raining heavily by the time Malcolm arrived at his condo. The sun was beginning to set; the clouds and lightning strikes over the ocean were moving in toward the beach.

"Welcome back, Mr. Tremell. Looks like a big storm is rolling in!" the valet Miguel said as he opened the car door.

When he saw the cuts on Malcolm's hands and the bruise on his neck, he frowned.

"Are you okay, sir?"

"I've been better, Miguel."

"Is there anything I can do for you?"

"Do me a favor and have the car washed and put the cover on it," he said and then tipped him with a one-hundred-dollar bill. "I won't be leaving anytime soon."

"Yes, sir."

A satellite cable company truck pulled in behind him. Malcolm heard Miguel giving the man directions. As he walked toward the sliding glass doors he saw the reflection of the truck speeding off in the direction of the service entrance.

"I got blown up, a hurricane is rolling in, and I don't even have cable—this is not my day," he said as he walked into the lobby. His body was aching and his head was light from drinking too much. While he waited for the elevator, he leaned against the wall and rubbed the bruise on his neck.

"That looks like it hurts!" a woman's voice said from behind him. It was the building manager, Angelita.

"It actually hurts worse than it looks," Malcolm chuckled, unenthusiastically.

"I heard about Alex; it's all over the news. Are you alright?"

"No, I'm not, but I will be after I get a shower and some sleep."

"You want some company? I'm off the clock."

"It must be nice to be off the clock whenever you want to be. I'm in the wrong line of work. Maybe I should've invested more into real estate."

"For your information, my grandfather started with one run-down hotel. Uno!" she emphasized. "By the time I was twenty-five years old I was running three resorts with a staff of four-hundred people. Trust me, I've earned this!"

"I'm sure you did. You're young, beautiful, and smart. You remind me a lot of Alex."

"Look, Malcolm, why don't I meet you up at your place after I file away some papers and lock up my office? You look like you could use a good rubdown and a cup of hot tea."

"You know what, that doesn't sounds half bad."

He grabbed her by the arm and pulled her toward him, but she pulled away at the last second.

"Not in front of the staff," she blushed.

"Trust me, the staff already knows we're having sex," he said while stepping onto the elevator.

"And how is that?"

"You have that fresh fucked look on your face every time I see you." Then the doors shut.

Malcolm breathed a sigh of relief as he peeled off the clothes he had been wearing for the past two days. He emptied his pockets and put his phone and wallet on the kitchen counter and then hung his suit in the closet. He went into the bathroom and turned on the shower and adjusted the water temperature to as hot as it could go. While he waited for the water to get hot, he wrapped a towel around his waist and stepped out onto the balcony.

"This is surreal!" he said to himself while he watched the rainfall over the ocean. "Did all that shit really happen?"

He reached his hand out over the balcony and felt the rain, as if to confirm that it was real. How could so many things be going so right and wrong at the same time? His businesses were booming. Melvin's was the hottest spot in town, and Maintenance Men International was franchised in four countries and still growing. All he had to do was be the face of the company, hire the right people, and collect the money. All of his dreams were finally coming true. He was on his way to the top. It wouldn't be long before he could pick and choose who to date and who to have sex with.

Simon is right. We've come too far. He thought to himself: I can't let my emotions dictate my actions. That was rule number one Melvin taught him. If you lead by emotions you are at a disadvantage to the man who is thinking strategically. He knew that Alex's murder was business—not personal. The senator's people were protecting their livelihoods. In their minds it was a matter of life and death and they pulled the trigger. It takes ruthlessness to do that. But even ruthlessness takes strength.

That was something he knew something about. He reflected back on his time in the Special Forces when he watched well-trained men freeze up when it was time to make the kill. It takes a certain mindset to kill a person and then go home and eat dinner with your wife and kids like you just punched out of the clock at the factory. That kind of man has to be detached, he has to be programmed, he has to be a cold-hearted son of a bitch. Malcolm was good at separation and he was even better at adopting beliefs that justified his destructive behavior. Cognitive dissonance, they called it.

As he looked out onto the city from forty stories up, he re-affirmed himself and set his mind on the business at hand.

"Don't be deterred, Malcolm," he said to himself. "We're almost there, stay focused!"

"Hey you!" a woman's voice said from behind.

Angelita was standing in the patio doorway holding a box of chamomile tea in one hand and a bottle of oil in the other.

"So, you just happened to have a bottle of massage oil stashed away in your desk, huh?"

"Sometimes a girl has to treat herself to a little maintenance every now and then. Besides, how can a woman tell you what she likes if she doesn't explore herself first?"

"Speaking of exploration...."

Malcolm picked her up and carried her into the shower. His towel was drenched and her clothes were getting soaked. Eventually they began to peel out of what they were wearing. Angelita tied her hair up in a bun and was about to go down on him.

"Wait!"

"Please don't stop me," she whispered seductively in his ear. "Let me take your mind off of everything."

Malcolm let down his guard again, this time to do what he

wanted to do anyway. Angelita was beautiful, young, tight, and enthusiastic. And he needed to get back on his sexual bicycle. Regardless of what happened to Alex, sex was how he made his living. Celibacy and the gigolo lifestyle were contradictions in terms. Why not tonight? he thought as Angelita wrapped her full lips around his shaft. When he tried to pull her up from her knees she resisted until he climaxed. After she was done, she walked out of the steamy shower, leaving him alone to relax and unwind.

Malcolm leaned his head underneath the showerhead and let the water run down his aching back for a few minutes and then he stepped out of the shower and wrapped a dry towel around his waist. As he looked at his reflection in the mirror he was surprised by how little damage there was to his face. His back and neck were bruised and his hands were cut in a few places, but from the chin up he was in good condition—good enough to keep getting paid. The bruises don't matter anyway, he thought while looking at the purple marks on his back. Women like men with scars.

"Here you go!" Angelita came back into the bathroom holding a cup of hot tea and wearing one of Malcolm's dress shirts.

"You look good in my clothes."

"You like?" she stepped back and modeled it.

"Well, since you've already raided my closet, allow me to show you my bedroom," Malcolm said, guiding her by the arm. When he made it to the bedroom, he turned off the lights and flopped down onto the bed with Angelita on top of him. As she began to massage his back, Malcolm reached for the remote.

"Ah, no you don't!" she slapped his hand. "No TV tonight, you're supposed to be relaxing."

"I guess you're right. Besides there's a problem with the satellite anyway."

"The satellite dish is fine. Whatever gave you that idea?"

"I saw the cable guy pulling up when I was coming into the building."

"We have a central dish for all the units and the only person authorized to call them for service is me," she said while squirting more oil in her hand. "And I'm positive I didn't call the cable company."

Malcolm closed his eyes for a second and then sprung up, knocking Angelina onto the floor.

"What did you do that for?"

"Shhh," he whispered while holding his finger to his lips. "Can anyone access this floor from the elevators?"

"What are you talking about?"

"Keep your voice down and answer the question!"

"No, the coding is updated every twelve hours to avoid unauthorized access to the units. The only way to make the elevators stop on your floor is with your pass or mine."

"Someone is in here, or they're coming soon. Don't ask me how I know, I just know."

Malcolm pulled a thirty-eight-caliber pistol out of the top drawer of the nightstand and took Angelita by the hand.

"Can you get into the stairwell from the service entrance?"

"Sure, that's the exit for the fire escape."

"Shit! That's what I was afraid of!"

"Why would anyone be after you? And why would they go through the trouble of climbing forty flights of stairs?"

"I haven't figured that out yet," Malcolm said while guiding her into the closet. "You should be safe in here."

He slid on a pair of pants and closed the door shut.

"Where are you going?" she whispered.

"Shhh, keep your voice down or we're both dead."

She instantly got silent.

Malcolm had to think fast. He tried to calculate how long it would take a man or men to get into the building, wait for the coast to be clear, climb forty flights of stairs, and cut through the thick metal door that separated his unit from the stairwell. He didn't have to wait long for his answer. A shadowy figure passed through the light coming from the open patio door. He chambered a round in his pistol and crept out into the living room. Judging by the amount of movement, he estimated there were two men. He looked back at the closet. He wanted to stay in sight of Angelita, but he knew that was a bad tactic. It would leave him too exposed.

His unit was large, over three-thousand square feet. The hallway leading from the stairwell was long and straight. The living room was on the right and the kitchen to the left. The master bedroom was in the back and had two exits; one into the living room and the other exit was through the master bathroom. That door lead into a short L-shaped hallway that circled back to the front entrance by the elevator. There was no way they could know about that hallway, he thought. It didn't show on the blueprints. His only way out was to use Angelita as bait. If they were in the living room they already figured they had him cornered in the bedroom.

He walked backwards into the bedroom and circled around through the exit in the master bathroom. When he came out at the elevators he saw two large men creeping towards the bedroom. He tiptoed into the kitchen and grabbed the pot of hot tea that was still boiling on the stove and threw it on the man who was closest to him.

"Ahhhh!!!" he screamed out. He fired off a shot at Malcolm, barely missing his head. While the man covered his face, Malcolm diverted the other man's attention from the bedroom by running behind the kitchen counter sofa to draw his fire. He fired a shot back at him and took cover. The killers had silencers on their guns, but even the sound of his gunfire wouldn't attract much attention. The walls were thick and it was thundering and lightning from the storm. There was no way anyone would expect gunshots and call the police. He was on his own.

He crept back out of the kitchen back down the hallway trying to lead them away from Angelita. Once the larger man took the bait, he rushed back through the master bathroom, through the bedroom, and crept up behind the man who he had burned with the water. He struck him in the back of the head with his pistol and caught him as he was falling and put him in a chokehold. He locked his legs around his legs to keep him from kicking. As he gasped for air, Malcolm put his hand over his mouth to keep him from making any sound, then tightened his biceps around the man's neck until he heard it snap.

When he rolled the man's body over to lay it down, something fell out of his pocket. It was too dark to see what it was, so Malcolm picked it up and put in his pocket. He crawled back into the bedroom and opened the closet door to get Angelita.

"Follow me!" he told her, "and be quiet, there's still one more in here!"

Malcolm kept low and led her out onto the balcony. There was a large sofa, plants, and a dining set for her to hide behind.

"Stay here and don't make a sound," he whispered to her as he slid the door shut.

When he turned around the other killer knocked his gun out of his hand, sending it flying into the corner. He punched Malcolm in the stomach and then lifted him off his feet by the neck and slammed him to the ground. Once he had him pinned down, he pulled out a needle and tried to stick him with it. Malcolm grabbed his hand before it pierced his skin. He kicked and punched, but the large man had him firmly against the ground. Malcolm reached around with his free hand and was able to pull the killer's gun out of the holster, but he knocked it out of his hand and went back to forcing the needle down on him. It was clear that it was supposed to look like an accident, just like with Marcia. Somebody wanted it kept quiet.

"I should have saved myself the trouble and did you in the hospital!" the man said as he leaned in closer trying to use his weight to press the needle into Malcolm shoulder.

When he got in closer, Malcolm recognized him. It was the same man he saw getting into the elevator right before the bomb exploded and killed Alex.

"It's you!"

"Say goodnight, pretty boy, your time is up!"

Suddenly the balcony door slide open and Angelita hit the man over the head with a large pot. He rolled off of Malcolm and staggered backwards against the wall,

"After I get through with him, you're next, bitch!"

Malcolm pushed back on his forearms and flipped up onto his feet in one motion. Both their guns were several feet away and he couldn't chance turning his back and getting stuck with the needle. Malcolm pushed Angelita out of the way as the man charged him with the needle in his right hand. Malcolm grabbed him by the wrist and twisted it until he dropped it. The killer elbowed Malcolm in the back, sending him to the ground, then he began stomping him. Angelita jumped on his back and tried to scratch his eyes out. He grabbed her by the hair and punched her in the face, sending her flying out onto the balcony and over the railing.

"Malcolm!" she yelled as she dangled forty stories up by one hand. The rain made the railing slippery and she was losing her grip. "Malcolm help!"

"I've had enough of this bullshit!"

Malcolm picked up the needle and rolled over onto his back

and kicked the man in the knee as hard as he could, breaking it. While he struggled to keep his balance on one foot, Malcolm rushed towards him while blocking his punches. Once he was close, he gave him two stiff uppercuts and then stabbed him in the neck with the needle.

"That's for Marcia!"

The man limped out onto the balcony losing consciousness. Before he passed out, Malcolm did a roundhouse kick that lifted him off his feet and sent him flying over the railing, barely missing Angelita.

"And that's for Alex!"

Malcolm quickly grabbed Angelita's hand and pulled her up and then sat her down on the sofa.

"Oh my God, is it over?" she said while hugging him tight.

Malcolm pulled the object out of his pocket that he found on the killer; it was Malcolm's own cell phone. First they switched out Marcia's SIM card after they killed her, now they were after his phone. They were looking for something.

"No, it's just getting started!"

CHAPTER 33

The coroner's vehicle was parked in front of the high-rise condo along with several Miami Beach police cars that had their emergency lights flashing. The streets were littered with orange traffic cones blocking off Ocean Drive for two square blocks. Yellow tape with the words: *CRIME SCENE DO NOT CROSS* was roped around the entrance and in the back of the building where the body was splattered on the pavement.

"This is a goddamn mess!" Agent Harris said as he boarded the elevator with two other agents. "I swear this guy is gonna give me a fucking heart attack!"

209

When the elevator doors opened onto the fortieth floor, the coroner was standing in the hallway with a dead body on a gurney. Agent Harris flashed his badge and unzipped the bag and looked inside. He recognized the man as one of Senator Nelson's bodyguards, but he kept it to himself. One of the agents with him took a photo and then he zipped it back up. "Okay, take him down!"

Angelita was in the kitchen being questioned by one set of detectives and Malcolm was standing out on the balcony with another officer. He had on a beige suit and a white shirt. Agent Harris had his men wait inside while he went to talk to Malcolm. He flashed his badge at the two cops as he approached them.

"Agent Harris, Secret Service, I'll take it from here!"

Without hesitation the two detectives walked away.

"That's a neat trick, can I have one of those?" Malcolm joked.

"What is it with you?" he said, closing the sliding doors behind him. "Every time I see you there's a dead body nearby."

"You didn't have any problems with me killing when it benefited you."

"That's different!"

"And how is that?"

"That was to protect a diplomat—you were helping me do my job."

"Bullshit! You can push papers in a cubical at the CIA and help save lives—but you choose to be in the field throwing yourself in front of bullets to serve your country. You're no different than me. You love danger."

Agent Harris smiled and leaned over the railing and looked down at the body that was being scrapped up off the pavement. Then he pulled a pack of Newports out of his jacket and lit one up.

"You want one?"

"No thanks, I'm trying to be more health conscious in my old age."

"At the rate you're going, you won't be around long enough to worry about getting old."

"So, aren't you going to play cop and ask me what happened?"

"I work for the United States Secret Service, not mall security. I already know what happened. I've been monitoring this whole situation since your name was mentioned on the 9-1-1 call."

"Did you know that the guy that's down there splattered all over the pavement was one of Senator Nelson's men?"

"I know that, too."

"So what are you going to do about it?"

"I told you, this is way over your head—and mine. You don't just walk up to a sitting U.S. senator, accuse him of murder, and start reading him his rights! It doesn't work like that, and if you think it does, you're living in a fantasyland. These men are protected by very powerful people, don't you understand that?"

"Then I guess I'll keep killing these bastards until I reach the guy who's pulling the strings!"

"These assassins come a dime a dozen. If you kill one, two more will take his place. It's just a matter of time before you run into someone who is faster and stronger than you."

"That may be true, but at least I'll go down on the right side—doing the right thing. I've been on too many missions where someone made a bad call. We simply traded one brutal dictator for another. Killing for hire, whether it's for the government or some wealthy prick on Wall Street, it's no different. At least I get to choose my enemies."

Agent Harris laughed sarcastically.

"What's so funny?" Malcolm asked him.

"For a minute you sounded like a soldier who was masquerading as a gigolo instead of a gigolo masquerading as a soldier."

Malcolm laughed, too.

"So, you know what I do, huh?"

"Hell, I knew that five minutes after we met in the lobby in Paris. I'm suspicious of everybody. Hell, I'd investigate my mama if she was acting suspicious," he laughed. "It took me less than thirty minutes to get your address, license plate number, military records, and your last urine sample. Do you think I would have trusted you in Paris if I didn't know your background?"

"So now that we got the charades out of the way, why do you keep checking up on me?"

"Let's call it professional curiosity. I've been trying to figure out how a guy with your training chose to go into this business."

"To be honest with you, it kinda chose me. I had a degree in music composition from a prestigious school, but it wasn't worth the paper it was written on. If you're not rapping or singing love songs you'll never get a record contract. So, I joined the service to put food on the table. But like everything else in my life, I had to be the best, so I signed up for the Navy SEALs for the challenge," Malcolm continued. "But even that wasn't enough, so I volunteered for assignments that nobody in their right mind would take, just for the sake of proving I could do it."

Malcolm paused and looked off into the distance. The rain had long since gone and a full moon was peering through the clouds casting a reflection on the ocean.

"You ever kill a man, Agent Harris?"

"Unfortunately, I have!"

"I'm talking about killing someone with your bare hands, not shooting at them from a distance like a goddamn video game. I mean cutting a man's throat and watching him bleed to death or choking someone until life leaves them. That's some spooky shit!"

"Sounds like you have regrets."

"No, just bad memories, but having memories means I'm still living—and they're not! In war it's either kill or be killed. Most people don't understand that politics is war; it's economic war without bloodshed and we all can choose to be either pawns or players—I choose to play!"

"So, is that what they're calling the gigolo lifestyle, a game?"

"No, I call it getting paid! Because when it's all said and done it all boils down to money. What's happening in Iraq and Afghanistan is about money. What happened in Paris was about money. And Alex's murder was about money. The adult sex industry is a three-hundred-and-twelve-billion-dollar a year business. That's real money, and I want my share!"

"You can't justify everything with money. What about morals and what about the fact that you're breaking the law."

"I'm amused by your condescending tone." Malcolm walked over and stood in front of him. "Where were your morals when you beat the hell out of that man in Paris who was chained to the chair?"

"I told you, that's different, it's my job!"

"And this is mine!" Malcolm said, raising his tone. "You think you're better than me because I get paid thousands of dollars by rich beautiful women to have sex?" Malcolm asked him. "I've got news for you, special agent Harris, everybody pays for sex! If you watch porno, spend money at a strip club, if you tip a woman more because she has large breasts, or even take a woman out for dinner, you, my friend, are paying for sex! The difference between people like you and people like me is that I'm honest enough to call it what it is! People like you are in denial or hiding. And the more people hide, the more they'll pay to keep those secrets safe. Professionals like me don't get paid just for having sex, we get paid to separate the emotional from the sexual and keep our mouths shut!"

"Three-hundred-and-twelve-billion dollars a year, huh?"

"Yep, three-hundred-and-twelve-billion," Malcolm replied. "That's more than the NFL, NBA, MLB, and NHL combined!"

"Damn! I'm in the wrong line of work."

"That's what I've been trying to tell you since we met!" Malcolm laughed.

Agent Harris took another drag off his cigarette, then put it out under his shoe. Then he walked over to the balcony door and grabbed the handle.

"Hey, before you go, I need one favor," Malcolm told him.

"I'm afraid to ask, but what is it?"

"I need you to set up a meeting with me and the senator."

"What! Are you crazy?" he shouted. "Give me two reasons why I should do something that stupid!"

"I know you don't want him to get away with killing Alex any more than I do."

Agent Harris paused for a second and put his hand on his chin.

"And what's the second reason?"

"I guarantee you he'll take the meeting. All you have to do is tell him that I've got the text and e-mail he's looking for."

"That's it?"

"That's it."

"What makes you think he'll bite?"

"I didn't share this with you before, but Vincent also killed Alex's hairdresser. When I found the body, they had replaced her SIM card and one of the guys they sent to kill me had my phone in his pocket. This guy is scared to death about something that Alex may have seen or recorded. And I think he'll do anything to get his hands on it."

"Sounds like a long shot to me!"

"Well, call me Larry Bird, because that's the best shot I've got."

"Okay, I'll get the message to him. But when this is over, if you're still alive, we need to talk about you joining the team," Agent Harris said. "You're a hothead, but we could use someone with your talents."

"How many times do I have to tell you, you guys don't get paid enough—and the hours are shitty, and the—!"

"Yeah, yeah, I remember, and you don't like our outfits," he said as he opened the sliding glass doors. "By the way, I know Mrs. Nelson's funeral is in a couple of days. Do me a favor and try not to get killed or kill anybody in the next forty-eight hours."

"You know I can't make you that promise, Agent Harris."

"I didn't think so, but it never hurts to ask."

CHAPTER 34

MAINTENANCE MAN II

The sun was just beginning to set in Las Olas, an upscale area of Fort Lauderdale just north of the airport. Senator Nelson insisted on meeting there since he was flying out later that night. Malcolm saw the black stretch limousine pulling into the parking garage where they agreed to meet. He stepped out into the open and waved his hand to make sure the driver saw him. The car slowly pulled up to him and came to a stop. The driver rushed out of the door and threw Malcolm against the car and began to frisk him.

"You don't think I'm dumb enough to wear a wire, do you?" Malcolm asked.

"I don't know what you're capable of, Mr. Tremell," a voice said from inside the car, through the back window that had been lowered. "So you will excuse me if I take every possible precaution."

"He's clean!" the driver said.

The back door of the limousine swung open.

"Get in!"

Malcolm looked around apprehensively, cupped the disk drive he had in his hand, and stepped into the car. There he was, face to face with the man who had caused him so much misery. Senator Nelson was only three feet away. There were two large bodyguards sitting in the back seat with him. One of them was pointing a gun at Malcolm. It took Malcolm every ounce of strength not to kill them all.

"So where is it?"

"You get straight down to business, don't you?"

"I don't have time for games, Mr. Tremell. Either you have something for me or you don't!"

"Before I give you anything, I just want you to know that Alex was a good friend of mine. Whatever it is that you think she knew, you didn't have to kill her for it."

"I don't have time for your speeches," Senator Nelson said to him. "You've got ten seconds to give me what I want or else these gentleman are going to throw you out."

Malcolm un-balled his fist and revealed a small flash drive. The bodyguard sitting next to him quickly snatched it out of his hand and plugged it into the computer he had on the seat next to him.

"You know, it's politicians like you who make people so cynical about our government. You stand in front of those cameras and lie to people about loving America and family values, but in reality you're nothing but a bunch of sick murdering bastards!"

Senator Nelson sat silently waiting to see what files came up on the computer.

"You shouldn't have killed Alex, senator, and you shouldn't have sent your goons after me."

"Shut your fuckin' mouth!" the bodyguard holding the gun on him said. "Or I'll shut it for you, permanently!"

"There's nothing on here, sir!" the bodyguard with the computer said. "This drive is empty!"

"What do you want, Mr. Tremell. I know you didn't have the agent set this meeting up just to see my handsome face."

"I wanted to let you know that I know what you're looking for and when I find it, I'm going to uncover all of your phony God Bless America bullshit!"

"You want me to kill him, sir!" the man with the gun asked.

"No, you idiot. The agent set up this meeting, remember? How are we going to explain him disappearing? Besides, this guy doesn't have anything on me, he's just bluffing," Senator Nelson said arrogantly. "Why don't you do yourself and your friends a favor, Mr. Tremell, and join the winning team? I guarantee you I can pay you a helluva lot more than you're making selling your ass on the streets."

"And what about the men I killed last night? You're trying to tell me all of that is going to be forgotten?"

"It was never my idea to kill you, I just wanted some information. Sometimes Vincent can go rogue and take matters into his own hands. The bottom line is you're still alive and they're not—to the victor go the spoils, right?"

"Yeah, but you're the one pulling all the strings. Just like you did with Alex and Marcia."

"Look, you naïve bastard, you can keep carrying this ridiculous grudge and end up dead or you can wise up and play in the big leagues. I'm a United States senator and soon to be president. No one is gonna give a shit about some made-up, unsubstantiated story by a high-priced male prostitute. Now, for the last time, do you want the job and the money or not?"

"Money can't buy everything, senator. It didn't buy Alex's love, it didn't buy Vincent's loyalty, and it's not going to buy your way out of me getting my revenge."

"Get this lunatic out of here."

The door swung open and the driver who was standing outside reached inside and pulled Malcolm out. Before the car pulled off the senator lowered his window.

"Next time you want to play high-stakes poker, make sure you're holding more than a joker!" He threw the empty flash drive at him. "And one more thing, don't forget to vote!" he said as the limo drove off.

Malcolm knew he was right; all he had was a story. No one was going to believe him over a U.S. senator.

"It's not over yet, you arrogant cocksucker," Malcolm said as he smashed the disk with his foot. "Guys like you always have secrets—you always make mistakes."

CHAPTER 35

The ride down I-95 was a long and painful one. As he watched the Miami skyline in the distance grow closer, the past week replayed in his mind like a bad horror movie. Alex and Marcia were dead, he almost got himself blown up, and Vincent sent his men to kill him in his own home. He balled up his fist and pounded the armrest. Malcolm didn't want to feel defeated, but he couldn't help it. He was used to being in control—in charge— but he had just been punked by a man who tried to kill him and laughed in his face. He knew it was only a matter of time before the senator finished what he started. Once the media attention subsided, the attempts on his life, and his friends, would start all over again. Living in that kind of fear is not living at all, he thought. Malcolm decided to call his men and warn them. As he was about to call Adam, his phone rang. The number was from an unfamiliar 954 area code.

"Hello?"

"Hello, Malcolm, this is Tanya, Marcia's sister."

"Look, I'm sorry I didn't get back to you about your sister. I never got past her security gate. Did you ever find out what happened to her?" He was playing naïve.

"The police found her dead in her garage later that day. They think she died of a heart attack."

He shook his head knowing that she had been murdered, but he kept his composure and continued to play the role.

"That's awful! Is there anything I can do?"

"Well, I'm in the process of closing the shop and I wanted you to have Alex's computer."

"I appreciate your calling but that won't be necessary."

"But she would want you to have it. I know how she felt about you. She would always light up whenever your name came up. Besides, she has all of her music and wedding pictures that she downloaded from her new iPhone."

"I'm amazed she figured out how to do that. She was so computer illiterate." Malcolm laughed.

"I know. She asked me one day, what did the 'i' stand for in iPhone? I nearly peed on myself," she laughed loudly.

It was the kind of laugh that relieved a lot of pain. Malcolm did not want to disappoint her.

"I'm headed in that direction now. I'll be there in twenty minutes. Can you wait for me?"

"Of course, I can."

"Okay, I'll see you then—bye!"

"Malcolm wait!" she shouted and then she paused. "Don't you think it's a crazy coincidence how they both died on the same day?" she said somberly. "I guess God wanted them to be together in heaven, too, huh?"

"Yeah, Tanya, that's exactly what I was thinking," Malcolm

replied, trying not to break down. "God wanted those two angels to be together in heaven. I'll see you in a few minutes!" Then he hung up.

• • •

When he arrived at the beauty shop, he pulled into the back and blew the horn. Tanya came out of the door with a black computer bag hanging over her shoulder and carrying a brown envelope. Malcolm stepped out of the taxi to greet her.

"I'm sorry about Marcia!" Malcolm said while hugging her.

"I'm sorry about Alex, too. I know you guys were more than friends. Women can always tell, you know?"

"Yeah, she was pretty special to me."

"Here," she said while handing him the envelop. "These are copies of her wedding photos. She looked so beautiful that day." Then she passed him the laptop. "She downloaded a song for you on this, but I'm not a Mac person so you'll have to figure out how to find it."

"Thanks, Tanya, I promise you I'll take good care of this." He kissed her on the cheek and stepped back into his car.

• • •

When he got home he opened the laptop and turned it on. He smiled when he saw the screen saver. It was a photo of him and Alex from their college days. He had a high-top fade haircut and she was wearing braces.

"The first thing I'm gonna do is delete this picture," he said, laughing.

He opened her iTunes folder and clicked on her music library. There were dozens of labeled songs with the word, DEMO, and the number next to it, 1 through 40. There was one song that stood out, it was labeled: DEMO For Malcolm. He clicked on it and it began to play. When he heard her voice, it gave him chills down his spine.

"Okay, Malcolm, this one is for you. Promise me you won't laugh, because you know how sensitive artists can be about their music." she laughed. "It's called, 'Let Me In,' and it goes something like this." The song began with a funky beat and then she began to sing.

> *Baby, I would like to get to know you bet-ter,*
> *What will it take for you to let me near-er?*
>
> *Don't be scared, I won't disappoint you*
> *Don't be scared, I won't try to change you*
>
> *My love is unconditional*
> *My devotion is immeasurable*
>
> *Let me in, baby, it's lonely out here in this cold world*
> *Let me in, baby, so I can stop being strong*
> *and play my role as your girl*

Malcolm couldn't listen to any more. It hurt too much. He turned the song off halfway through and started scrolling through the other songs. He noticed there were four files with no names, only dates and different times. The first file was labeled 11/11/5:35 AM. He clicked it and heard Alex's voice.

"Testing one-two, testing one-two. Is this thing on?" she laughed. "I'm home alone playing with myself. Where is a good vibrator when you need one?" Then it stopped.

The second file was labeled 11/11/12:15 p.m. He clicked on

it and heard Alex's voice again.

"I hate this phone, I can't tell if I'm recording or not, where is the fucking manual? Hello, hello! I knew I should have kept my Blackberry. Dammit!" Then it stopped.

Malcolm smiled just thinking about how raw Alex was. That's what he missed most about her. He scrolled down to the third file labeled 11/11/4:44 p.m., and clicked it. This time Marcia and Alex were talking.

"Hello, this is Marcia! We're here at Marcia's Hair Salon trying to teach this grown-ass woman how to use her own phone. Isn't that a shame?" Then Alex jumped in. "I know what I'm doing, give me that! Hello, America, this is Alex Nelson, wife of the very serious and anal Senator Gary Nelson of Florida. Please don't judge me by my stuck-up husband; he has a serious pole up his ass. Anyway, watch me tonight on national TV during the election. Win or lose, I will be looking fabulous." All the women in the salon were cracking up in the background. Then it stopped.

"I'll be damned!" he said to himself. "That was recorded on election night." He pulled out his phone and frantically scrolled through his call history. When he found Alex's call from that night, the information read November 11, 7:22 p.m. The last file on Alex's computer was labeled 11/11/7:25.

Malcolm turned the volume up as loud as it would go and clicked the file. The voices in the background were faint, but he could hear every word.

"Mr. Kross, the senator will be up shortly," he heard a man's voice say. "Can I offer you gentleman anything to drink?"

"No, thank you, we won't be here long."

"Gentleman! Glad you could make it!" It was Senator Nelson's voice.

"Let's cut the bullshit and get down to business," Randall Kross said. "We want you in Washington first thing tomorrow morning to start pushing through our prescription drug legislation Senate Bill HP 1189. We have a man inside the FDA who will make sure we get fast approval."

"I was told the president threatened to veto it."

"You let us worry about that. We have new data that shows that our new drugs are safe."

"You mean the drugs that cause cervical cancer and eventually kill people five or ten years later?" Gary responded. "And according to the confidential reports I read, your company is also manufacturing the drugs to treat the side effects that your drugs will cause. As you can see, I've been doing my homework."

There was an extended pause. Then Malcolm heard one of the men clear his throat.

"Since when did the truth ever get in our way?" Allan Kross asked. "That's what you said at our last meeting, remember?"

"Yes, sir I do."

"There'll be lots of money in it for you. It takes a lot of cash to run for president."

"Understood. I'll be on a flight first thing tomorrow. Let me check with my staff on what's available."

"Why wait for tomorrow? We have a jet fueled and ready to go tonight. Let's meet at the West Palm Beach Airport. We've got a few things to pick up at our Boca Raton estate before we go. Our driver will pick you up. How does midnight sound?"

He stopped the audio at that point and frantically pulled out his phone and called Adam.

"What's going on, Boss?"

"Adam, drop whatever you're doing and get over here right away!" Malcom told him. "I've got something to tell you, but you need to know in advance, it could get us both killed."

"Man, at my age, I don't fear nothing but erectile dysfunction and the IRS—shoot!"

"Alex accidentally recorded the Kross brothers and Senator Nelson discussing some back-door deal—I have it right here. I'm loading a copy into your dropbox file now," he told him while he was typing. "And there's something else I never told you. The explosion that killed Alex at the Palladium Hotel was a cover-up by the Senator! I was there—I watched her die!"

"I knew that son-of-a-bitch was dirty! That story sounded bogus from the jump!" Adam stated. "So, what do you want me to do?"

"I need you to reach out to our political contacts and get a meeting with the Kross brothers."

"Are you talking about *the* Kross brothers? The ones that own half the country?"

"Yes, that's exactly who I'm talking about."

"What do you want me to tell them it's about?"

"Just tell them I have some information about Senator Nelson and Senate Bill HP 1189."

"That's it?"

"Trust me, that's all it's gonna take."

"I'm on it, boss, but—," he stopped mid-sentence.

"But what?"

"How do you know the Kross brothers don't already know this audio exists? How can you be sure?"

"If the Kross brothers were the ones after me, I'd already be dead! Just trust me on this one and set up the meeting." Then he hung up.

Malcolm reclined in his seat and listened to the audio file again and again.

"Now we'll see who has the best poker hand!" he said out loud. "I've got all of you by the balls now!"

CHAPTER 36

It was 10:15 the next morning when Malcolm approached the gate of the Kross Brothers' estate. He stopped at the security gate and showed them his I.D. A large man with a heavy Polish accent gestured for him to step out of the car. "Put your hands up, and turn around," he said to Malcolm. While he was being frisked, another man went through his car looking for anything that seemed suspicious. He checked Malcolm's pockets and found a small digital recorder. He turned it on and off and then handed it back to him. "Okay, let him in!" the guard said.

The wrought iron gates slowly opened and Malcolm drove toward the large mansion determined that his meeting would bring an end to the attempts on his life. The Kross brothers were ruthless, but they were businessmen first. If he could convince them that it was in their best financial interest to do what he wanted them to do, why wouldn't they? Senator Nelson and Vincent, on the other hand, were reckless bullies. They killed first and asked questions later. But killing always has consequences; those who are impacted often respond and draw unwanted attention. Malcolm was banking on the Kross brothers' obsession with privacy to make his enemy, their enemy.

As he drove up the driveway of the posh ten-acre estate, he felt a degree of respect for the Kross brothers. Yes, they were crooks and killers, but they always did it by proxy. They were always three to four people removed from the crime. Instead of pulling the trigger, they pitted people against one another to destroy themselves. Instead of breaking the laws, they purchased the lawmakers. It takes more balls to hijack the congress of a nation than to knock off a liquor store, he thought. Their story was the American Dream: money, power, and influence. The wealthiest people in this country made their fortune off of other people's sweat or by stealing it from someone who had more than they did. As Malcolm pulled up to the front door, he admired their strength to do what most other men are afraid to do—build an empire and do whatever it takes to protect it!

"Good morning, sir," the butler said while opening his car door. "Mr. Kross is expecting you." He closed the car door and walked ahead. "Follow me."

He led Malcolm down a wide hallway through the living room and past a lavish art gallery. The décor screamed old money. The furnishing was traditional and antique. The large paintings hanging on the walls resembled an art museum. Malcolm was no art expert, but any novice could tell the paintings were worth millions. When he entered the library, a large man dressed in a black suit patted him down again. Once he determined that Malcolm was clean, he gestured for him to walk inside, then he closed the door behind him. The Kross brothers were sitting in two leather chairs behind a large oak desk looking relaxed and self-confident.

"So you're the man who's causing Senator Nelson so much trouble," Allan Kross said.

"I see it the other way around."

"We'll just see about that. Play the recording."

Malcolm pulled the digital recorder out of his pocket and pressed play. As it played, they whispered in each other's ears while staring back at Malcolm. Thirty seconds later, they heard what they needed to hear.

"Okay, that's enough!" Allan Kross said.

"Don't you want to know where I got this from?"

"What does that matter now? You have it, don't you?"

He whispered in his brother's ear again and then stood up from the table.

"What is it that you want from us, Mr. Tremell?"

"I want Senator Nelson out of the picture."

"So, go pay a hit man. We're businessmen, not gangsters," Randall Kross told him. "We overcome our opponents by calculation, not by force."

"That's a philosophy shared by the ancient Chinese military philosopher Li Quan."

Randall looked over at his brother with a sly grin. He tried not to show it, but he was impressed.

"Come have a seat, Mr. Tremell," Randall Kross said to him. "And let's get down to business."

Malcolm walked over to the table and took a seat opposite them. There was a pitcher of water on the table and a tray of lemon wedges. Randall Kross poured Malcolm a glass and set it down in front of him.

"Don't worry, it's not going to kill you."

Malcolm apprehensively took a sip and put the glass down. Their cordialness caught him off guard.

"So what were you expecting, a room full of Ninjas and a torture chamber?"

"To be honest with you, I didn't know what to expect."

"I'm impressed that you're familiar with *The Art of War* by Sun Tzu."

"Yes, sir, I read it in boot camp. I pick it up every now and then to refresh my memory."

"Then you should know that we don't take people out of the picture—as you say."

"Gentlemen, you can call it anything you want, but you know he's a dangerous and reckless man who loves killing people, and he doesn't care what innocent people get caught in the middle."

"You're the one who's dangerous, Mr Tremell." Allan Kross pulled out a thick folder and slammed it down on the table. "You have no children, no significant relationships, no close relatives, and no personal property."

"And how does that make me dangerous?"

"Because you have nothing to lose."

Malcolm stood up from the table and placed the recorder down in front of them.

"Then you should know that I have every intention of going through with my threat of making this public."

"That recording means nothing, we'll just deny it. Our lawyers will never allow it to be admitted in court!" Allan shouted at him.

"Who said anything about court," Malcolm said while walking toward the door. "I'm sending this to MSNBC, FOX, and CNN. Oh yeah, and my one million Facebook friends and Twitter followers. By the time I get through with you, your stock won't be worth ten cents." He grabbed the doorknob. "Have a good day, gentlemen."

"Mr. Tremell, wait a second!" Randall Kross shouted. "What assurance do we have that you won't go public after we do what you ask?"

"Because it's the only insurance I've got not to end up like Senator Nelson's wife, whose funeral I'm already late for!" he said looking down at his watch. "It only appears as if I have nothing to lose, gentleman, but I do enjoy waking up every morning—and breathing."

They huddled together and then Randall Kross walked over to him.

"Can we give you our answer in forty-eight hours?"

"This man is a psychopath. I could be dead in forty-eight hours," Malcolm said while opening the door. "Make it twenty-four." Then he walked out.

ACT IV

AN EYE FOR AN EYE

CHAPTER 37

Dozens of media satellite trucks lined the streets outside of Flagler Memorial Park. A white truck with Channel 2 Action News painted on the side was parked closest to the gate as the funeral procession drove past.

"Senator Nelson, do you have any comments about the bomb explosion that killed your wife?" one reporter shouted at him.

"Is it true that the terrorist group Al Qaeda is responsible?" another added as he shoved his microphone at the senator's black stretch limousine.

Senator Nelson and Vincent were smiling behind the tinted glass window as they passed through the cemetery gates.

"You were right, sir, the terrorist story worked like a charm."

"I never had a doubt!"

"What made you so sure?"

"Since 9/11 all you have to do is mention terrorism and people will believe whatever you tell them. And that's exactly how we'll win the White House; keep showing the president's black face every chance we get and blow something up every now and then. Racism and fear can be a powerful combination in getting out the white conservative vote," he said while watching the FOX News channel. "Now, tell me what happened last night. I thought I made myself clear that this was supposed to be handled quietly."

"This guy is a lot better than we thought! Whoever trained him did one helluva job. He took out two of my best men without firing off a shot. He's a tough son of a bitch, I'll give him that!"

"Okay, that's enough! I don't want to hear any more of your professional accolades. I want you to take care of this personally, do you understand?"

"Yes, sir. Everything is already in place. We got a tip from one of his rivals. It will all be taken care of tonight!"

"Good!" the senator said while rubbing his eyes to make them red. "Now, try to look depressed and let's go bury this Puerto Rican bitch!" he laughed.

Malcolm was watching the procession through his binoculars from across the street. There were too many reporters around for him to try to get any closer. He decided to wait until everyone was gone so he could show his respect. While he watched the parade of limousines pull up to the gravesite, his cell phone vibrated. It was a call from Helen.

"Glad to see you arrived on time," Malcolm said.

"Yes, darling, and this Miami humidity is destroying my expensive hairdo."

"I think you can survive twenty-four hours on South Beach," he said to her. "Did everyone else get in on time?"

"Yes, everybody's here! The meeting is set for seven o'clock sharp in the conference room at the Fontainebleau Hotel, so don't be late."

"The Fontainebleau, huh? Isn't that a little retro for your taste?"

"I beg your pardon. I'm checking into the Four Seasons. But I do have a date at the Fontainebleau before the meeting."

"Don't tell me you're dumping me again for some new young meat."

"What can I say, sometimes you feel like a smooth ride in a Bentley and other days you want to speed in a Lamborghini. Men exercise their options all the time so why shouldn't women?"

"You know my motto, live and let live," he told her. "Enjoy yourself, Helen, and try not to hurt those young boys too badly."

"For the amount of money I'm spending his young ass will be in traction before the afternoon is over. Toodles."

Malcolm went back to looking through his binoculars at the funeral party. He could see Alex's parents being helped out of one of the limos. Her mother was so distraught she was barely able to stand up as they walked her over to be seated. There were several local and national politicians in attendance, as well most of the senator's wealthy friends. Even the mayor was there in his black suit and tie to show his support and for a photo op. Malcolm zoomed in on the senator's car as it pulled up. Two men jumped out of the black Cadillac Escalade and stood in front of the door while the chauffeur opened it. One of them was Agent Harris. The sun bounced of his sweaty bald head as he looked around to make sure the coast was clear. When the door to the limo opened, a tall muscular man stepped out wearing an earpiece. Malcolm couldn't make out his face; Agent Harris was standing directly behind him next to the car door blocking his view. Once Senator Nelson stepped out, he took a step forward and the man's face was exposed. It was Vincent. The ragged scar on his right cheek was impossible to miss. Malcolm felt a rush of adrenaline. In his mind, Vincent was the one responsible for Alex's death. Senator Nelson was pulling the strings, but Vincent was the one who pulled the trigger.

A few minutes later, the service began. The preacher said a few words over the grave and then Alex's body was lowered into the ground. Senator Nelson grabbed the shovel and placed the first pile of dirt over the coffin. He was sobbing and looked depressed.

"And the winner for best actor is—," Malcolm said to himself. "Gotta hand it to him, he's playing the role to a tee."

When the service was over, Senator Nelson hugged Alex's parents and got back into his limousine. Agent Nelson and another man jumped into the Escalade and led him out of the cemetery, accelerating once they got out of the gate. Malcolm waited for a few of the stragglers to leave, then he made his way into the cemetery from the back. He was carrying a dozen yellow roses and a DVD with a copy of her first performance at Melvin's. He walked over to her grave as the funeral workers were covering it with dirt and threw the flowers and DVD on top of her casket.

"I wish I could hear 'Smooth Operator' just one more time," he said. "What a waste—what a fuckin' waste! I'm gonna miss you, my friend."

He sat down in one of the chairs and pulled out the photo of Alex that Simon had given him. It was the one of her wearing the Armani dress the first night she performed. He closed his eyes and tried to reflect back on the good times of that night, but the vision of Alex reaching out to him just before the bomb went off kept replaying in his mind over and over again. He put his hands over his face and took a deep breath to clear his mind, then he took another deep breath and exhaled. He put the photograph back in his pocket and was about to leave when he sensed someone was watching him. He knew who it was.

"Don't you just hate funerals?" Vincent asked. He was sitting in a chair a few rows behind Malcolm. "All the tears, reminiscing, and all that other depression shit. Makes you wonder why they don't just cremate people and get it over with."

"After last night, it looks like you may have two more funerals to attend," Malcolm said, turning around to face him. "Vincent, I presume."

"In the flesh! And you're the man with seven lives. You're a hard man to kill, Mr. Tremell!"

"Maybe you're just not trying hard enough."

"Or maybe you don't realize you're already as good as dead."

Vincent stood up and walked closer to him while reaching inside of his jacket pocket. Malcolm sprung up from his chair and reached for his gun.

"Easy, Piano Man, I'm not going to kill you in front of all these nice people." He pulled out a pack of cigarettes and a lighter. "Besides, that wouldn't be any fun, now would it?" Then he lit one up.

There was another funeral procession making its way through the cemetery and people were beginning to gather at a gravesite close to where they were standing.

"So this is some sort of game to you, killing innocent people," Malcolm said, still holding on to the butt of his nine-millimeter. "The woman you buried today was innocent!"

"How the fuck do you know that she was innocent?"

"She didn't deserve to die!"

"Is that your emotions talking or your head?" Vincent tapped the top of his head. "What happened to her was about business—plain and simple. You, of all people, should know better than to attach your feelings to your work."

"What's that supposed to mean?"

"It means that you had no problem fucking her brains out at that romantic hotel in the Keys knowing full well she was engaged to a powerful man, but you didn't let that get in the way of business, now did you?" He walked in closer to Malcolm. "That's right, I know everything. That stupid bitch didn't realize she had her phone turned on all the time you were together. GPS is a wonderful invention, isn't it?"

Malcolm smacked the cigarette out of his mouth and grabbed him by the collar. When the people around him reacted, he let him go.

"You just think you know everything, smart ass. You don't know that she was a friend, not a client. And you don't know that I figured out that you're looking for something that you didn't find on my phone or Marcia's." Malcolm moved in closer and whispered in his ear. "And you don't know that I'm going to be the one who kills you—soon! Enjoy the rest of your day, Scarface, you don't have many more left." Malcolm shoved him slightly and turned and walked away.

"Hey, Piano Man! You should be careful about who you threaten when you have so much to lose," he shouted at Malcolm as he was walking away. "I know who your friends are and I know how to get to them."

"Leave them out of it, Vincent, they're off limits. This is strictly between us."

"Nobody's off limits in war, there's always collateral damage!"

"Well, then I may as well kill you now!"

Malcolm pulled out his gun and pointed it at his head. The people from the funeral party behind them scattered. The pallbearers dropped the body they were carrying and took cover. Vincent went for his gun, but Malcolm had him cold.

"You're pretty good with that thing! I see the government trained you well," Vincent said.

He calmly lit another cigarette and blew out the smoke hard in Malcolm's direction. "I'll tell you what, since we're both prior military I'll make an exception and leave your friends out of it. As a professional courtesy." He turned and began walking away. "But your time is running out, pretty boy," he laughed. "Tick Tock, Tick Tock!"

CHAPTER 38

MAINTENANCE MAN II

It was 6:45 when Malcolm arrived at The Fontainebleau Hotel. The area inside and outside the hotel was buzzing with activity. College kids were out on winter break and the snowbirds had arrived for the winter from all over the country and around the world. Malcolm waited outside as all of his gigolos pulled up to the valet one by one. First Darius, then Carlos, Juan, Ramon, and Adam. Finally, Jason pulled in. They stood out from the casually dressed hotel clientele in their business suits and polished shoes.

"Let's get this show on the road," Malcolm said as he led them through the thick crowds single file. As they made their way past the eclectic groups gathered in the lobby, they could hear chatter in several different languages: French, Italian, Russian, Spanish, and German. It was still in the upper seventies and most of the women were scantily dressed and checking them out as they paraded by. Adam and Carlos still had bruises on their faces from the fight at the club, but that didn't stop them from attracting attention.

"Hey, sexy!" a young Latino woman shouted at Carlos from the bar. "I'll be here all weekend!"

"What can I say, women love scars!" Carlos joked.

"Yeah, but just wait until she gets your invoice!" Adam said. "She's probably sharing a room with three other women just to pay for it."

"In that case, I'll fuck them all!"

"Nobody's fucking anybody tonight. This trip is strictly business. Stay focused and let me do all the talking," Malcolm said as they walked toward the conference room. "These gigolos have flown in from all over the world to take this meeting. They're the best in the business and we need them on our team."

"Ten-four, boss!" Darius said. "I want to see what these hot shots look like anyway. It's always good to size up the competition!"

"Put your dick back in your pants, Darius, we're all on the same side."

"That all sounds good, Malcolm, but being a gigolo is a competitive sport—it always has been and always will be," Darius went on. "If they have a client that's earning them ten-thousand a month and mine is only paying me five, I'm going to make my pitch and may the best man win!"

"He's got a point, Malcolm," Adam added.

"That's exactly what this meeting is about, setting prices, setting standards, and setting boundaries."

"All I want to know is which country has the freakiest rich women!" Juan said.

"I'm with you, bro, women in Paris and Russia like to get peed on, too!" his twin brother, Ramon, joked.

"I swear, you are two of the nastiest motherfuckers I've ever met," Darius joked. "You'd probably suck a donkey's dick if the price was right."

Ramon looked at Juan, Juan looked back at Ramon. There was a brief silence and then they all burst out laughing.

"Every man has his price," Ramon said to Darius. "Hell, for a million dollars I'd suck your dick. But if he wants to hold my head, it'll cost you another million!"

They all burst out laughing again.

Suddenly, Helen poked her head out of the conference room door with a look of annoyance on her face.

"So, are you guys coming inside or are you staying out here in the hallway to finish your comedy show?"

"We're right behind you, Helen," Malcolm said.

"Boy, she's a feisty old broad, isn't she?" Adam said.

"Man, you don't know the half of it," Malcolm replied. "Let's go!"

The conference room was brightly lit with a long rectangular table in the center. As Malcolm entered the room he shook each man's hand as he walked by them and then took a seat at the head of the table. The five top gigolos sat at the table with their five best men seated behind them. Each man was strikingly handsome, in excellent shape, and distinguished looking, most of them in their late thirties and early forties.

"Gentleman, let me begin by thanking you for coming such a great distance to be here," Malcolm said. "Paul from London, Ricardo from Italy, Michael from Brazil, David from Cape Town, South Africa, and Jonathan from Toronto, Canada. I asked you all to be here because our little enterprise has taken off. Thanks to our mutual acquaintance, Miss Helen Daniels, as well as a good friend of mine, Alex Garcia, who is no longer with us, Maintenance Men International has built a clientele in the U.S. that is estimated to net more than ten-million dollars over the next year. And it's nearly double that in Europe. We need your markets to completely shut out the competition, and we need them now!"

"What's in it for us?" Michael asked. "We already own Brazil and Latin America. No disrespect, but how does it benefit us to join your organization?"

"The same goes for Canada," Jonathan added.

Malcolm looked back at his men, who were relaxed and confident. They already knew his game plan and had already heard his pitch. They were certain the other gigolos would buy into it the same as they did. Malcolm turned back around and stood up from the table.

"The only thing you gentleman control is the male prostitution business. What I'm offering you is more valuable than sex, I'm offering you access."

"Access to what?" David asked in a strong South African accent.

"Access to everything: insider trading information, political and judicial access, and the methods of extortion, if necessary!"

"And how do we get this access?" Paul asked.

"Simple! Listen and collect data."

"What the hell is that supposed to mean?" Michael asked.

"It means start thinking with your heads and not with your dicks! These women we lay down with have money, power, and influence, and if they don't have it they're associated with people who do." Malcolm went on. "Look around this room. There's a reason I choose the best in the business because, collectively, we have the most affluent clientele in the world, and that, my friends, is worth something! If you join me, I'll teach you how to monetize those relationships and quadruple your money."

"And where are we going to get this valuable information, pull it out of our asses?" Ricardo joked.

They all laughed. Malcolm's men sat stone-faced and assured as Malcolm drove his point home.

"Women talk in the bedroom, especially when they're sexually and emotionally frustrated, which is why they call us in the first place. And the more frustrated they are with their men, the more they talk." Malcolm started to pace back and forth. "Hell, I can get more information out of a woman eating her pussy than the CIA can from waterboarding."

"And what do we do with the information?" David inquired.

"We hold onto it until we need it to get one of us out of a jam! If we pool our resources together we can exploit our contact's information for more than a one night payday. It'll be worth millions. Maybe even tens of millions!"

"That's unethical!"

"Fuck ethics! This is about making money, which is why we're all here! If you want ethics, go join a goddamn monastery. Oh, sorry, they're too busy raping little boys."

Malcolm calmed himself down and took a seat.

"Look, we have to start thinking beyond sex. My man Adam is a former stock trader. He can invest our money for us using the tips that we're getting from our clients. But we have to move now and move together so that The Maintenance Men brand is strong enough to stand out by the time they legalize prostitution."

"Get the hell outta here!" Ricardo said. "Estáis locos."

"Legalized prostitution in the United States is never going to happen," Michael said. "Your country's leaders depend too much on religious fear to ever pass that kind of legislation. It will never happen."

Malcolm laughed sarcastically.

"What if I told you I heard it from a reliable source that marijuana and prostitution will be legalized in the next two years?"

"I would say someone is lying to you," David said.

"Come on, Malcolm, this is every gigolo's pipe dream," Jonathan added. "But it's never going to happen. Besides, who is this so-called source anyway, some horny-ass senator's wife that you're fucking?"

"No, it's some horny-ass senator that I'm fucking," Juan said, jumping in.

"That's bullshit. There are only seventeen women in the Senate and I know for a fact that none of those stuck-up wenches are paying for service. I have my resources, too, and they're all clean!"

"Who said I was talking about a woman, mi amigo?" Juan asked.

The room got quiet. The other gigolos sat back in their chairs and took a long sip of water. Malcolm reached back for a folder that Adam handed him. He passed out a piece of paper with statistics and graphics on it.

"Look at the top of the page," Malcolm directed them. "This country is in debt. By last estimates, more than fifteen-trillion dollars and counting. The unemployment rate is over ten percent; double that for our African-American and Latino brothers. Now, I'm not here to give you gentleman a history lesson, but the prohibition of alcohol ended in nineteen-thirty-three, a year after the worst period of the Great Depression, and guess why?"

"Money!" Ricardo yelled out.

"That's right, money! The government needed those tax dollars on booze. And now that the economy is jacked up, they're about to start taxing sex, marijuana—and a whole bunch of other shit!" Malcolm continued. "The question is not if they're going to legalize it, but when! The tobacco companies already have the marketing and packaging in place. Twenty-four hours after that legislation passes, you'll be able to buy Jamaica Gold Buds and Orange Crush Blunts at your local 7-Eleven!"

They were all on the edge of their seats taking in every word. Some of them were taking notes on the pads in front of them.

"Now, stop thinking about how to fuck more women and think about how we're going to fuck the government, because it's only a matter of time before the government starts running brothels and whorehouses, too. Trust me, if there's money in it, Uncle Sam is gonna find a way to get his hands on it. So, who's with me?"

"Where do I sign up?" Ricardo asked.

"I'm in!" David told him.

"Sign me up!" Michael added.

"What the hell, let's do it!" Jonathan joined in.

Paul was still sitting back in his chair with his hand on his chin. After everyone signed their contracts, Malcolm walked over and placed a contract down in front of him.

"So what are you waiting for?" Malcolm asked him.

"To hell with being a gigolo, put me in touch with your contacts so I can invest in some weed!" he laughed.

CHAPTER 39

MAINTENANCE MAN II

While Helen and Malcolm celebrated with drinks at The Fontainebleau Hotel Bar, the other gigolos were scattered around the lobby and pool area taking in the sights and enjoying the attention from all the beautiful young women.

"A toast!" Helen said to Malcolm as she lifted her glass. "To the man with the plan. I knew you would hit a home run! Looks like you have another piece of the puzzle in place."

"Yeah, too bad Alex wasn't here to see this happen. She helped me get my business back off the ground. I couldn't have done it without her—or without you."

He leaned over and kissed her on the lips, she blushed.

"What was that for?"

"For being you!"

She put her arms around him and kissed him back.

"And that's for being you," she said. "I've met a lot of men in my life, Malcolm, from presidents on down to dope dealers in Colombia, and I have to tell you, you are the best of them all. Yes, the sex is great and you're handsome, and strong, and charismatic, and confident, but it's this," she pointed at his heart. "This is what separates you from the rest."

"A gigolo with a heart, now that's funny."

"Well, it's true, and you know it. That's why women come back to you, Malcolm. That's why they want to be with you. They can get sex anywhere, from anybody, but you don't pay a man for sex just to get you off, you pay him to connect with you. And you know how to connect. That's what makes you special."

"Can I get that in writing? That's one helluva endorsement."

"You can make fun of me if you want, but I've known you for a long time and I know what I'm talking about."

She took a sip of her drink and set it down on the bar. She moved in closer to him and put her hands against his broad chest.

"I've also been close enough to you to see what most women will never see."

"And what's that?"

"I've seen you get your heart broken; once with that beautiful young dancer, Toni, and now with Alex."

Malcolm's expression became more serious. He stepped away from Helen and took a long sip of his champagne.

"I know you're going to try to act all hard, but you know it's true. Those two women somehow got past that suit of armor, didn't they?" she said while poking him in the chest. "You really do have a thing for those artistic types, don't you? I guess it's true what they say, birds of a feather—"

"Flock together," Malcolm said, finishing her sentence. "Yes, I loved them, each in my own way. And I know that's shocking for you to hear me say, but I'm stronger now than I used to be—more mature. Time and pain will do that to a man. It also teaches him about who he really is, and that's why I will always leave myself open for love, but I will never fall in love again."

He took another long sip of his drink.

"You men are so typical. You get your feeling hurt and you run into your emotional caves like scared little rabbits," Helen said, jokingly. "Women on the other hand, we keep coming back over and over and over, until we get it right."

"Is that what you do, Helen? You open yourself up emotionally for every man who makes you feel all tingly and lightheaded?"

"Hell naw! I was talking about those other dumb broads. My days of falling for the banana in the tailpipe are o-v-e-r! I learned my lesson twenty years ago. Fuck love, I just want to have fun!"

"Now, I'll drink to that!" Malcolm said as they bumped glasses. "Helen, you've been the one constant in my life for past 15 years. I don't know how you put up with me."

"Because I love you, Malcolm, didn't you know?" she said bluntly. "Not in the school girl kinda way, but as a true friend—without expectations, or boundaries, or rules. I let you be Malcolm so you won't ask me to stop being Helen. I've known you longer than any other woman in your life, but I let you do what you want and see who you want, because I know when I call you, you'll always be there for me, even if I do have to pay for your time. After all, I can afford it! And you're worth every dime, baby, inside and outside the bedroom." She put her hand gently on his face and kissed him again. "And I put up with your wise ass because you've got one of the prettiest dicks I've ever seen!" she laughed. "And it's so heavy!" she grabbed him in the crotch. "What do you do, tie a dumbbell to that thing every night?"

Malcolm pulled away and grabbed her hand.

"Helen, you'll never change," he laughed.

"You're right about that, I'm going to party and screw—and sleep—and party some more until I die or until my money runs out!"

"Okay, that's enough champagne for you for one night," Malcolm said, signaling Carlos to come over. "Let's get you back to your hotel in one piece."

Carlos broke off his conversation with two Asian women and rushed over to the bar.

"What's up, Malcolm?"

"Go outside and see if Helen's car is out there."

Carlos ran off while Malcolm paid the bartender and gathered Helen's purse and wrap.

"You better be glad that young stud Blake wore me out this afternoon. I would've rocked your world," she slurred.

"So, that's who you went to see this afternoon? I told you that guy was trouble." Malcolm wrapped her arm around his neck. "That's what you get for messing around with these youngsters. I told you they don't know what they're doing."

"You got that right, he was going like a jack rabbit, bam, bam, bam!" she said while pushing her fist in and out. "I think he tilted my uterus." She grabbed her stomach.

Carlos signaled that the car was waiting. Malcolm walked her to the door and Carlos grabbed her hand.

"Oh shit!" Malcolm said. "I think I left my credit card at the bar."

"Don't worry about it, I'll make sure she gets to the car okay. He's parked just around the corner."

"Thanks, Carlos. I'll go round up the guys. I'll meet you inside Club LIV in the VIP section. We're not done celebrating yet!"

Malcolm gave Helen a kiss on the lips and patted her on the behind.

"Good night, you old Cougar."

"Good night, man with the pretty dick!" she laughed.

Carlos walked Helen down the driveway of the hotel toward the street where a man was holding up a sign with her name on it. The driver opened the door and Carlos helped Helen inside.

"Good night, Ms. Daniels."

"Good night, young man. You be careful with these fast young girls tonight."

"Yes, ma'am."

When Carlos lifted his head up out of the doorway, he was struck on the back of the head and thrown into the back seat.

"You should have listened to the lady and been more careful, lover boy!" Vincent said. "Now you're both going for a ride. And it's a one-way ticket."

"Okay, I did what you asked me to do, now give me my money," Blake said.

He was the gigolo that Malcolm kicked out the night he had his first meeting at the club.

"Here's your payment, you fucking snitch!"

Vincent shot him twice in the stomach with a silencer, jumped in the front seat of the car and drove off.

CHAPTER 40

MAINTENANCE MAN II

Club LIV was jam-packed and the music was loud. Malcolm, Jason, and Adam were sitting in the VIP area surrounded by a group of beautiful Jamaican women they had invited over for drinks. Malcolm waved a hundred dollars in the air to get the attention of the waiter to bring over more champagne. Ramon, Juan, and Darius were on the dance floor bumping and grinding to "California Love" by Dr. Dre. Darius raised his hand to get their attention. He was dancing in the middle of three tall Latin women who were rubbing him all over his chest and ass.

"Show off!" Ramon yelled at him. "What is it with black guys, they always seem to attract the biggest freaks?"

"Because women think they have the biggest cocks, that's why," Juan jokingly replied. "But we know that's not the truth, don't we, ladies?" He showed the women sitting in the booth with them the imprint of his large penis and then began slowly unzipping his pants.

"Take it off! Take it off! Take it off!" they yelled.

Juan started dancing and doing a striptease that got the attention of the women in the area who were standing nearby. Pretty soon, they were all chanting along.

"Take it off! Take it off! Take it off!"

He jumped up on the stage and started working the crowd. Not to be outdone, Darius started unbuttoning his shirt and doing a striptease, too. Pretty soon all the other gigolos from the other countries started to compete to see who had the best body and who could get the most cheers. The DJ saw what was going on and he quickly changed the record. When he played the song "Pony" by Ginuwine, the club went wild! All of the men made their way to the stage and started performing. They each took turns strutting to the front of the stage to see who could get the most cheers, and the most tips. Malcolm and the other top gigolos sat on the sidelines recording video with their cell phones and placing bets on which guys would win. In the end, Darius came out the winner.

"This is racial!" Juan shouted playfully, "Somebody call Reverend Al Sharpton, I want a recount!"

The crowd erupted with laughter. Even Malcolm had tears in his eyes as he collected his money on his bets.

"That was the most fun I've had in years," he said to Adam.

"That goes double for me! But what happened to Carlos? He would've given Darius a run for his money?"

"He's probably still talking to those two Asian cuties in the bar. Do me a favor and take care of the tab. I'm going to step away from all this noise and call Helen to make sure she got back to her hotel okay."

"You might want to give her a minute to get there!"

"Why is that?"

"Her driver called fifteen minutes ago and said he was going to be late."

"What?"

Malcolm made his way through the thick crowd back into the hotel lobby and then into the bar area. He didn't see Carlos or the Asian women. When he turned toward the front entrance, he noticed the flashing emergency lights reflecting off of the hotel's glass doors.

He rushed outside and saw that a large crowd was gathered down the street. It was the same direction Carlos went to escort Helen to her limo. Miami Beach Police had the area roped off and an ambulance had its doors open ready to load a body inside. Malcolm took off toward the street knocking people out of the way. He broke through the police barricades and ran over to the body and lifted the sheet. "Blake!" he said to himself. "Goddamn you, Helen!"

Malcolm dropped the sheet and ran back toward the hotel. He felt a sense of both relief and terror. Carlos and Helen were still alive, but he was sure Vincent had them. What is he up to? And why hasn't he called? He snatched his keys out of the valet box and jumped into his car headed for Melvin's. If Vincent went for Helen, he would definitely try to grab Simon and Ariel, Malcolm thought. He reached for his phone as he swerved through traffic to call Simon. Just as he was about to dial the number, his phone rang. It was from Helen's cell.

"I know you have them, you piece of shit," Malcolm said. "This was supposed to be between you and me."

"I lied!"

"What do you want?"

"I want you, pretty boy! And you've got ten minutes to get here or else they'll be serving them up in the hamburger meat at the next Dolphins game!"

"Just give me an address and I'll be there!"

"I've already texted it to you. And if I see even so much as a bicycle riding by, I'll shoot first and ask questions later. Now, don't be late, your time is running out! Tick Tock, Tick Tock!" Then he hung up.

The address was in an abandoned warehouse district, not far from Melvin's Jazz Club. That was another thing that bothered him as he sped down the highway; the distance between the warehouse address and the club was only six blocks. There's no way that was a coincidence. And there's no way he could be in two places at the same time to save Simon and Ariel. For the first time since his military days, he knew he needed help, and there was only one person he could trust. He reached into his wallet and pulled out Agent Harris's card and dialed his number. He picked up on the first ring.

"So, Malcolm, who did you kill this time?"

"Cut the comedy. I need your help!"

"Okay, shoot!"

"Vincent just kidnapped one of my men and a lady friend of mine. And I think he's gonna make a play for my partner Simon at the club. I need you to get some of your men over there and take him and my manager Ariel into protective custody."

"My men and I are driving in the motorcade right now with Senator Nelson on our way to a fundraiser. I'll call my guy at the Miami PD to go by and pick them up."

"Look, goddamit! This guy has already killed two people that I know of, and he tried to kill me. I don't trust anyone else but you. Besides, there's no telling how many Miami cops he has on the payroll. It's gotta be you, Agent Harris. So get off your ass and help me save my friends!"

"Ok, I'll get my men on it. What are you gonna do?"

"I'm going to meet up with Vincent. He wants to trade them for me."

"You know it's a trap, don't you?"

"No shit, Sherlock! Of course, I know it's a trap! But I don't have any choice. If I don't go, they're as good as dead."

"And if you do go, so are you."

"I still have a few tricks up my sleeve. You just make sure you get to Simon and Ariel. If I know Vincent, his men are probably already at the club!"

"I'm on it!" Agent Harris signaled his driver to pull over. The truck behind him carrying his other men pulled behind them. He took a small device out of the pocket of the backseat and jumped into the second truck and instructed his men to head over to Melvin's, and then he sped off. "By the way, I have some good news for you; I found that small door latch you told me about from the hotel bombing. It may not be enough to get a conviction, but at least it corroborates your story."

"Thanks for following up," Malcolm said. "Not bad police work."

"What can I say, I'm a stubborn, hard-headed boy from Brooklyn. I told you, I'm suspicious of everybody! Now tell me where this trade is taking place and I'll meet you there!"

"No chance, this guy is psycho! He'll kill them both if he even suspects I have company. I have to ride or die alone on this one, chief."

"He'll never let you leave there alive!"

"What would you do if you were me?"

"I would call the cops and wait for me to get there."

"I said, what would you do it you were me, not you, re-member? Good-bye, Agent Harris and thanks for everything!" Then he hung up.

CHAPTER 41

Malcolm dimmed his car lights as he drove into the warehouse district. Abandoned buildings ten stories tall lined the streets on both sides for blocks. There was one way in and one way out. It was a strategic nightmare. He thought about allowing himself to be taken and then plot a way out. That was his specialty in the military; enemy insurgence and close encounter combat. That's what he was trained to do. That's what he was the best at. But Vincent was a cold-hearted killer. He might shoot him on site. There had to be another way, he thought.

As he grew closer to the address, he saw a man standing outside signaling him with a flashlight. Malcolm drove in slowly, looking around for every possible exit—every angle—and any advantage. There were men on the rooftops; he couldn't see them, but he knew they were there. He had to think fast, there was no way Vincent was going to allow Helen and Carlos to go free and report what happened to the police, if they were even still alive. As he got closer to the man waving the flashlight, the reality of his situation became grimmer. Once they had their hands on him, he knew it was over. He had only one chance.

Malcolm slowly lowered his hand between his legs grasping the handle on his pistol and then stepped on the accelerator, ramming the man into the building. Bullets from automatic rifles with silencers ricocheted off the walls as he jumped out of the car and took cover behind a steel beam. He was inside, but he was cornered. The man he ran over slowly got up off the ground and limped toward him with his gun drawn; Malcolm coolly shot him in the head and dragged his body in front of him, using it as shield to get into the stairwell. He knew Vincent would be on the top floor where he would have a tactical advantage. Malcolm sprinted up the stairs determined to kill anything that moved.

His strategy was working. They didn't expect him to take the offensive. They were in disarray; he could hear men shouting obscenities as he made his way to the third floor, then the fourth. He shot one man who rushed into the stairwell as he ran past the fifth floor. Once he was at the tenth floor, Malcolm put his ear to the door and could hear the sounds of someone being beaten. Instead of charging in, he ran up the next flight of stairs and out onto the roof. He crept to the edge and leaned over as far as he could and peeked inside the room. Carlos was handcuffed to a chair and two large men were taking turns beating him. Malcolm looked around for something to lower himself down with. He noticed an old ladder to the fire escape a few feet away. He put his pistol in his waist and was about to lower himself down, when, suddenly, Vincent walked out of the shadows with a rifle pointed right at him.

"Good job, soldier boy. You did exactly what I would've done, look for an alternative access point. You Navy SEALs are so fuckin' predictable!" Then he hit Malcolm in the head with the butt of his rifle, knocking him out.

• • •

One of Vincent's men threw a bucket of cold water in Malcolm's face to bring him back to consciousness. When he opened his eyes, Helen and Carlos were sitting across from him with their mouths gagged. They were both handcuffed to steel chairs. Malcolm's arms were handcuffed, too, as were his ankles. Vincent pulled up a chair right in front of him and lit a cigarette.

"You want a smoke?" he said mockingly to Malcolm.

"No, thanks, it's not good for your health."

"Glad to see you've still got a sense of humor—you're gonna need it!"

He blew smoke in Malcolm's face.

"I bet you didn't expect to find yourself in this situation when you woke up this morning, did you?"

"Let them go, Vincent. You got me, that's what you wanted."

"What I want is for you to suffer!" he said, grabbing Malcolm by the throat. "This is no longer about business, it's personal! You killed two of my best men and you've been a pain in the ass since I blew up your whorish little girlfriend, Alex."

Malcolm jerked at the chains on his arms and feet.

"Save your strength, Piano Man. Those chairs are solid steel and so are those handcuffs. As you can see, this is not the first time we've had a going away party up here," he laughed while pointing to the bloodstained floors. "So, let's get this party started, shall we?"

He stood up from his chair and pulled a thirty-eight revolver out of his waist.

"I'm sure you all know this game, it's called Russian roulette. Which one of you wants to go first?"

"I'll go first!" Malcolm said.

"We can't let the guest of honor go first, what fun would

that be?" he said while taking five bullets out of the gun and then spinning the cylinder. He slapped it back into place and pointed it at Carlos's head.

"Don't do it, Vincent!"

Malcolm looked at Carlos, who was bleeding from the mouth, nose, and ears. His eye was so badly battered it was nearly hanging out of the socket. Vincent took a pull off his cigarette, smiled at Malcolm, and slowly pulled the trigger.

"Click!" The chamber was empty. His men cheered and placed bets.

"Okay, it's the old bitch's turn!" Vincent said, spinning the chamber. He slapped it back into the gun and then pointed it at her. "It's times like these that really make you appreciate the little things, isn't it!"

Helen was shivering, crying, and praying.

"Goddammit, Vincent, don't you do it!"

"I don't believe in God!" he said and then he pulled the trigger again.

"Click!" That chamber was empty, too.

Helen breathed a sigh of relief, but it was Carlos's turn again. He was nearly unconscious from all the beatings. Vincent's men threw water on his face to revive him. Vincent stood in front of him and pointed the gun at his forehead. He didn't even bother to spin the cylinder.

"Look at me!" he ordered Carlos. "Now, look at Malcolm. You can thank him for this." Then he pulled the trigger. *Bam!* Carlos's brains splattered all over the back wall.

"Arrggh!" Malcolm screamed and jerked at his handcuffs. "I'm going to kill you! I'm going to kill all of you dirty bastards!"

Vincent stood in front of him. Calmly, he loaded the other five bullets into the revolver and then took another drag off his cigarette. "Didn't I tell you that you would need your sense of humor?" he said with a devious grin. "Gag him and bring him over here!"

Vincent's men put a gag in Malcolm's mouth and dragged his chair over to the window.

"I choose this spot especially for you, Malcolm. I wanted you to have a front-row seat to watch everything you've ever cared about be taken away. In about fifteen minutes, Melvin's will be in ashes. And if your friend Simon survives, I'll hunt him down in Atlanta or Chicago and beat him to death with a ballpoint hammer. And you don't even want to know what I have planned for sweet little Ariel. I'm going to take care of her personally," he said, licking his lips. "After that, it's all downhill. You're going to watch Helen get her throat cut. And last but not least," he reached behind his back and pulled out a long hunting knife, "they're going to cut off your balls and suffocate you with them."

He handed the knife to one of his men and walked toward the door.

"I'm sorry I can't be here to catch the show, but I need an alibi—just in case. By the time the fireworks start, I'll be at the Intercontinental Hotel with the senator and hundreds of distinguished guests. Nice sparring with you, Malcolm, but it's the end of the fifteenth round and you're out of time! Tick Tock! Tick Tock!" he said while looking down at his watch.

He blew Helen a kiss and walked out, leaving two of his men behind.

"Well, looks like it's just the four of us!" one of the men said while unbuckling his pants. He was blond and wore a thin mustache.

"She's a little overdressed, don't you think?" the stocky Latino man holding the knife added.

269

He cut Helen's dress down the middle starting at the bottom and splitting it up to her breast and then he ripped her bra and panties off, leaving her completely naked. She struggled and tried to kick at them.

"Smack! Smack! Stay still bitch!" he struck her in the face, bloodying her nose and lip. Then he took the handcuffs off her wrist and flipped her over onto her back. "You should try to enjoy this, it's the last piece of dick you'll ever get!"

Malcolm's chair was facing the window, but he could see the men raping Helen in the reflection in the glass. He struggled to get his wrist through the handcuffs, but they were on too tight.

"Look at the ass on this old broad?" the blond man said as he raped her from behind. "She's tighter than a teenager, and trust me, I know," he laughed.

"Don't be greedy, save some for me," the Latino man said as he pushed the other man off and jumped on top of her.

Malcolm scooted the chair close to the wall and pushed his feet against it. He tilted the chair up enough to free his ankles. He stood up in the chair and charged the blond man, who was still buckling up his pants. Malcolm knocked him to the ground and then head-butted him.

"What the—," the Latino man said as he jumped off Helen and dove for his gun.

Malcolm was struggling to stand up. The heavy metal chair was still handcuffed to his wrists. Just as he was about to rush the Latino man, he got to his gun and pointed it right at Malcolm's chest.

"I know Vincent wanted me to cut you after the bomb goes off, but there's been a change in plans!"

He cocked the trigger, and then, *Bang*! A shot rang out, but it wasn't his gun that fired. Agent Harris emerged from the shadows with a gun in his hand. *Bang*! *Bang*! *Bang*! Three more shots rang out, hitting the Latino man, twice in the chest and once in the forehead. His gun dropped to the ground as he fell to the floor, dead. Agent Harris rushed over to Malcolm and uncuffed him from the chair and took the gag out of his mouth.

"What took you so long?" Malcolm asked sarcastically.

"The traffic on I-ninety-five is a bitch!" he laughed.

"How did you find me?" Malcolm said as he rushed over to Helen and wrapped his jacket around her.

"I put a tracking device on your Ferrari while it was impounded at the police station the night of the explosion. You didn't think I was going to let a loose cannon like you move around without a chaperone, did you?"

"We'll talk about that later. Right now I need your phone to call Simon."

"Don't worry, my men have him and Ariel in protective custody. They should be on the way to my office by now."

"What about the club?"

"The club is still open. You didn't say anything about shutting it down!"

"Give me your phone, quick!"

"What's wrong?"

"There's a bomb at the club and it's set to go off in less than five minutes!" Malcolm said, looking down at his watch.

While Malcolm was dialing the number, Agent Harris went over to check on the Latino man who he had shot. By then the blond man that Malcolm knocked out with the chair was regaining consciousness. He eased his hand over to his gun and pointed it at the back of Malcolm's head. *Bang, Bang, Bang, Bang*!

"And that's for calling me an old broad, you dirty son of a bitch!" Helen shot him with the Latino man's gun.

Malcolm and Agent Harris took cover; seconds later they realized where the shots had come from.

"That's my girl!" Malcolm said to her. They looked at each other and smiled.

"Go help your friends, Malcolm, I'll be alright," she said while trying to stand up.

"Lay still, the paramedics are on the way," Agent Harris said, holding her in his arms. The sounds of sirens could be heard in the distance. "Malcolm, she's right though, you can make it to the club if you leave now. Here are my keys." He threw them over to him. Malcolm caught them with one hand and took off.

"Call Simon and tell him what's happening!"

"I'm on it, and try not to run my car into a building, too!"

Agent Harris's car was right outside the warehouse; Malcolm jumped in and sped off. He frantically dialed the number to the club, but all the lines were busy. His watch read 10:56 as he raced down the side streets trying to make up time. He only had four minutes to drive six blocks. It was Saturday night and the traffic in downtown Miami was bumper to bumper. There was a Prince concert at American Airlines Arena and the traffic going to Melvin's only added to the challenge. He finally gave up on calling the club and tried to reach the head bartender, Big Mike, on his cell phone. When he picked up, Malcolm could hear the loud music playing in the background.

"Mike, it's Malcolm!"

"Hey, Mr. Tremell, what in the hell is going on? Some feds just came and picked up Ariel and Simon!"

"I know about that, but I need you to listen closely!" Malcolm shouted as he ran through a red light, barely missing a young couple. "There's a bomb in the club!"

"You got that right, Mr. Tremell, there are some bomb-ass women in the club tonight!" he laughed.

"No, you idiot, there's a bomb in the club. Get everybody out now!" Malcolm yelled.

Big Mike put his finger over his other ear and walked away from the music into the back room.

"Say that again!"

"I said, there's a bomb in the club, and it's going to go off in a couple of minutes. Get your big ass outta there, now!"

"A bomb? Holy shit!"

Malcolm heard the phone drop. He could hear Big Mike screaming in the background.

"There's a bomb in the club! There's a bomb in the club, run for your fuckin' lives," Big Mike screamed. "Hey you! Get your goddamn hand outta my tip jar, you cheap bastard!"

After that all he heard was screaming and the sound of breaking glass.

Malcolm looked down at his watch, it read 10:59. He drove onto the curb with Agent Harris's police siren blaring, sending people leaping onto parked cars and diving into the street. Once he couldn't drive any further, he jumped out of the car and starting running. "Not again!" he said to himself as he sprinted down the middle of traffic on Biscayne. His heart pounded as he turned the corner down the side street to Melvin's. He was a block away and he could see people rushing out of the doors and crashing through windows to get out. It was complete chaos. He was twenty yards away from the driveway when it exploded. Malcolm went flying backwards and onto the ground. It sounded identical to the bomb that went off when he saw Alex killed. Bodies were scattered everywhere! Most of the people were just knocked unconscious, but he knew that there were some who didn't make it out alive.

Malcolm watched as the business that was passed down from his mentor, and through three generations, went up in flames. Just then, Simon and Ariel drove up in a black Escalade and rushed over to him.

"Malcolm, you okay?" Simon yelled.

"It's gone! Melvin's is gone!" Malcolm said solemnly while lying on the ground.

Ariel was in tears as she watched the historic building go up in smoke. Police sirens could be heard in the background as strangers rushed over to help the wounded.

"Don't worry, partner, we can rebuild."

Malcolm stood up and walked closer to the building. The sign that read Melvin's had been blow to pieces and was dangling over what was left of the front entrance.

"There won't be any rebuilding," Malcolm said with conviction.

"What—?"

"You heard what I said, this is the end of Melvin's, and the end of our partnership," Malcolm said while turning toward Simon. He walked over and gave him a brotherly hug and then he grabbed Ariel and brought her in with them. "They'll always use what I care about most to hurt me and I can't allow that to ever happen again."

"Malcolm, please don't do this." Ariel cried.

"All of these people are dead because of me, my lifestyle and my choices. I've tried to live a normal life, but it's never going to happen. I tried. Simon, I really tried!" He stepped away from Simon and began to walk backwards. "Take the insurance money and disappear, both of you."

"Malcolm, I love you, thanks for everything."

"I love you, too, partner. That's why I have to do this. Now get the hell out of here!"

"What are you going to do?" Simon asked as the agents rushed him and Ariel back into the Escalade.

"I'm going to finish this!"

CHAPTER 42

Malcolm drove up to the Intercontinental Hotel and snatched the security pass off the seat that Agent Harris left in his car. He flashed it to the hostess to gain access into the ballroom where the fundraiser was taking place. Just as he was walking in, Senator Nelson was being introduced. The crowd applauded as he took the stage. A red and white banner with the words Fight Against Domestic Violence hung over his head. What a damn hypocrite, Malcolm thought. He looked around for Vincent. He spotted him standing offstage near a back exit with three of his men; he recognized them from the warehouse. Two of them went through the exit doors and Vincent and the other man stood guard by the stage. As the Senator began to speak, Malcolm made his way out of the ballroom and headed to the service area of the hotel. Most of the hotel security officers were off-duty Miami cops. He flashed Agent Harris's badge and walked right by them. Once he was in the laundry area, he grabbed a waiter's jacket and put it on. He blended in with the staff and wandered around the kitchen until an order came in from the ballroom. When the chef called a waiter to refill the filet mignon on the buffet table, Malcolm hurried over with a cart. "I got it, Chef!" he said while keeping his head down.

Two of Vincent's men were guarding the narrow corridor that led from the kitchen to the ballroom. As Malcolm approached them, he slid a steak knife under his sleeve and bowed his head. When one of the men looked under the napkin to do an inspection, Malcolm slit his throat and threw him into the other man. When he tried to go for his gun, Malcolm rammed the cart into his knees, pressing him against the wall. Then Malcolm grabbed him by the wrist and twisted it; the gun dropped to the floor. "Arggh!" he yelled out! Malcolm quickly moved behind him and kicked him in the back of the legs, dropping him to the floor. He gripped his head with both hands and twisted his neck until it snapped.

Malcolm crept up to the exit door that was near where Vincent and the other man were standing. He tucked the steak knife back under his sleeve and tapped lightly on the door to get their attention. When one of the men came through the door, Malcolm pistol-whipped him and then knocked him unconscious. "Three down, one to go!" he said. While he was pulling the man out of the way of the door, Vincent came in from behind him and pulled out his gun.

"Don't move! Turn around and put your hands up!"

As Malcolm was lifting his arms up, he let the handle of the blade slide down his sleeve.

"It's you!" Vincent said with a stunned look on his face. "You're a hard man to kill, Mr. Tremell."

"And you're dead and don't even know it!"

"We'll just see about that!" Vincent said, moving in closer and pointing the revolver at his head. Malcolm noticed it was the same one he used to play Russian roulette with Carlos. "Get moving down that corridor. I don't want to shoot you here; it would raise too many questions."

They walked down the darkened corridor until they reached

the last door. It was the trash compactor room. The words Big Ben were written on the door with a red marker.

"Open it!" Vincent ordered Malcolm.

"I'll have to put my hands down for that," Malcolm said.

"Just do it!"

Malcolm slowly lowered his hand to turn the knob. He pushed the door open and walked inside.

"Now put your hands back up!"

"Make up your mind," Malcolm said while turning around. "Do you want them up or down?"

"It doesn't matter, pretty boy!" He lifted the gun up toward Malcolm's head, "because you're dead. Say goodnight!"

Just as he was about to pull the trigger, Malcolm flung the knife at him, cutting Vincent on the wrist. The gun went off and dropped to the floor. Malcolm dove for it, but Vincent kicked it out of the way. The gun disappeared into the shadows of the large, damp, dimly lit room. The only light came from the street lamps shining through four small rectangular windows. A huge trash shredder was in the middle of the room. It had a ramp that lead to the top, where the garbage was loaded into the shredder.

"Looks like it's just you, me, and Big Ben over there," Vincent said while taking off his jacket. "They won't even be able to find your teeth when I get through with you."

Malcolm calmly took off the waiter's jacket he was wearing while staring at Vincent with a look of hate and determination. When he spoke there was not even an inflection in his voice.

"I can't wait to kill you."

Malcolm went straight at him, throwing three quick punches that hit Vincent twice in the face and once in the stomach.

"Is that all you got?"

Vincent wiped the blood off his lip and came back at Malcolm. He kicked him in the chest, sending him crashing into a row of garbage cans. While Malcolm was down, he elbowed him in the back and kneed him in the forehead, sending him flying back into the garbage cans again.

"Get up!" Vincent said as he pulled Malcolm up off the ground by his shirt collar. "This is too easy!"

He threw a haymaker, but Malcolm caught his fist in mid-air and bent his arm behind his back.

"Now, it's my turn!" Malcolm said.

He kicked Vincent in the groin from behind, then rammed his head into the control panel for the shredder, splitting Vincent's scalp open. Blood poured down his face. Struggling to get up off the floor, Vincent reached for something to help hold himself up, accidentally flipping the switch for the industrial shredder. The loud motor kicked in and the sharp blades began to spin.

"It's time to take out the garbage!" Malcolm said as he hit Vincent in the stomach and kidneys until he was spitting up blood. With every punch, he spoke to him.

"Now–you're–going–to–feel–the–pain–that–Alex felt!"

He stood him up straight and punched him in the jaw, sending him staggering, dazed, into the corner. Malcolm felt around on the floor and found the steak knife and went after Vincent, who was lying against the wall in the shadowy corner. When he took a step towards Vincent to finish him off, two shots rang out! One of the bullets grazed Malcolm on his left shoulder. He dove for cover behind the trash cans.

"Enough of this karate bullshit, it's time to die!" Vincent yelled over the loud motor of the shredder. "Come out, come out, wherever you are," he playfully called out.

Malcolm made a dash for the exit. Vincent shot at him twice, forcing him back into the room. He was dripping blood, leaving an easy trail for Vincent to follow.

"You're like a wounded thoroughbred. Come out into the

open and I'll put you out of your misery."

Malcolm spotted a janitor's toolbox at the top of the ramp of the shredder. He found a bottle in the trash and threw it in the opposite direction to distract Vincent while he crawled up. He pulled two screwdrivers out and put them into his pocket, then he pushed the toolbox over the edge of the ramp. Vincent fired two more shots; one ricocheted off the metal railing and grazed Malcolm in the thigh."Aughh!" he screamed out! Vincent quickly ran to the top of the ramp toward Malcolm's voice. He found him lying on the ramp bleeding next to the conveyor belt of the shredder. His right hand was in his pocket.

"Ah, ah, ah, don't move!" Vincent shouted while pointing the gun right at him. "Just so you know, I'm going to track down Helen and finish her off, along with the rest of your friends. Think about that when you're taking your last breath!" Then he pulled the trigger. "Click"

"Next time count your bullets, asshole. You used the first shot to kill my friend Carlos. Think about that while you're taking your last breath!"

Malcolm pulled the two screwdrivers out of his pocket and in two swift motions, flung them at Vincent, hitting him in the chest and throat. He fell back onto the conveyor belt and slowly descended down into the shredder. Malcolm leaned over the railing and watched as Vincent's head was about to hit the shredder blades and he yelled.

"You're time is up. Tick Tock, motherfucker!"

Blood sprayed everywhere as the blades cut him up into pieces. Suddenly the lights flashed on and Miami Police and Secret Service agents stormed into the room. Agent Harris walked over to the power switch of the shredder and shut it off, then he leaned over the rail and looked inside the shredder at Vincent's mutilated body.

"I thought I told you not to kill anybody else for forty-eight hours," he said to Malcolm.

"It's after midnight, Agent Harris. Check your watch!"

EPILOGUE

The next morning Malcolm was released from the hospital. He took a taxi over to Melvin's Jazz Club and sat on a nearby bench and watched as the demolition crew began removing the debris. A few minutes later, Agent Harris drove up in a black town car and walked over and sat down beside him.

"I thought I might find you here," Agent Harris said to him. "I just got a call over the radio about Senator Nelson."

"What about him?"

"A bomb exploded at his home in Coral Gables, he's dead! The news reported that it might be the work of the terrorist who's responsible for the bombing that killed his wife."

"Is that what they're reporting?" Malcolm smiled as he looked down at his watch counting back from the twenty-four hours since he met the Kross brothers. "Well, I guess it must be true if it's on the news, right?"

"Yeah, right!" Agent Harris said with a sly grin. "Speaking of bombs, your club is a disaster. I hope you've got good insurance."

"Shouldn't you be out chasing bad guys?" Malcolm asked, trying to change the subject.

"There are no bad guys left. You killed them all."

"I didn't kill them soon enough. Five people died in that explosion. Not to mention, Carlos got killed."

"I'm sorry about what happened to your friend. I wish I could've gotten there sooner."

"I'm glad you got there at all. You saved my life and Helen's, too. I won't forget it." Malcolm reached out and shook his hand.

"How is she doing, by the way?"

"Helen's a tough old bird. She's already on a plane to Las Vegas to see the Chippendales and attend an adult movie Expo," Malcolm laughed.

"What about Simon and Ariel?"

"They're both gone. I told them to get as far away from me as possible. I don't want anyone else getting killed on my account. Sometimes you have to let go to move on, and that's exactly what I'm doing. I'm letting go of old relationships, old memories, and old guilt."

"Does that mean you're done with the gigolo game?"

Malcolm suddenly stood up from the bench while holding the sling on his left shoulder. "Hold that thought, I'll be right back." Malcolm rushed toward the heavy equipment operator waving his hands and whistling to get his attention. "Hey, hey, hey! Stop for a second!"

Malcolm climbed over the charred wood and broken glass and brushed the dust off the top of a shiny brown piece of wood; it was his Steinway piano. It was scratched up badly, but it was still intact.

"Well, I'll be damned!"

Agent Harris rushed over and stood next to him.

"This must be pretty special to you."

"It was a gift from my dad on my eighteenth birthday! He always wanted me to be a musician. I wish he was here now."

"That's right, he died four years ago. And you lost your mom early this year to cancer."

"Damn, you do know everything, don't you?"

"I told you, I'm suspicious of everybody," he laughed. "By the way, you never did answer my question? Are you going to stay in the gigolo game or get yourself a real job?"

"A real job? What—like yours?"

"Sure, why not?" he said while walking back toward his car. Malcom walked alongside him. "What other job allows you to kill people, tear shit up, and get paid for it?"

"For the last time, you guys don't get paid enough—the hours are shitty, and the—!"

"Okay, I got the picture—but that's not gonna stop me from revisiting this conversation after your shoulder heals. There are a lot of bad people in this world and I'm only one man," he laughed as he opened his car door.

"I'll make you a deal. If you can convince the president to allow me to wear my own clothes, I'll think about it."

"Deal!"

"And I want to drive my own car!"

"I can make that happen!"

"And I want to keep my escort business; it's the perfect cover."

"You know—that's not a bad idea."

"And I want a million-dollar salary!"

"Okay, now you're pushing it." He laughed and then they shook hands.

"So, you're gonna be alright? You need a ride?"

"No, I've already got one."

Just then, Angelita pulled up in a white convertible Lamborghini and then got out and walked around to the passenger side. She was wearing a white halter top, low-cut blue-jean shorts, and stilettos.

"Um, um, um!" Agent Harris said while staring at her. "You know, Malcolm, I've been married to the same woman for over fifteen years, and I'm lucky if we have sex once a month."

"Now you know why women need a Maintenance Man," Malcolm laughed as he stepped into the driver's side of the Lamborghini.

"I hate to admit this, but I envy you—you lucky bastard!"

Malcolm took off his sling and threw it into the air and kissed Angelita on the lips.

"Most men do, Agent Harris, most men do!" Malcolm said before speeding off.

MICHAEL BAISDEN

How Much is One Night of Passion Really Worth?

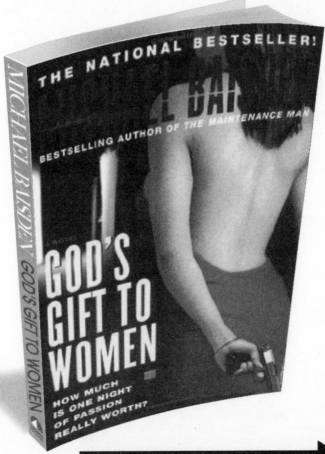

THE NATIONAL BESTSELLER!

BESTSELLING AUTHOR OF THE MAINTENANCE MAN

MICHAEL BAISDEN

GOD'S GIFT TO WOMEN

HOW MUCH
IS ONE NIGHT
OF PASSION
REALLY WORTH?

Turn the page to read an excerpt.

New York, NY
New Year's Day 2012

I WAS FIGHTING to stay conscious as the paramedics rushed me down the corridor of my office building. In the distance I could hear gunfire and horns blowing.

"You chose one hellava way to bring in the New Year, Mr. Payne," the paramedic said.

"Where's my daughter?" I asked while trying to sit up. "And where's Terri?"

"Please lie still. You'll only make the bleeding worse."

The radio station was on the twenty-fifth floor. I didn't feel strong enough to make it to the ambulance—let alone the hospital. The bullet had penetrated my left side and exited through my back. It burned like hell.

"Am I gonna die?"

They both paused, then looked at one another as if to seek the other's opinion. That terrified me. Once we boarded the elevator, they began broadcasting my vital signs into the radio. I didn't know the significance of the blood pressure and heart rate numbers, but judging by the urgency in their voices, I was in trouble.

287

"Where's my daughter? And where's Terri?" I asked again.

"Relax, Mr. Payne, your daughter is—"

He stopped in mid-sentence as the elevator doors opened on the lobby level. Suddenly, a wave of photographers and reporters rushed towards me. A barrage of flashing lights blinded me. Although my vision was blurred, I could see the outline of several husky policemen clearing a path.

"Julian, can you tell us what happened?" a reporter yelled out.

"Who shot the security guard?" another shouted while shoving a microphone in my face.

"Fuckin' vultures!"

I tried to lift my hand to shield my bloody face but my arms were strapped down. The yelling was deafening—like a continuous roar. The paramedics tried to move faster, but it was no use. The lobby was packed with policemen, reporters, and nosy fans who had come to watch. The atmosphere was festive, like a circus.

"Get out of the way, please!" the paramedics yelled. "This man is in critical condition! Move, move, move!"

The paramedics fought through the main doors, but once we made it outside we came to an abrupt stop. The crowd was even larger. People were jumping up on the hoods of their cars trying to get a better look. As the brisk night air blew across my bloody face, their loud voices suddenly faded—replaced by sirens and the humming of the helicopter blades. I could feel the blood soaking through the bandages.

It was obvious from the paramedic's expression that we were running out of time. The ambulance was only a few yards away but the crowd was out of control. When they continued to push, the cops pushed back—violently. People were knocked to the pavement and trampled.

"I love you, Julian!" A woman screamed as she struggled to get off the ground.

"I'm your number one fan!" another woman shouted as she lifted her blouse, exposing her breasts.

Suddenly a woman lunged towards me and ripped the sleeve off my blood soaked shirt.

"Aarrgh!" I screamed.

"Now I'll always have a piece of you," she said. Her hazel eyes and deranged stare were all too familiar.

The stretcher seemed to move towards the ambulance in slow motion. I was growing weaker. I fought hard to stay conscious—to stay alive. I gazed up at the flashing lights from the squad cars as they danced across the dark sky and against the nearby glass buildings. It reminded me of the Fourth of July in Chicago.

I wish I had seen the fireworks on Lake Michigan this summer, I thought to myself. And I never did see the view from the top of Sears Tower. I wish I had gone to Sam's first basketball game when she was seven. I wish I could be with Terri when my baby is born. But most of all, I wish I had never met Olivia Brown. She was the reason I was bleeding to death in New York City on New Year's Eve.

How could she go this far? I wondered as they lifted me into the ambulance. And *why* did she choose me?

ABOUT
MICHAEL BAISDEN

Michael Baisden is undeniably one of the most influential and engaging personalities in radio history. His meteoric rise to #1 is redefining radio with the numbers to back it up. The show is syndicated by Cumulus Media and is heard in over 78 markets nationwide with over 8 million loyal listeners daily. His career began when he took a leap of faith to leave his job driving trains in Chicago to self-publish his book, and began touring the country selling books out of the trunk of his car. Through the power of his sheer determination, Michael carved a unique niche as a speaker, radio personality, and social activist. He is always in the lead when it comes to helping those who don't have a voice. "I'm not one for just talking; either do something or get out of the way!"

Baisden, who now has four best selling books to his credit, has hosted two national television shows, and has recently produced three feature films.

Nationally Syndicated
Radio Personality

Baisden Communications: His radio career began in 2003 when 98.7 KISS FM in New York City offered him a position as the afternoon drive-time host. Because of budget constraints the station was unable to offer him a salary. Michael's response was, "Just give me the mic!" And sure enough, within six months, their afternoon drive ratings went from number 9 to number 1.

After eight months of consistently high ratings, Michael suggested taking his show national, but management was apprehensive, suggesting that New York wasn't ready. A few months later, Michael threatened to quit if management did not pursue a syndication deal. "There was no doubt in my mind that I could have one of the hottest shows on radio! I knew the impact it would have on people all across the country and I wasn't taking no for an answer," Michael rebutted.

Since his radio show debuted nationally in 2005, Michael has captured the hearts and minds of millions of Americans with his provocative mix of relationship talk, hot topics, politics and the best of old school with today's R&B. When it comes to entertaining, enlightening and educating, no one in talk radio compares. His high energy and love for interacting with his listeners are just two reasons for the popularity and success of "The Michael Baisden Show." Michael ignites heated discussions with explosive episodic themes like: Infidelity In The Church, Deadbeat Parents, Talking To Your Children About Sex, and Do Women Know What They Want?

BEST SELLING AUTHOR

Baisden Publishing: According to Simon & Schuster, Michael Baisden is "probably the most successful self-published African-American male author out there today." With nearly 2 million books in print, both hardcover and softcover, his books blend the perfect combination of entertainment, humor, provocation and sexuality. Michael's vibrant personality on and off the air has made him a people magnet.

He began attracting attention with primarily female followers as author and publisher of the highly successful best selling books: *Never Satisfied: How and Why Men Cheat, Men Cry in the Dark, The Maintenance Man, God's Gift to Women* and, most recently, a hot new book, *Never Satisfied: Do Men Know What They Want?* Two of his titles ultimately were adapted into stage plays playing to sold-out crowds across the U.S.

TELEVISION SHOW HOST

The author and relationship expert previously hosted a nationally syndicated talk show, "Talk or Walk," which was a compelling and fast-paced reality series that combined the

emotion of talk, the conflict of court shows and the fascination of a relationship series.

Another dream was to host a Late Night Talk show. He got that chance in the fall of 2007, when he partnered with TV One to host and co-executive produce *Baisden After Dark*, featuring comedian George Willborn and band leader Morris Day. The show was a smash hit, breaking records for viewers on the network. The show currently airs weekdays.

PRODUCER / FILM MAKER

Baisden Film Works: Michael has two successful national stage plays (based on his novels), which toured the U.S. playing to sold-out crowds; an award-winning feature-length film presentation documentary titled *Love, Lust & Lies* that deals with relationships and sexuality based on the perspective of people of color; and two seminar tapes, *Relationship Seminar* and *Men Have Issues Too.*

His television career kicked off in 2001 with "Talk or Walk" distributed by Tribune Broadcasting, which was a nationally syndicated Daytime TV Talk show he hosted that dealt with relationships. In 2006 he created, hosted and executive-produced a Late Night TV Talk show with co-host comedian, George Willborn, and band leader, Morris Day, which still airs on TV One titled "Baisden After Dark". In 2011 Michael produced a TV Special titled "Do Women Know What They Want?" that is currently airing on Centric of the BET Network and is based on his upcoming film. In 2011 Michael struck up a distribution deal for 3 feature films with TimeLife: *Do Women Know What They Want?*, *Love, Lust & Lies*, his two relationship films, and a comedy show titled *Turn Around* featuring his radio show co-host George Willborn.

In 2011, Michael continued to expand his media reach when he produced, wrote, and directed a groundbreaking relationship film titled, *Do Women Know What They Want?* The reviews have been amazing! "It was time for something new and exciting, and no one else was doing it, not like this!" Michael said. Get ready! It looks like the baddest man on radio and late night TV will be in theaters near you soon!

Michael continues to entertain, enlighten and educate as he pursues one of his first dreams, to have his novels adapted to major motion pictures.

Motivational Speaker

Baisden Entertainment: The Love, Lust & Lies Relationship Seminar Series attracts thousands of standing-room only, sold-out crowds nationwide as he tours the country. As a motivational speaker he has been an inspiration to hundreds of thousands attending his seminars and events. As well as numerous national Baisden Live Tours, he has also produced international Island Jam events in Jamaica and has an exclusive upcoming trip to South Africa.

Philanthropist

The Michael Baisden Foundation: A non-profit organization was formed with a goal to eliminate illiteracy as well as promote technology and is dedicated to education, support and advancement in our communities. Michael's own passionate testimony as to how books changed his life gives hope to those who have been enslaved by the shackles of illiteracy.

In December 2009 Michael called for a National Mentor Training Day and announced his plans for a 2010 nationwide campaign. He pledged up to $350,000 of his own money to be donated in over 72 markets he would visit on a bus tour. The outreach was named "One Million Mentors National Campaign To Save Our Kids." Michael challenged his listeners to match or beat his donations and get involved.

In October 2010 President Barack Obama publicly congratulated Michael on his efforts. He founded the Michael Baisden Foundation focusing on education, literacy and mentoring.

Michael believes "books change lives" and he is living proof!

SOCIAL ACTIVIST & COMMUNITY LEADER

Baisden's proudest moment came on September 20, 2007, when he passionately and skillfully spearheaded the famous Jena 6 March in Jena, Louisiana. This historic and momentous occasion garnered tens of thousands of citizens of all races to peacefully march in support of

six young men who have been unfairly treated by the justice system. In addition, he urged millions of listeners to wear black on September 20 in protest of unequal justice. The news traveled throughout the country. Everyone from college students of all races to corporate executives wore black in support of the Jena 6.

Another historic year was 2008. In late January Michael endorsed Sen. Barack Obama in the Democratic Primary. He celebrated President Obama's victory with over 4,000 fans at a watch party in Miami on election night. The Obama camp along with millions of listeners credited Michael with being one of the major forces behind this historic victory to elect the first African-American to the Presidency of the United States.

In 2009 he again stepped up and answered the call of the National Association of Free Clinics. With Michael's help they were able to get more volunteers than they needed and get the word out to the countless thousands that needed the free health services.

In March 2012 Baisden along with Rev. Al Sharpton held a rally in Stanford, FL to protest the injustice over the lack of an arrest in the killing of Trayvon Martin, an unarmed teenager who was just walking home from the store. Over 30,000 people attended the rally along with the teenager's parents and other leaders.

One Million Mentors National Campaign to Save Our Kids Tour went to over 72 cities nationwide in 2010 with him donating over $350,000 of his own money while recruiting mentors and working with organizations. While impactful only 15 percent of the nationwide mentoring network's male mentors are Black, with African American boys disproportionately represented on waiting lists. In 2012 Baisden partnered with Big Brothers Big Sisters of America and its national African American fraternity partners [Alpha Phi Alpha, Kappa Alpha Psi and Omega Psi Phi] for *Mentoring Brothers in Action*, an initiative to recruit volunteers and raise funds to provide mentors for African American boys. Baisden has contributed $10,000 to the initiative, making $105,000 his total donation to BBBS. "If you can't become a mentor, invest and support mentoring programs with your dollars. These children need our help," Baisden says. Go to www.MentoringBrothers.org for more information.

Stay tuned—it's just the beginning of the Baisden legacy.

Follow Michael on Facebook, Twitter
or YouTube @ BaisdenLive.
www.MichaelBaisden.com
www.BaisdenLive.com

THE MICHAEL BAISDEN SHOW
Informative, Engaging...Funny!

The show is syndicated in nearly 80 markets nationwide making it easy for you to get connected and  stay connected with Michael no matter where you are! Keep up with all of the latest and get first notification of exclusive online events, contests, activities and tours. The show airs weekdays from 3-7 p.m. EST. Listen live online or via app, download podcasts and check out the daily show features.

For more information, go to the office show website at: **www.BaisdenLive.com**

SOCIAL NETWORKING:
www.MingleCity.com is the online community for drama-free adults. It is a place for singles, couples, groups and friends to interact with other  like-minded members in their area, across the country and the world. Create your own personal webpage, invite your friends, start or join groups, find events, chat, blog, post your favorite photos and videos.

SOCIAL MEDIA @ BAISDENLIVE:

Follow Michael @ Twitter:
BAISDENLIVE

Be A Facebook Fan @
BAISDENLIVE

Tune In on YouTube @
BAISDENLIVE

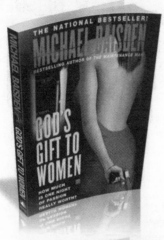

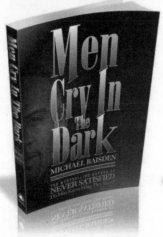
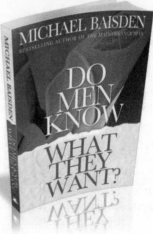

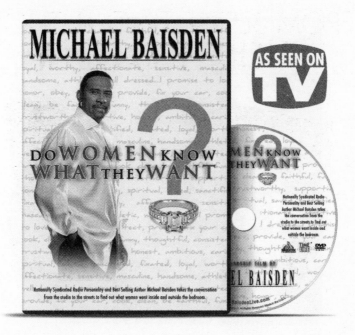

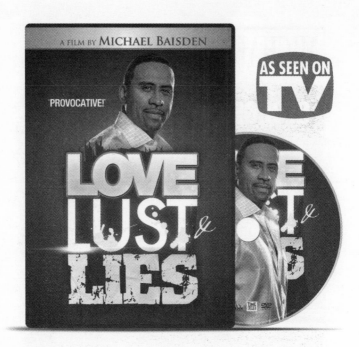

LOVE, LUST & LIES

We've all seen documentaries that deal with relationships and sexuality, such as "Real Sex" on HBO. But if you're like me, you've thought about how exciting it would be to experience a program that deals with these issues from the perspective of people of color. Well the wait is over.

"It's amazing to me how many people are afraid to be open about what they want inside and outside the bedroom," Michael says. "Hopefully, after watching these interviews they'll be more willing to explore their sexuality and to discuss issues such as infidelity, adult toys, and the swinging lifestyle."

Suggested Retail Price: $16.95
Available in Cut and a *Too Hot for TV*, UN-CUT version!

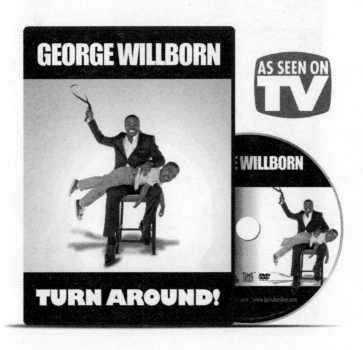

TURN AROUND!

"Turn Around!" Comedy Show featuring George Willborn aka The "Stress Reliever" and Co-Host of the Nationally Syndicated Michael Baisden Radio show takes the stage to deliver his unique brand of cruelly honest comedy with Special Guest comedians including Vanessa Fraction, Damon Williams, Alex Ortiz, Tyler Craig and Deon Cole.

Suggested Retail Price: $16.95

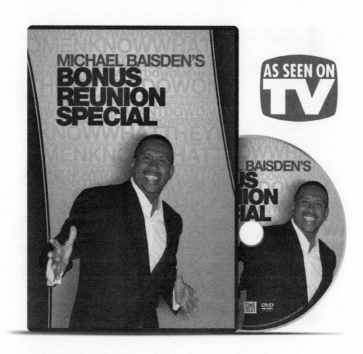

MICHAEL BAISDEN'S
BONUS REUNION SPECIAL

Filmmaker Michael Baisden digs even deeper into what women really want in this special reunion DVD. He unites some of the most outspoken men and women interviewed from across the country for one hot night of up close and personal Q&A!

Only Available Online
Suggested Retail Price: $16.95